COLD NEW CLIMATE

Cold New Climate

ISOBEL WOHL

WEATHERGLASS BOOKS

To my mother, Lisa

PART ONE

Chapter One

The hillside is dry. Across the road the variegated tans of shrubs and grasses and bare dirt, dark and milky and sun-faded, purple-tinged and yellowing, seem to glide the land into the distance. If she turns around and looks out of the back of the house she can see other homes and greener, rising hill ranges, and then where the ridge meets the sky the white linear intervention of a wind farm. Blades turn where the wind allows something to be generated.

On her second day in the village Lydia hears from the young woman who works at the bakery that there was a long debate about the wind farm, that the older people did not want it because they thought it would deface the hillside and that the tourists would not like it, that the tourists would not come, and sometimes tourists do ask why they didn't put the farm somewhere else, somewhere where it wouldn't ruin the view. Lydia says she does not think it ruins the view at all, that in the morning she likes to watch the white propellers turn. If you are putting turbines on a hillside you are trying to secure a future, and the wind farm, Lydia tells the young woman, makes her feel as if everything will, perhaps, be all right, because we will, perhaps, do something in time. The woman says yes, this is what the young people think: that they should try to preserve their part of the Earth, because everything is changing. And so the young people, by and large, supported the local government when they put in the wind farm.

Besides, the woman says, there is always a view. Everywhere. So if you don't want to ruin a view you can't have any turbines.

Her dark eyes are serious and hopeful. Lydia feels herself smile and is surprised, is pleased, keeps speaking although her order has been filled and she has already paid.

Did you hear about the wildfires in California? You can see pictures online, it's terrifying. Google *California wildfires*.

But now the woman is looking out the window at the front of the bakery, past Lydia, who feels sweat on her chest. The woman wipes the counter and looks up.

Yes, she says. Her smile is pronounced and careful.

Thank you, says Lydia. And with her white bag of pastries she walks back to the house.

Two weeks ago Lydia was on the crosstown bus on her way to dinner at Bobbie and Dan Philbrick's. She did not want to go but they were old friends of Tom's so she went. When she came in Bobbie asked her how her son was and Lydia had to correct her.

Sorry, said Bobbie, you've been with Tom so long I just thought it was nicer. Doesn't Caleb call you Mom anyway after all these years?

No.

What does he call you then?

Lydia.

Hmm, said Bobbie. Anyway, how's he doing?

Fine, thank you.

Gosh, it's so good to hear that. I'm so glad.

Before long they sat down to dinner. It was halibut. A voice at the far end of the long table said, He's only been in office for what, eight months, we ought to give him a chance.

4

Nine months, another voice said.

Lydia was supposed to be talking to Kathleen Delaney about her garden.

When they had almost finished eating Tom leant back in his chair and hooked one thumb into his belt and looked down the table at Lydia. She was following something that the man next to Kathleen was saying, the journalist, and when Tom tried to catch her eye she was annoyed and knew that the journalist could tell that she was annoyed. The journalist continued talking about how much data advertisers were collecting from them all.

Did you know – the journalist leant in, he seemed to look at her with interest, something about the angle of his head – that the way you swipe on your phone is as unique as a fingerprint? The way you use your finger on your phone.

Tom smiled at Lydia, and she realized that she had expected him to have something stuck in his teeth. He didn't. She looked at his mouth and could not decide what was wrong with it. She turned away.

Really, she said to the journalist.

The journalist asked if she had heard of Scribd. She had. Tom stood up and asked if he could do anything useful. Bobbie Philbrick said to sit back down. Dan Philbrick poured more wine. The journalist said that Scribd collected data on how fast you read, on where you stopped, because it wanted to know what you enjoyed.

But how does it know? Kathleen Delaney brushed her hair from her face with one hand. I mean, how can it tell what you enjoy?

Well it knows where you stopped, he said, so it figures you didn't like that part.

What if you just ran out of time?

Lydia got up to help clear.

Or if someone interrupted you, Tom said. His voice was too loud.

Bob Mackenzie said he wished there were cigars. No one lets you have cigars these days. Tom touched his face and laughed.

Lydia took the journalist's plate. She saw the clean line at his neck where his dark hair was neatly buzzed and between that line and his starched collar an inch of olive skin.

A few days later she told Tom that she was still in love in the place sense but out of love in the shopkeeping sense, by which she meant that she was near love or around love or adjacent to love but had no love to give. After much pleading he agreed to six weeks of separation.

She would go to the seaside and eat and be alone and think, except for the time she would spend with a man. She would meet one or more than one. She did not tell Tom this in so many words but got him to agree that when she was back neither of them would ask the other if during the time apart there had been other people. She knew she would have no real need to ask him but it was important to pretend otherwise.

I *don't* want to cheat, she said, if I did I wouldn't be talking to you about this.

She told him she was sure that she would come back replenished and carefree and committed and affectionate. She told him how badly she wanted to be all of those things.

In the mornings Lydia looks out over the hills at the wind turbines and watches each crisp white blade move across the blue behind it and become perpendicular to the horizon. As each one passes the zenith of its motion another blade follows, and another, as the first blade is coming back up. Lydia watches and drinks coffee. She decides not to read the news. Stray cats rub past her lower leg and occasionally climb onto her breakfast table. There are tortoiseshells, black ones, white ones with brown and ginger spots. Some are fat and glossy. Others are bony and irritable. These hiss.

Don't feed them, Liz said that Marty's cousin said, when Lydia called to say she'd arrived at the house that the cousin had agreed to lend her. It's cruel. Apparently people do it all the time, people feel bad for them and feed them for a while but soon the cats show up expecting it and of course no one wants them around pestering so they stop and the cats starve, by that time there are kittens and that's why there are more and more and more of them. Taking over the town. Robert says feeding them's like hurting them. The future ones who will be more likely to be born, that is, because they'll suffer. Do you want me to tell Tom you made it all right?

When the day gets hotter she goes into the house and opens her laptop and begins to work at the kitchen table. She can hear the cats rubbing against the wooden door and meowing to be let in. The current project is an energy drink called ENGINE. The company board says that they do not want the packaging to look too industrial because they do not want anyone to associate ENGINE with engine fluid, so Lydia comes up with can designs in pale green and silver, evasive and full of pep. There is no Wi-Fi but she has a dongle and most of the time this works all right.

She cannot entirely stop herself from Googling in fits of boredom the weather this coming week and double-checking how to say Hello, how to say Do you speak English and May I sit and With you. May I sit with you. Someone will say that to her soon. She would like to understand it, and then she can say I don't speak Greek, possibly in Greek but also possibly in

English to underline the point. Anyone who will be able to speak to her in English will understand if she says in English I don't speak Greek.

She tweaks a design and sends an email suggesting that the brand reconsider biodegradable material and receives in reply an email with a reiteration that the material suggested is outside of the packaging budget. Would she please stop going over old territory. Lydia apologizes. The cats sound lonely.

In the late afternoon she walks up stony paths and into the town. She goes to the bakery, where she says hello to the girl who told her about the wind farm dispute. They no longer speak about the climate.

On the way home Lydia sometimes stops at the convenience store, where in the back of the glass cold case there is good yogurt in a round terracotta dish covered in plastic wrap. This yogurt, the label says in English, is locally produced. She buys some, and also eggs and cheese and sometimes gummy worms, which are near the register and difficult to resist. When she gets home she puts these items away in her cupboards and refrigerator.

I don't want to check in with you, she texted Tom back on the fourth day of her absence, that's why I'm away.

The Aegean is a darker blue than it was in the pictures she saw on the internet. She eats anchovies and whitebait alone at the seaside cafe.

One day a man in a Panama hat sits at the table next to hers.

I don't speak Greek, she says.

He looks at her quizzically and says, Okay. Then he opens his newspaper. When the waiter comes he orders an ouzo in English.

The bodies of the anchovies are silver-white on the back.

When they were cleaned they were sliced open along the long tapered belly and there is a groove where the spine was. Lydia likes the salt and the lines in the white flesh pattern. The sun sets. When the striations of color are close to fading Lydia walks back up the road to the town, past kittens, who follow her for a few minutes before giving up and lying down by the roadside.

Each night Lydia orders a small beer at the town's only bar and sits on a stool near the high table in the sandy front yard. La Isla Bonita and Africa and Romeo and Juliet play on repeat. From the television near the open door Lydia can sometimes hear a brisk commentator announce some sports event she cannot see and cannot understand. She can tell when there's a goal because of the cheering that blares from the speakers. She tries to use her peripheral vision so that the people exiting and entering cannot tell that she is watching them.

Across the street she can see the unfinished new town hall and sometimes, once it is dark, teenagers who step past the slices of unused white stone. The girl at the bakery told Lydia that the government started to build this new building but then quit halfway through because they found they did not need it and also they had no money. Lydia asked if this was connected to the cost of the wind farm. The girl scoffed and asked if Lydia had heard of the debt problem. She said she had.

Well, said the girl, and shut the case of pastries.

Often at night a pair of moonlit adolescents enters the structure one after the other; often one offers the other a hand as they make their way up unfinished steps, giggling, and pass through gaping doorless rectangles; often it is the boy who offers a hand to the girl but not always, and one night Lydia believes there are two girls but she cannot say for certain because it is very, very late and they are fast and careful.

Lydia wonders who will sit at her table.

The young men who enter the bar, Lydia notices, generally come in groups with young women. The older ones sometimes come alone.

On the third night a man comes up to her and asks, Do the Americans really like Trump?

Lydia says that some do and some don't.

When the bar closes she walks again down the winding path to the house. It is very steep.

Around one a.m. she wakes up hungry. In the anodyne light of the fridge she puts a slice of wet white cheese on a chipped plate and eats it with her fingers.

When Lydia met Tom she was very young and he was middle-aged and knew Italian. He still knows Italian but now Lydia sometimes notices that there are small drops of clear or yellow sputter on his pillow. When she wakes up in the borrowed house she's glad not to see it. She sits outside on the terrace and sees the sun come up in pinks and wafty blues and oranges.

Sometime in the past couple of weeks he went to a faculty meeting, unless it was cancelled or he decided not to go. At any rate there was a faculty meeting scheduled on the whiteboard calendar that hangs on their metallic fridge door on the Upper West Side. Caleb's birthday was circled in blue, a big 19 scrawled on top. She won't be there.

On the ninth of October Lydia was supposed to have a drink with Liz, and she hasn't seen her in months, though that's not unusual. Now that Liz and Marty have kids it's tough, or that's why Liz says she doesn't have time. Still Liz

was instrumental in the Greece plan for emotional reinvigor-
ation, even if she did not entirely understand why it was necessary. In her most affected moment Liz said, Lydia, boredom
is the price of intimacy.

Lydia remembers when they were inseparable.

By the roadside she finds what she thinks is wild oregano
and picks a few sprigs. When she gets back to the house she
checks online to see if she is right before she eats it. She is. She
picks the leaves off and puts them on sliced ripe tomatoes. At
least she does not have to go to dinner with Tom's friend Bob
Mackenzie, who has a habit of spitting in flowerpots.

Sometime in the second week she realizes she wants to text
Tom about the sunrise but does not have service, and anyway
she has said she will not do that. On Caleb's birthday she
sends him an email and embeds a photo of the landscape. It
shows the turbines.

On the twentieth evening of her stay in Greece Lydia arrives
at the bar later than has been her custom. Again she orders a
beer, again she sits outdoors at the high table. The usual girls
enter, with their soft curved shoulders and painted lips, with
charming and effective distance in their eyes and in the casual
tilt of their chins. Young men follow them. As on the nights
before, they walk past Lydia.

Tonight there is a man who looks at her. She looks back.
He is not young but younger than Tom is now and as they
continue to speak she notices an Australian accent's strange
heights and attenuations. At the house she offers him something to eat and without waiting for a response opens the
refrigerator door. An arm reaches around her waist and she
stumbles and grabs a chilled plexiglass shelf. She stands up
and turns around. She takes off his shirt. Not far from his

hip there is an inch-long horizontal scar. What's that from, she says.

You should close the fridge.

Oh, said Lydia, and closes the fridge, just as the man is saying Appendicitis. Now the house is very dark and Lydia feels with utmost sensitivity how cool the terracotta floor is on the soles of her feet and how warm by comparison the worn wooden floor of the bedroom and then cool again the sheets on her shins, thighs, back, face.

Vomit on me, says the man.

What?

The man says again what he wants her to do. Put your fingers down your throat, says the Australian man, and vomit on me.

I don't want to do that.

Please. Please at least put your fingers down your throat. Please at least gag for me.

Chapter Two

The next morning Lydia does not watch the sunrise but instead feels its diffuse light coming through the curtains, passing over the form of the man sleeping behind her to touch the back of her left ear. Across the room she can see the low wooden table and on it the red lamp, tan cord curled around its base and its plug lying to the side, unused. On the wall above hangs a painting of globular and emotional peaches encircled by a blue mark meant to indicate, expressively, a bowl of the kind one might find on a kitchen table in a house like this. In a countryside like this you might expect to find a rough-hewn kitchen table and on it a bowl of ripe fruit on which bumblebees and wasps might land. There are no wasps in the painting. Lydia wonders if the artist feared that if he or she painted a wasp or a bee or a fly it would come out a black spot. And a black spot could look like mold or some other damage. A hole made by a worm.

Outside a bird caws. The man's arm is heavy on her side. Lydia can see the sun in the lashes at the outer corner of her left eye.

Then again Lydia has not taken the trouble to look closely at the painting when walking from the doorway to the bed or when leaving the bedroom in the mornings. There might be, invisible from this distance, a wasp with thin flat wings, neat head and thorax, long curving abdomen and brutal point.

Awake, the man embraces Lydia. Afterward she lies on her right side with his forearm under her neck, his belly against her back, and soon with his free arm he reaches for his phone and retrieves it from the windowsill. He mentions work. Things at work are very urgent now. Then he reaches his arm back around Lydia and holds the phone in both hands near her face. Lydia is not sure if she should look down into the sheets or up at the ceiling or unabashedly at his phone as he inputs his passcode and opens his Gmail. She closes her eyes.

Do you have service? she asks. I don't have service.

Did you get a Greek SIM?

Yes.

Then I don't know. What carrier?

The man has marks on his back, long pink ones. In the light spilling in from the still-curtained window Lydia notices them as he puts on his shirt.

Oh, she says, I'm so sorry, and he says, About what, and she tells him she has noticed pink marks, shallow tender excavations.

Don't worry about it. He pauses, then says, Oh I know what you're talking about, that's not you, they're old. When I was a child I was attacked by an eagle at the Adelaide Zoo. Did I ever tell you about it? It came out of nowhere.

We only met yesterday, says Lydia. They have not talked about his childhood or the zoo.

Right, of course, says the man. He tells her a story:

He was a child in Australia in the late '70s. His mother and his father worked long hours and did not have much time off. When they did they took the family to the zoo. On one of these occasions he and his brother were walking across the Central Lawn on their way to see Greater the Flamingo, having spent the morning with the gibbons and the stick insects, when he felt the cuts by which his shoulder and upper back opened into the lines she now sees. He could not see the eagle but he could see his brother, who saw the eagle. The boy who was being attacked by an eagle felt points of claws first over his scapulae and then crossing the back of his neck and finally in the delicate hollow above the clavicle. His brother did not know what to do. They are called fossa, the doctor told him later, those vulnerable soft bits, because the boy asked. As he was getting stitches he thought Fossa. When he emerged from the doctor's office his red-eyed mother was sitting on the low beige sofa clutching his brother, her face in his neck and one hand grasping at his blue striped shirt. Then she took them both for lemon ices and on the way home in the car she cried again and said they should not have gone to the zoo.

But it wasn't even a zoo eagle, the man says, it was just there.

Then how did it get in? asks Lydia.

Open-air zoo, says the man.

After the man leaves Lydia looks at the peach painting again. There is no wasp. She goes from room to room, looking at seashells, books in English, books in Greek, books about Greece, torn magazines, stones, bits of paper that testify in small purplish print to the purchase of things that are to her unreadable, snapshots, more paintings. Paintings of the beach. She looks at the shape of the sofa from across the den and from close up at its abraded and sun-worn fabric. She told herself she would not call Tom while she was away and more to the point she told him she would not. Downstairs, she finds a tortoiseshell cat asleep on a shelf of white linens. She carries it in her arms to the front door and places it outside, shuts the door and leans against it and listens to the yowling.

Later, Lydia opens her laptop and uses the dongle to get online. She Googles the Adelaide Zoo, Googles *vomit fetish* and finds a Wikipedia page for emetophilia that traces the fetish's increasing popularity to the video 2girls1cup, does not watch 2girls1cup but reads the Wikipedia page about it, watches one reaction video and then another. A young man looks at the camera and says, Damn, while his friend is typing in the link. They cannot get it to work. Don't put a dot com on, another friend is saying in the background. The man who is typing furrows his brow. The music starts.

Lydia discovers that the greater flamingo Greater was the oldest living member of the species *Phoenicopterus roseus* when it died in 2014. Six years earlier the blind bird had been attacked and beaten by teenagers. Its beak was damaged. Its caretaker was encouraged, days later, that it could hold up its head.

In the spring of the year she met Tom, Lydia went back home for the weekend. Why don't you bring the professor, her mother said, and Lydia said that he was busy. His name was Tom and he was busy.

I bet, said Lydia's mother. He sounds like a nice man.

He is, said Lydia.

Remind me again how old he is? And the little boy?

Lydia said that the boy's name was Caleb and did not tell her mother Tom's age.

For the rest of the weekend they prepared and ate meals and cleaned the plates on which those meals were served and the sheet pans, roasting pans, bowls in which the meals had been made. When they spoke to each other the sentences were over too fast, and they were not sure what had happened. Lydia noticed the brown wallpaper, its spots and flowers and the shine of its lamination, the spatters and stains of oily accidents, the places where it had begun to peel. She was a new person now, she told herself then. A person like her had never before been in this house.

You watch out, her mother said when she saw her looking at the wallpaper. But she did not say what to watch out for. Instead she told her again the story about her grandfather's arm.

The next day she dropped Lydia at the bus and said, You bring him out here sometime, and the boy. Lydia said she would, but they both knew that she would not, even though, she reflects now, Tom would have come, Tom would have been perfectly nice, Tom would not even have said anything about the wallpaper, which really did need to be replaced, and perhaps Lydia in her new circumstances could even have convinced Tom to lend money to spruce things up if she could have convinced her mother to accept it and then she could have brought Tom out, except that her mother was dead within the year and couldn't accept anything anymore and in any case had no need of wallpaper. They sold the house for next to nothing. Lydia gave the plates to her cousins.

Lydia spends her remaining time in Greece alone. She watches sunrises and sunsets and starts to design packaging for another energy drink and various snack foods and some cleaning products. She orders prototypes. The weather continues to cool but she still likes to sit at the beachside cafe and eat anchovies. She no longer goes to the bar. At home she feeds the cats and hopes for the best for the kittens.

She fantasizes about smuggling one onto the plane, flying home with a tiny tabby hidden in the front of her shirt, hot and fuzzy, crawling and mewling. On further reflection she likely wouldn't have to smuggle anything. She Googles *bringing a cat from EU to US*. It seems easy. She could ask Tom. She almost calls him.

But she would have to take the cat on the ferry, on the bus, then through security, and she has no cat carrier, realistically you need a cat carrier, there is nowhere near here to get a cat carrier and what if the cat dies in transit. And maybe Tom would rather get a dog.

A week before Lydia leaves the island the woman at the bakery mentions another place to drink in the town.

I thought there was just that bar, Lydia says.

It turns out that on a side street there is a local taverna.

You should come, says the dark-haired young woman. I will, says Lydia.

That evening Lydia walks down narrow and uneven streets. She reaches the edge of the town and finds she is at the path back to her house, so she returns to the main street and tries another way. She thought she knew the street the girl meant but it appears that she was wrong. On the far side of the town she finds a stand of quince trees from which ripe yellow fruit have already fallen and almost gives up. Eventually she finds the place by the music that pours out into the street and by the light in the windows.

Inside the taverna families sit at round tables with red tablecloths. Lydia sees an old man dancing with his arms outstretched. He takes small steps and everyone is clapping in rhythm.

There might be a storm, no boat until tomorrow, says the man who sells the ferry tickets.

How do I get to Athens? Lydia asks. I have a flight. I have to get home.

Your best bet is a taxi.

The taxi driver is available. In halting English he explains that they will have to go up the coast of the island and over the bridge at Chalkida. It is expensive but cheaper than missing the flight. They drive away from the port and up the hillside and as they leave the town the road grows straight and the driver speeds up. Then Lydia sees the ridges of the land dissipate as if the spines of hilltops, before tired and slumped, can now stretch to their full and pleasurable extension.

Chapter Three

I think you ought to have a baby, says the woman in the seat next to Lydia's. With her spare hand she arranges the coverlet. Lydia looks at the blue fabric where the child's head was just now visible and sees the dinosaur print move and hears the sucking noise.

Now the woman is looking up at Lydia. Do you want to have a baby?

Not really, Lydia says. She pulls the sleeve of her cardigan down past the joint of her wrist and over the pad of flesh at the base of her hand. Anyway, she says, my partner has a child. A teenage child who has had a lot of problems and still needs a lot of support. It's too air-conditioned, don't you think? The air conditioning is too much.

Well, you should have your own baby. You know what they say.

What?

Children keep you together.

We're actually all right, says Lydia.

How old are you? asks the woman. I know you're probably worried you're running out of time. But let me tell you, it is possible!

Thirty-seven.

Thirty-seven, repeats the woman. Hmm.

When do they come by with the pretzels? asks Lydia. I hope they have those little pretzels, you know, the sour cream chive ones. And then I'm going to watch a movie.

Look, says the woman, here's the thing: when you become a mother, you realize you are just like a horse or a cow or a tiger or a goat. But if you haven't had children you don't know. It's not just giving birth and breastfeeding and all that, it's how you'd do anything to protect them. I'd do anything to keep Ethan safe.

Oh.

I mean absolutely anything. I'd tear someone's arm off. I don't want to have to but I would. I would kill someone. Really, I am an animal. You are too. But *you* don't know.

I'm very cold, says Lydia, are you cold? She reaches into the pocket in the seat in front of her and takes out the plastic-wrapped blanket, rips the packaging open and arranges the gray polarfleece over herself. She undoes and refastens her security belt so that it's visible. Next she grabs the package of earphones and tears it open, puts the earphones in her lap, stuffs all the clear plastic back in with the evacuation maps and free socks with rubber treads on the bottom and her used plastic glass, which has cracked under the pressure of the elasticized flap.

Besides, she continues, I'm worried about the environmental impact. I want to do my part. And also we may get a dog.

Oh I see, says the woman.

Yes. We've got to do something.

The flight attendant comes by with the small pretzels.

Anyway, just like a horse.

They have Blue Planet II, Lydia says. Excuse me. She puts her headphones over her ears and plugs the copper endpoint into the jack in the armrest.

What to text from baggage claim?

I'm at the airport. Home soon. I love you. I can't wait to see you.

Can't wait to see you. Home soon. I've got so much to tell you.

Home soon!

On the belt Lydia's brown suitcase comes into view.

Home soon, I missed yellow cabs and your old body and I can live without hunger. I've got a lot to say.

I know we said we wouldn't talk about things with other people but I almost fell into the fridge. I didn't like it.

Let's get a cat. Or a dog. Or a cat.

When she gets home the apartment is empty. She is pleased to see the green carpet, mirror over the mantel, gold clock in front of it, brass floor lamp in the corner. Spare keys on the hook near the door. She rolls her suitcase into their bedroom and begins to unpack.

That evening they do not go out. Tom sits across from her and after some initial difficulty explains himself with tremendous calm. He has been preparing for this. He knows when to take a sip of wine and when to take a sip of water and when to refill Lydia's glass and when to look her in the face. He pronounces all the words very clearly, especially *unexpected*. He is executive and compassionate. When Lydia raises her voice he takes his square glasses off, cleans them, and puts them on again.

What does Lydia hear? What will Lydia remember? Later, in the hotel, she revisits it:

Let's have a drink, said Tom. Why don't you tell me about Greece?

Okay, said Lydia. She followed him into the kitchen. Two long-stemmed glasses were waiting on the kitchen island. He must have set them out earlier.

He was opening a bottle of wine and she was supposed

to start talking about Greece. She would tell him about the starving cats but not about the man with the scars from the zoo, she had planned to describe the sunrise and the open glistening bodies of marinated anchovies and the seaside café but she could not find the words, she needed Tom to understand how happy she was to be home and that she knew how wrong she had been to leave him.

She began by saying, I know. Then she stopped speaking.

Tom was having trouble. He worked the corkscrew out and centered it on the cork and drove the screw back in again.

When's Caleb coming home? asked Lydia.

Out for the evening.

Oh. Is that a good idea?

Tom succeeded in opening the bottle. He twisted the damaged cork off of the corkscrew and turned it over in his hand.

Anyway, said Lydia, I know that it's been difficult, my . . .

Tom pressed a finger into the ragged groove the screw had made in the cork. It split lengthwise. With flicks of his thumb he made grains from one half's dry shorn area. They scattered on the countertop. Lydia watched. After a few seconds she asked if he was going to pour the wine.

Yes, he said.

Anyway. I am trying to say that I —

Tom threw the broken cork in the trash. I thought you were going to tell me about Greece, he said.

He ruffled his hair with one flighty hand. She was aware then, she remembers now, that she had missed that hand. She was going to say so, or rather that she had missed him and not only the hand, or not the hand in particular.

Tell me about, you know, he said, did you meet anyone while you were away?

We said we weren't going to talk about that.

Could he be jealous?

I fell in love.

Tom said it as he was pouring the wine. Tom asked her to tell him about Greece and then said it and says it again when Lydia thinks or drinks or turns over in the hotel bed.

I was going to wait to tell you but I can't wait. I'm sorry. It was completely unexpected. I thought you were going to leave.

Now Lydia opens her mouth and inhales. Air settles on her tongue and stings.

If you leave your mouth open like this you look like a fish. If you close it and open it again without speaking and close it and open it again you will look like a fish. Open your mouth when you've got something to say.

In the new world air is painful and Tom has fallen in love.

Ideally, he said, scratching the skin over his cheekbone, I mean, I didn't want to bombard you with it, I was going to wait and tell you later in the evening, but then I just. Well now I've done it. I also didn't want to lie to you or let you go on thinking.

I was going to tell you about Greece.

In the fish world eyes are made of water and the light from the overhead fixture is beginning to tremble itself all over the room.

You didn't let me tell you about Greece. You asked but then you told me something else.

She was going to tell him about the cats and the wind farm and the rotating blades and the peach painting with no wasp and the future, she wanted to, she still wants, but Tom said Let me get you a tissue. You need a tissue.

I don't need a tissue.

Lydia went to the counter and brushed the particles of cork

into the sink. She turned on the faucet and rinsed the stuff down the drain and into the sewer and into some ocean. For a minute or two she was alone in the room, and with the water off it was quiet, and she listened. Then Tom returned with the tissue and wiped the area under her eyes. When he removed the tissue she saw black mascara smeared on it. He blinked and looked down and did not smile. She could feel paper and emollient.

I didn't think it would happen. I didn't even try to meet anyone. But I'm in love.

Not with me, Lydia said, thinking about the wind farm.

No.

They went to the table and sat across from each other and Tom finished pouring the wine.

When Lydia could not hear more she went into the living room and sat on the sofa. Tom followed her.

You were the one who wanted this, Tom said. You wanted to see other people. It was your idea. You said you were bored. Don't you remember?

Yes, said Lydia. I was bored. Obviously you were too, you just didn't say it.

Fine, yes, so I was too. I was too. Thank you for being the one to say it. He winced and touched his forehead, covering his eyes with one hand. Wait, no, I'm sorry. I didn't mean that the way it sounded. He sat down next to Lydia and put the hand on her knee. Honestly, thank you.

Lydia looked down. The hand's back was wrinkled and hairs interrupted the pattern of Tom's freckles. In recent years the skin there had begun to settle over dark veins fat as worms. Blood was coursing back from the pads where Tom's hands, touching things, made fingerprints. It moved through capillaries in the thin casing of sagging flesh that mobilized the dashes of bone in his fingers, then along the blue protrusions she could see now, up the arm and past the angle of the elbow, back toward the lungs, the heart.

Lydia placed a thumb over one thick vein and pushed down to pinch it shut. She looked at Tom's face and waited to feel pressure. His eyes were large and bewildered. Again she sees them now with her own eyes closed. His eyelashes are gray.

What did she expect to happen?

She pushed his hand away and walked to the bathroom, where she repacked in the small gray case eyedrops, toothpaste, tweezers, toothbrush, floss, small round cotton pads, makeup remover, mascara, various balms, colors for eyes cheeks lips.

Tom poked his head just past the open door.

You're going now?

Yes, said Lydia. I am going now.

Hence the colors, removers, small round cotton pads.

You don't have to.

You want me to go too, you're just not saying it.

Tom took a step into the bathroom. You're taking this very well. Relatively.

And not long ago Tom was planning this while she ate pretzels and was told she did not know how like a horse she was. A horizon of water halved the small screen inset in the headrest in front of her. She watched a large silver animal prepare to surge from its blue hiding place, to leap, to grab and devour a low-flying baby bird. Then she came home to tell Tom about the sunrise and how much she had missed him and how happy they were going to be.

In the mirror her face and behind her Tom's face watching it. If she told him now she would see his reaction. She could say now, if she wanted, about the eagle-scarred man. She could put in or leave out the gagging. She could embellish the gagging or be in love too.

Carefully, slowly, Tom stepped closer to her.

You saved us, he said, with your honesty. You knew it was time to move on. I appreciate it.

Lydia zipped the case of toiletries.

The hotel phone rings. Liz's voice asks how Lydia is and why she has not been picking up her cellphone. Lydia says everything is as one might expect and asks if Liz knew and if Liz has met her and how Tom met her. Liz has not met her and dodges the question about knowing but says that Tom said that they met at a dinner. Apparently she's a friend of Bob Mackenzie's.

Bob the flowerpot-spitter.

Did Tom tell you where I was, Lydia says, or who told you.

Late or early in the dark. She turns on the light, dresses quickly. In a moment she will go down to the hotel lobby, to the hotel bar which, she assumes, is accessible from the hotel lobby, to the bar where cheap disinfectant glistens on black countertops, where chemicals not yet evaporated may wet the skin of her forearm, elbow, edge of hand, resting with palm open toward the imagined man. He has yet no face.

But no guests in the hotel have Tom's face, which is against Tom's pillow, sleeping soundly near another face or perhaps not yet. Perhaps she's not there. Arm wrapped around.

In the mirror Lydia puts brown liner on the eyelids of a devastated woman.

She leaves a big gap between the mark and the lashline and has to remove it. Then she has to wipe droplets of remover from her cheeks.

She puts the liner on again, more carefully this time, and then she adds mascara and the dress. Her lips are chapped. She zips the dress up the back.

When she gets in the elevator a drunk woman is saying to a man in a suit, Whereas I'm a big emotional, you know.

What time is it?

You know. Tom knows. She is a big emotional you know. Not everyone does.

See for me when I need to work I'm really disciplined, the woman is saying.

Lydia hasn't checked the time since the first eyeliner deba-cle and now she can't remember and the dress has no pockets and there is nothing in her hand, should she go back up in the hotel to the room to get the phone but then again there is nothing in either hand and earlier the keycard opened the hotel room door and the door clicked just now, shutting, and the man in the suit is asking if she is all right.

I've locked myself out.

Well that's all right.

Spots of light gleam on his brown shoes. Lydia looks up and meets his eyes.

They'll help you in the lobby. They'll let you back in.

When the elevator door opens Lydia does not go to the front desk but instead out the automatic door which star-tles into motion when she nears it like something long ago wounded and never put right.

It is dark out except for the streetlights. She begins to walk. She should have brought a coat. She did not anticipate leav-ing the hotel. Tom has left her. She has left their apartment. The movers will come to the apartment and take her things from it like she has already taken herself and swabs of cotton and her body. Christ it's cold. Tom adores her, she knows he adores her, he always adored her, she wrapped his wife's things in tissue paper and wiped the snot from Caleb's nose while Tom was mediating media in journals and lectures and lately decentering heavens between the thighs of spitters' friends.

She rounds the corner, she wraps her arms around herself.

Tom was always generous. It seems now that she adored him. Someone leaves an office building, someone hails a taxi-cab, a woman in a miniskirt is looking at her phone and slips almost off the edge of the curb and catches herself with a quick short step before she falls.

She adored him. Adores. Adored. She mouths the words and in a pool of gutter water iridescent with gasoline she sees office lights and soggy advertisements and her face and chicken bones, work for some fortune-teller.

It seems to her now, it seems.

Chapter Four

Caleb has no idea what Dr. Antonelli just said. But he says it makes him think of Wayne.

Who? asks Antonelli.

Caleb explains that as a child he played at Wayne Waldroff's house at least twice a week. Wayne wore green shirts and large glasses and wanted to be a paleontologist. Plastic pirates with hard blue chests and devilish black print beards stole hoards of treasure from one another on the floor of the Waldroffs' living room, hid their stash in the cave under the brown sofa.

The session is almost over, Caleb has almost made it to the end and all he has to do is keep the doctor talking about his toys from years ago.

Playmobil, says Dr. Antonelli.

No, says Caleb. Legos.

Dr. Antonelli makes a note. He looks up and waits. His head is slightly tilted. Caleb would like to ask Dr. Antonelli if he learned that tilt of the head in graduate school.

Instead Caleb says that their pirates could not swim because of the sharks in the carpet. Caleb and Wayne had one tan plastic island from the official island set and as a second they had the base of a chrome floor lamp. When a captain needed to get from one island to the other he could swing over on the cord that hung from the blinds.

Dr. Antonelli waits.

We were both captains, says Caleb. You could use the rope to swing from the lamp base to our plastic island. The cord wasn't really that long but we just allowed ourselves to, you know, go for it.

Caleb waits for Antonelli to say something, but Antonelli rests his hand on his notepad. Caleb cracks his knuckles.

I mean we pretended the blinds cord was longer than it was.

Antonelli is still quiet. He wants to see Caleb change the subject. See what he changes the subject to. Caleb won't let him. Antonelli makes a note.

So we could use the blinds rope to swing from one island to another or from the lamp island to the, uh, ledge.

Ledge?

I'm forgetting the word for some reason. For the actual thing.

Dr. Antonelli waits. Caleb has the feeling he is not running out the clock.

That's all right, says Dr. Antonelli. His brown eyes are large and compassionate through square glasses. After the last time Caleb got out of the hospital his father decided that finding someone younger might be smart, Caleb might connect better with someone younger than he had with Klingman, who always wanted to talk about the tennis player Novak Djokovic and kept asking questions about Caleb's mother's death even though she has been dead since he was tiny. His father also thought it was good that Antonelli was a psychiatrist, so they wouldn't need a separate prescriber and maybe the care would be better, maybe the reason treatment was not working was that until now something had been getting lost in translation between the two members of the team. At the time Caleb was sold on the idea of fewer appointments. But the mild-mannered young doctor bothers him with his exact and gentle attention. It was not so bad, talking about Novak Djokovic.

31

Dr. Antonelli leans back in his chair.

Windowsill, says Caleb.

When Dr. Antonelli does not move Caleb says that he remembers overhearing Wayne's mother on the phone to some representative of something or maybe it was a machine. She said, No, W. A. L. D. R. O. F. F. Not like the salad. R. O. F. F. That's R. O.

But Caleb won't tell the doctor that he and Wayne were going to found a new country where pirates ran free. Their money was going to be a cryptocurrency called the septillion, and the coins for it would look like gold doubloons. When Wayne's brother Jeff asked how they were going to reconcile the operation of the blockchain with the parallel presence of a cash system they had no answer and Jeff said they didn't know what cryptocurrency was, and besides, septillion was already a number, so how was anyone supposed to know whether ten septillions were ten units of their money or seventy million of some other thing? And then the Waldroffs moved to Macon, Georgia, when Wayne and Caleb had never even agreed on the name of the pretend country. Caleb tried to finish it on his own but it was not the same.

He had always imagined that in their country there would be a valley whose slopes were carpeted entirely with blue-bells. He kept this valley secret from everyone but Wayne for some reason he did not understand. For a long time the boys tried to keep in touch. By the time they got their own phones Wayne had forgotten all about the country and so the blue valley was not part of any place.

Lydia, Lydia.

Her name sounds different now in her imagination of Tom's voice. Anyway he is not saying Lydia, is saying some other name in his room with the lights off or on and another loved body.

The sheets are crisp like a hotel and white. They are hotel sheets crisply. She is staying in a hotel.

Last night she returned very late from the street. The man from the elevator was sitting on the sofa in the lobby with his white shirtsleeves rolled up so that she could see on one forearm a tattoo that read *Il était une fois* and on the other a bold ampersand in black ink. She asked him if he was waiting for her. In her own ears this sounded ludicrous and then the man said yes and it was ludicrous no more. She still did not have her keycard so they went to his room. On his bed nine ties were laid out in differing shades of crimson vermilion and scarlet all lapping cheap gloss from the overhead light which he turned out around the time he said Just dump the ties on the floor. Lydia gathered the ties in one hand and dumped them on the floor and said Can I vomit on you. She had to repeat it. That's disgusting, said the man, who does that, there's something wrong with you. He was right, she felt ill, there was no chance he'd really been waiting for her in the lobby, she felt worse, she lunged for the wastebasket and missed it. He called the front desk and told them about the mess and asked them to come with her keycard and take her back to her room. I've been helping a fellow guest, he said, she was locked out. Can you come clean this up. There was a pause. Lydia turned the light back on. The pile of red ties was slippery underfoot. The man said, They say you have to go down to get the keycard. They say they can't send someone up immediately unless you won't leave and then they'll send security. I think she'll leave, he said into the hotel phone, but can you still hurry because of the vomit. She put her shirt on.

Lydia, Lydia.

Lydia now means something like *Be reasonable.*

The whole thing is not to overthink it. Or not to think about it at all. To stay in the hotel sheets, occasionally to open her laptop. Common-law marriage has not existed in the State of New York since 1933. Her inbox is overflowing. She sets up an out-of-office that says she has had to take time off for a family emergency but does not give details about when the emergency will end.

Tom answers his phone on the third ring and says hello.

Do you have a picture of her? Lydia asks.

Lydia.

Do you have a picture?

In the space that follows Lydia is embarrassed that she could have thought Tom might not have a picture.

Why?

I want to see, says Lydia. I want to know what she looks like. Send it.

What does it matter to you what she looks like?

Lydia starts to laugh.

Doesn't it matter to you what she looks like? She lies back in the bed and stares up. The bright O of the overhead light burns into her vision and she closes her eyes and puts one hand over their lids. In the darkness she sees a violet dot and hears Tom say:

I am in love with her. It hurts me that you assume it's anything else.

Fine then, says Lydia to the violet point, how old is she?

Fifty-four, says Tom. And beautiful.

Lydia opens her eyes and coughs. No she's not.

Tom takes a slow breath. She is. I suppose that was gratuitous, forgive me. I do have a picture of Diane if you want me to send it. But she's also very accomplished, she's not just beautiful, it's really not like that.

No, says Lydia, I mean she's not fifty-four. She can't be.

What do you want, her birth certificate?

No, says Lydia, no, that's not what I want. I mean, no, I do not want to see your picture.

She ends the call. The spot of violet light has disappeared so when she closes her eyes again it's dark but she can't keep them closed, it's too lonely.

Tom and Sarah's friends, the Philbricks and Delaneys and the rest of them, all thought Tom was having a midlife crisis when not long after Sarah died Tom started bringing some student around. Lydia put Sarah's things in boxes and gave them to Housing Works and told Tom to turn the master bed to face the opposite way. She helped him lift it. You're my crisis, Tom joked. She laughed because she was sure he was joking. They were laughing together behind the backs of his friends, the backs of his colleagues, the backs of naysaying strangers who understood neither sex nor love. They enjoyed it.

And now he prefers accomplished Diane, who is fifty-four and not his student. He says he is in love with her. No one will say she is a crisis. It is embarrassing even to type *moving company* into Google. *Movers. Hotels.* She types also *hotels* and *best hotels.* How should Lydia or anyone imagine what Tom likes or wants anymore.

It is easy with a few clicks to book, afterward to call downstairs and notify the front desk, to get in the taxi and look out the window at children opening bright umbrellas and women hiding their hair from the rain and carefully shaped bushes in tall pots. It is easy to slip the right piece of plastic into the slot in the machine, tip the cabbie generously, tip the man who puts her suitcase onto the rack. There are fresh flowers everywhere and the entire check-in experience is tremendously agreeable and the minibar luxuriously stocked. This new place has a marble floor. The bathtub has claw feet.

Liz calls Lydia's cellphone and says she's been looking for her, she tried that little hotel where she thought she was and they said she'd checked out. Where is she?

Lydia tells Liz where she is staying.

How can you afford it?

Lydia replies that so far she has been charging it to Tom.

That's not right, says Liz.

He hasn't called, says Lydia, so clearly he's fine with it.

She takes another bath. Soon she gets a call from Tom, who says that she has to move out or he is going to dispute the charges, bad as he feels about everything, and he does feel bad about everything, to be sure he never meant it to wind up like this and if she recalls she was the one who left in the first place and will she please move into at least a cheaper hotel. Wasn't she in a cheaper hotel at first?

But Lydia likes the very clean carpet here. She likes the marble floor and the men downstairs with their small stupid hats. She tells him this and is waiting for him to respond when the call ends and suddenly she's just listening to nothing, not sure what happened.

On her iPad, alone in the darkness, Lydia finds as much information as possible about the ADX Supermax facility in Florence, Colorado. This Supermax is in the desert, she reads, and the windows are angled so that prisoners can see nothing but the sky. That way they have no idea where they are in relation to the rest of the building. The cells are made of poured concrete and soundproofed to prevent words or Morse code from traveling.

Lydia reads about the prisoners held in Florence (Theodore Kaczynski, Dzhokar Tsarnaev, Ramzi Yousef, Michael Swango) and then a link brings her to a page for the Administrative Unit of FMC Carswell, near Fort Worth, Texas. FMC Carswell houses prisoners at all security levels but the Administrative Unit functions as the sister unit to the ADX. Because she has just read that much of the ADX is designed so that no prisoner ever sees another she is unsure why there can be no female prisoners there and why it therefore needs a sister facility but she guesses that this is general corrections policy resulting perhaps from staffing issues, strip-searches, and disciplinary concerns. Anyway, Wikipedia tells her that prisoners include Squeaky Fromme and Reality Winner.

The only female inmate on death row in the federal prison system also resides at FMC Carswell. Lisa Montgomery cut a child of eight months' gestation from Bobbie Jo Stinnett's uterus in 2004 and left Stinnett to die. The child survived and was returned to her father. In the images Montgomery wears wire-rimmed glasses and does not meet the eyes of the cameraperson. In one image she is holding a small dog. It lies on its back in her arms and touches its raised hindlegs with its raised forelegs.

Another link brings Lydia to Andrea Yates. She remembers the magazine covers and her mother's voice saying, How could she.

According to the internet, Yates's original conviction, since vacated, rested on the argument that she must have known right from wrong, in part because she waited for her husband to leave the house and also because she caged the dog. The dog was not usually caged. Andrea knew, the prosecutors argued, that the dog might have tried to save the children.

In order to drown Noah she moved baby Mary's body from where it floated in the bathwater to the bed where it joined the neat little bodies of John, Paul, and Luke, with their clean faces. This freed up the tub.

Lydia checks her phone. Tom has not called back. She orders room service.

After Andrea finished, according to Wikipedia, she called the police but would not say why she needed an officer. Lydia imagines the police car pulling into the driveway, the faces of the officers as they see the quiet children in the bed, find quiet Noah facedown in the water.

My journey now will be to learn about myself and conquer my demons, writes Harvey Weinstein in an apology statement Lydia finds on NYTimes.com. *Over the last year I've asked Lisa Bloom to tutor me and she's put together a team of people . . . I am going to need a place to channel that anger so I've decided that I'm going to give the NRA my full attention. I hope Wayne LaPierre will enjoy his retirement party.*

Tom opening the door for her, Tom closing the door, Tom in the shower in the mornings, their days together once pallid and lackluster and in her mind now enervated, Tom leaving a lone black sock in with the whites.

She's left her winter coat at home so she treats herself to a new one, shimmering emerald wool in an elegant cut. Downtown she counts empty shopfronts and loses track of spending on seemingly reasonable happy hour oysters. When she walks back to the subway the air is wet and not cold enough for November. She remembers the spring tulips and their long green leaves, the white pear trees, the pink riot of the flowering cherries. It is almost warm enough for them all to come back out. She leaves the coat open.

This past spring she was so dissatisfied.

In April Tom drove to Grove Acre to see Caleb with Lydia in the passenger seat. She watched the woods go by and they exited the woods. She heard him breathe as if he was about to try some topic so she said How about some music and looked out the window at mud and new grass. Now she remembers the vigilance and care with which he drove, how for a second his hands shook when he took them off the wheel and his voice when it said Caleb's name at reception was tense with adoration and restraint.

Just this way, said the receptionist, and they were shown to the waiting room. They sat in orange chairs that had their backs to the wall.

Caleb walked through the white door. It swung shut behind him.

I told you not to come. I didn't want you to come.

I know, Tom said. Lydia wondered what he was looking at, something on the ground, and then he looked up toward his son's face again. She watched Caleb slip his thumbs into his pockets, looked at his heavy and beautiful hands. She did not know if she was blushing or going pale.

I didn't have to let you in, he said.

Yes, Tom said. Thank you. I know that, and I'm grateful. How are you?

Fine, Caleb said. Better.

I'm glad you can have visitors now, said Lydia. Caleb looked at her. He looked at her too long and she thought he was angry.

I'm going to go back upstairs, he said. Thanks for coming. Please stay, said Tom. Please not yet.

But Caleb was already back through the door. In the car Tom said, Do you think he's okay, he seemed okay, he said he was better, and Lydia said, He seemed better than the last time we saw him, at least.

Tom drove silently for a while, then said, What is he going to do when I am not here anymore?

Next to them the valley rolled from the roadside down swiftly into lawn and planted rows of crop and then, far off, Lydia saw the treeline and in front of it a red house and a silo containing something.

Liz calls Lydia's cellphone to ask where she's staying now and how the move went.

I haven't moved. I'm paying now, so there's no problem.

But you can't afford it on your own.

I emptied the joint account.

Lydia walks to the bed and picks a foil-wrapped chocolate up off her pillow. She unwraps it and puts it in her mouth. She chews, tastes the mint at the center, and swallows.

Oh, Lydia, says Liz.

It was a joint account.

What did Tom say?

Nothing, Lydia says, and he must have noticed by now, so it's fine. He's fine with it. He hasn't called me to say anything, he said he didn't want to pay for the hotel, so I listened, and now he's not, and he hasn't called. Lydia throws the foil wrapper in the trash.

But it's half his.

No. All of it was both of ours.

Liz changes the subject. She says that in Phoebe's class at

school there is a boy who never grew teeth and never will. When he was a baby his parents waited for milk teeth to come in but it just never happened, he was all gum in the mouth, slick, pink. They brought him to the doctor, who offered them water. This surprised the parents. They said, Water? The doctor said, Yes, a glass of water, and smiled reassuringly. The mother wondered if the gesture was intended to calm her down and if she should therefore interpret it as an indicator that the son was in fact very ill. She tried to catch her husband's eye. They both said, No thanks, no water. The doctor said that some kids get teeth early and some kids are a little later and their little boy was just in the late-tooth group. The teeth would most likely come in soon.

They never did. Apparently, says Liz, it's a very rare disorder.

So then what does he eat?

They still have to mash everything up.

Later Tom texts. Lydia wonders if Tom even noticed what's in or not in the joint account or if Liz told him. Lydia does not respond to the text or to the first call but she picks up on the second ring of the second. Tom says he's shocked that she didn't even tell him she was planning to do this, and Lydia says that she is shocked and embarrassed herself as a matter of fact. Tom has other accounts. Yes, he says, but that is not the point.

She asks if he remembers when they went to visit Caleb at Grove Acre and that they stopped on the way home at a stand by the roadside for barbecued brisket on soft rolls. They were both so scared. She was as scared as he was. The sandwiches helped. They both got sauce on their chins.

Could we please try to stay on topic, says Tom.

Fine, she says. Although she is not entirely clear on the numbers she is guessing that his other accounts are very healthy and that the money in the joint account should therefore go to her. Tom says that does not follow. Lydia says that he is sidestepping the question about the other healthy accounts and what about his parents' estate. Tom says that none of that has anything to do with her. He's got to think of Caleb. Lydia says she knew he would say that which is why she has taken all of the money in the joint account. Tom asks if she will please just give half of it back, and she says no and asks exactly when it started with Diane, how long she had been out of the country, how many hours, give or take, and Tom says he could very well ask who she fucked while she was off by the sea but he doesn't, and Lydia says that falling in love with other people was never mentioned in their original negotiation and says she will give back twenty percent and that's it and how does he know, really, that he's in love with Diane? How can he be sure? Tom says to keep the money.

The young people who show Lydia spare rooms in their apartments are friendly enough. On each visit she hopes one of them will open a door onto a dark secret corridor lined with framed photographs. She would walk past them and Tom would lean forward into the rectangle of light at the end. Tom would beckon her into the big front room. She would see the expanse of green carpet. Tom would have just made coffee. All these young people must know which door is the right one but somehow no one opens it.

Chapter Five

Caleb asked his father once, When does memory start?

I think around the age of five or six, his father said.

Then Caleb knew that his memories of his mother could not be real.

When Caleb was thirteen he woke up in the hospital and was asked if he understood what had happened. He started to say what he'd said to the school counselor: that he could not shower and that since summer the world seemed far away from him.

The man in green gloves said, I'm not asking about that, I want to know if you know what you did to get yourself in here.

The lights were very bright. The man that Caleb had thought was a counselor pulled at the edges of his green rubber gloves. Caleb thought of the frost on evergreens in pictures of Norway he had seen on the internet. He felt dizzy and tasted the charcoal in his mouth. The taste was sweet and full of acid. He heard the smack of rubber released from the hand of the man. He said that he had tried to kill himself. The man pressed the screen of a device Caleb had not noticed until that moment. His father and Lydia were anxious to see him, he was told. His father asked him why he'd done this and he had no answer. The next day he was transferred to a nearby facility where he was formally diagnosed with major depressive disorder and not allowed to go outdoors.

He looked at the blue sky through the windows. The day afterward he was put on some capsules that were roughly the same color as the gloves the psychiatric nurse had worn in the emergency room.

Soon his heart beat too quickly and scared him. The psychiatrist, who wore no gloves, told him that most side effects would probably go away or lessen after a few more weeks or months and also that the flutterings might be related to the presence on the unit of a blonde girl two or three years older than Caleb. She had an aloof manner, freckles, and bulimia. The psychiatrist said that when walking from Meeting Room East to the front door he had seen Caleb drinking juice and watching the girl from the peach vinyl sofa in the lounge. The girl's hair had been half tied back in a loose bun and wisps fell around her face. She was reading an old copy of *Jughead*. Caleb protested that he had not been watching the girl. The doctor ripped a piece of ragged dry skin from the outer edge of his own hand.

When the palpitations got worse the doctor switched Caleb to pale blue tablets. The freckled girl was soon transferred to a specialist eating disorder unit.

When he was able to return to school the other students looked away after they looked at him, so he went around the corner and vaped and missed classes. He tried to keep in touch with his hospital friends, who understood him, but they did not text him back and he did not know if they were okay. He woke up afraid for them in the night. He went back to the hospital and came home again.

The pills were white and blue and green and yellow, they were round or oval. Some split easily between his fingers or his father's fingers and others needed a pill cutter so he could go slowly up to the right dose. He went back to the hospital. He ate chocolate ice cream in styrofoam cups with paper lids. He was afraid to go back to school, where they would laugh at him.

But in his second week back Kenny Vaunt said, Sounds like you've got some stories to tell, and sat with him vaping on the steps of the old church around the corner, and two eighth graders with light blue backpacks saw them and began talking to each other in low voices. Caleb kept his mouth shut about how he'd never liked Kenny and the next day Kimmie Luback and her four best friends saw them in the same spot. Then no one made fun of him, and Beau, who was new that year but had gone to the same camp as Caleb two summers before, started sitting with them too, and at least he was not alone.

They began to take vodka from Beau's parents' freezer. Before long they pooled allowances to buy their own liquor from hairy men in sympathetic bodegas. They brought the drinks to parties and before long even the seniors greeted them warmly, and on Caleb's fifteenth birthday Josh Slit of all people clapped him on the shoulder. When Caleb looked around the room at all the happy and drunk and forgetful faces he thought he was like other people.

The doctors and his father sent him to a hospital called The Tamaracks. Through the sealed window in his small room full of white furniture meant to calm him he watched his father's car drive away. Caleb did not tell the staff there that he drank. He did not tell them about the pills at the parties either, because they looked just like the pills he was supposed to take, and those were not doing much anyway.

When he got back, his father said he had a curfew but for the few months of sophomore year when Caleb was in school he did not pay attention to phones or clocks at night. When he came home around dawn his tearful father made strong statements about trust, and Caleb saw how terrifying his own sadness was. He could do what he wanted and his father still would not stop him, his father was too afraid of the gross sad boy, and who would make it better? The doctors had helped other kids but they could not help him. Soon his father found a baggie of Percocet 5s hidden under the fuzzy leaves of a potted violet.

At Las Palmas-Bridges Caleb made collages with statements like I AM IN CHARGE OF HOW I FEEL. After about six weeks he was allowed to move into a less secure dormitory.

One Thursday he and another boy and a girl decided to find a spot on campus to vape and talk without everyone watching, at least that's what he thought they wanted, so he went with them to the new lodge building, which was under construction and named after some rare weather pattern, and they all sat on the floor. The boy and the girl were almost eighteen and had been hospitalized more times than he had, and so Caleb was the newbie, which was a weird feeling, kind of fun and embarrassing at once, and then the girl and the boy only talked to each other and he was a little annoyed. The boy and girl went together behind a half-built wall covered in Tyvek. He wasn't sure whether or not he should leave so he wandered around the construction site feeling awkward and found a pile of broken glass to play with near the cord of an abandoned drill and then the girl came out from behind the wall and said that she had a way to get Oxycontin. Then on Friday he failed urinalysis and they told his father he was kicked out of the program and that he would have to come get him.

They shouldn't leave drills lying around with all these unhappy people, he told his father, drills and broken glass.

The next day he was supposed to wait for his father and Lydia in the front room. He sat in the red leather armchair and thumbed through books that no one ever read. No one was watching him. Caleb walked out to the street and then to the interstate, and when he called his father two weeks later from the passenger seat of Ellen's Honda on some road outside of Tuscaloosa he would not say what had happened in between and his father had to make a resentful peace with those secret days. You don't understand how crazy you made me, his father said.

Ellen drove him to New York and decided to stay. She told Caleb she wanted to see if she could get anyone to take a look at the movies she made on her smartphone and also to be near him, because he was her best friend.

He downloaded Tinder and added two years to his age because you had to be eighteen to open an account. The next week he went for coffee with a girl called Casey. She asked him about college and he said that actually he was still working on high school. Casey, who was in her first year at Pace, said, Oh, that's cool. She scratched her knee. The coffee shop was quiet except for the sound of a waitress laying a fork on a table. Caleb said that he'd gotten a little behind because he'd had some difficult things to deal with. Again Casey said, Oh. Caleb had not planned on talking about this and wished that he'd come up with something else to say. He watched Casey's manicured hand scratch her knee again.

Are these stools comfortable enough, he said, we could sit somewhere else.

The stools are fine, said Casey.

Caleb said that he'd gotten into pills when he was younger and just not been able to stop, that one thing had led to another, that he'd had to go to rehab. As he was saying it he knew that it was not a story he believed but he had no idea what the real story was. He could have gone back to what happened when he was thirteen but he was not sure how to tell that story either.

So you did the thing where you stand up and say, My name is So-and-so and I'm an addict, said Casey, rapt.

Yeah, he said, I mean, we did a version of twelve-step.

So tell me you're an addict.

My name is Caleb and I'm an addict.

Casey started to laugh.

I'm sorry, she said, I'm so sorry. I know it's bad. So many people nowadays, actually some people I went to school with had the same thing, and I know it's not funny. Actually I had a moment where I thought things were going kind of that way myself.

Really, said Caleb.

Yes. I was sixteen and I got a Vicodin prescription, for something, a little, a minor surgery I had to . . . anyway, I was supposed to take them for pain, but then I started wondering what it would feel like to take more, so I took two at a time. And after a couple of weeks I'd gone through almost the whole month of pills. And I counted that I had just a few left, and I thought, This is not good, and I threw them out.

And then what happened?

I just threw them out, repeated Casey, I flushed them. But I scared myself.

Yeah.

And after that I never forgot it, I never forgot that, you know, I have that in me. She was looking directly at him.

Although she was backlit her green irises were very bright. Caleb was tired.

It was difficult, she said, but I knew if I didn't . . .

She paused once she had said this. She blinked and tilted her head to one side and seemed to be choosing her next words carefully. The sun moved through her bleached hair. Caleb understood that she was telling him something that was very important to her and then she shook her head.

Do you have any tattoos? Casey asked him.

Yes, he said. But he did not elaborate. When she kept asking they went to her dorm room and in the days and weeks that followed, when she texted that she wanted to see him again, then that she didn't understand why he wouldn't reply, then that if *that* was all he'd wanted he should have told her up front, he reminded himself that she had wanted to see the shark on his thigh, the initials at the top of his bicep, the eye on his back.

Whose initials are those? Casey had asked.

I think she was jealous, Caleb told Ellen later, when I told her they were yours.

Do you want me to do you another one?

Yeah. I want a ghost.

Where?

But Ellen never made the ghost.

Over the next few weeks Ellen and Caleb drew pictures and discussed where the ghost could go. Once Ellen suggested that the ghost could go on the left side of his back just below the shoulder blade. There it could look at the eye on his spine.

They can be friends, she suggested.

But the eye on the spine was looking straight out behind

him. They could not make it look back toward the ghost.

Poor ghost, said Ellen. Then she glanced at him, tucked her hair behind her ear, and said, Fuck it, let's go for pizza.

They got slices and sat on a bench under a red awning. As they ate he wanted to tell her to put the ghost on the sole of his foot. When he was barefoot in the house the ghost would be exposed each time he took a step, exposed but almost certainly unnoticed. His father would almost see and almost see again but never pay enough attention. Ellen got sauce on her face and wiped it off and said she was thinking about moving back to Ohio. Then Caleb did not care where the ghost tattoo went.

He pleaded with her and got her to promise to stay in the city at least a while longer. From then he visited her almost every afternoon at the shop where she sold black semi-transparent dresses and dark glitter accessories to depressive thirtysomething women and the occasional teenage girl or twentysomething.

Once when they were alone in the store they made a short video. Ellen filmed while Caleb held lace and silk and tulle dresses up to the window to see what effects they could create with the daylight pouring through. He watched her soft arms. She zoomed in and asked him to overlap the fabrics. The manager came in and told them to stop. Another time Ellen hid her phone and Caleb played a lonely customer.

After Ellen finished work they went for drinks with Kenny and Beau, who had fake IDs now. Caleb ordered soda or sparkling water with lime.

Sparkling water, said Kenny, chuckling. Beau chuckled too.

The lime was important. It made it look like he had gotten

what he wanted or at least more like he might have. To be honest he didn't think a beer would be so bad for him, he didn't really think the way he drank was so far off the way everyone else drank, the only thing was that he was also on all these other pills, the ones he was supposed to be on and also the other stuff, but that didn't necessarily mean anything. Still at the bar he swallowed water because he could not find a way to be sure that he was right.

He wanted to ask, How do you know if you are right about yourself?

But Kenny and Beau would not stop joking about the sparkling water and about how Caleb was doing sophomore year over again. So one night he had a beer, and then he went with them to a party at Kimmie Luback's, where he drank more. Before dawn he came out of the bathroom with a swift and shaky group of new acquaintances and someone he hadn't realized he knew said Man, are you supposed to be doing that?

He did not know.

Caleb has not been to see Ellen at the dress shop since the four months he spent at Grove Acre, even though she was the one who had called his father to say that she did not think that he was okay which was how after too many long conversations he wound up back in the hospital. For a while he was furious with her. Now he sees that you could call that love, what she did, friend love or sibling love maybe but love. And it is true that at least so far the meds they put him on seem better than the old ones. Besides it was Ellen who when he got out talked to her boss who talked to a friend who got him the job at the greeting card store. No one else understood why he would not go back to school.

It'd be so humiliating, he told her. Then he asked if she was still thinking of leaving.

No, she told him. I'm staying in the city.

Caleb wonders if she still drinks with Beau and Kenny now that he does not join them.

This time out of the hospital has to be different. Otherwise he will soon be back there, trying to convince doctors he's stable enough to be allowed on the Group Walk, waiting in line at a medication window where nurses hand him pills in paper cups, trying to make do with the hospital nicotine patch and desperate for his vape pen.

Besides this is better for Ellen, who cannot help that she does not feel what he wishes she did. It was hard the first few times he didn't respond to her messages but now he just doesn't open the chat and the hurt is lodged somewhere in him, cold and not bad so long as he keeps his mind busy.

Some days when he gets home from the greeting card store his father is still at the university. More often he is sitting in his armchair near the entrance of the living room, reading a book and having an evening whisky, gray hair flopping forward in the lamplight. Often now he reads with his phone in his lap or tucked between cushions in the armchair. Every so often he puts the book down and checks his phone and says, I don't think I can read like I used to be able to read before these things.

They optimize the colors on the screen, says Caleb. They up the contrast.

Sometimes when Caleb enters the room his father is reading something on his phone and has forgotten all about the book, which lies open and overturned on the sofa or the chair arm or is splayed between the armchair and the floor, one cover on each surface and stray pages hanging between them. When his father sees him he puts the phone away and says hello with enthusiasm and unacknowledged nerves and every possible hope for Caleb's future.

How was your day?

Caleb's day was generally fine, which is enough these days.

Next his father asks what he's been up to. When Caleb responds his father watches him too carefully, and Caleb knows he is collecting his words and the movements of his face. I ate a great burger, I want to see the new BoJack Horseman, I'm trying to get into running, I'm not playing Journey because I'm into Plague Inc now. All of these are parsed, turned over, opened like oysters. It is exhausting to be with his father, who cannot see how greedy he is.

He can never ask his father, What is going to happen to me, because his father would try to open that too.

Last Caleb heard Kenny was having an alright time at Wesleyan and Beau was finding NYU okay. Maybe by the time Caleb goes back to high school everyone who knows him will have graduated and then the strange and lumbering boy can be ignored. Alone in his room he reads Reddit for hours but never finds anyone who can tell him what is wrong with him.

One day last year, after he had started missing school again but before he was sent to Grove Acre, he was in his room when he began to cry. Because he believed that he was alone in the apartment he did not try to stop or to be quiet. Then through his sobs and gasps he heard the door open. He imagines now that Lydia's face showed first alarm and then compassion but he can't be sure because when she opened the door his eyes were pressing against his wet pillow. He wiped his face on the sheet. By the time he sat up her expression was wary.

She watched him and came to his bed and lay next to him. He put his face on her chest. He was still crying but was no longer loud and could take slow breaths. Her sweater was navy. Her breast was soft under his cheek. Did something happen, she asked, and he said no, and they stopped speaking. The light from the window was pale and bright as scanner light. It moved over the bed slowly and over their bodies but did not reach the foot of the bed before they got up.

Do you miss Lydia? his father asks one evening.

Caleb says he does not know.

I hope it's not too hard on you that I've asked her to stay away, says his father. I don't know why she's taking it like this.

Caleb says that he understands. His father says, I appreciate that.

In the kitchen Diane splits leeks lengthwise down the center. She puts them in a bowl of water and when Caleb asks why she tells him she has to get the sand out. He watches her run her thumb across the close-packed leaves of the vegetables' cut hearts. Her divorce was difficult so she knows just how it is but she didn't have anyone to talk about it with. She was all alone.

Chapter Six

Here's to living together.

Jane raises her glass of red wine and holds it in the air, waiting, her brown eyes bright and eager. Lydia raises her glass too.

Cheers, she says, and they both drink.

As they go to sit on the futon Lydia notes the ratty orange armchair. On the far wall the blue paint is flaking. But there are hardwood floors. The alcove kitchen is appealing in its way. And Jane Brent, a paralegal from Westchester, seems very kind. In any case Lydia needed a room.

Jane asks earnest questions. Lydia says she thinks she's settling in fine so far, thanks. She looked in Windsor Terrace because of the park. Before this she was staying in hotels and before that with Tom. Jane furrows her brow and nods in sympathy when Lydia tells her the relationship just burnt itself out, no one can account for why, most of her stuff is still in storage.

Jane tucks a loose strand of dark hair behind her ear and says, That must have been so painful. I'm so sorry.

Lydia takes a sip of her drink so as not to recoil.

But moving to a smaller place can be good, Jane continues, think of it like Konmari. Have you heard of Konmari?

I think so, says Lydia.

I'll have to lend you the book.

Jane starts explaining the method with obvious enthusiasm: you touch all of the things you own and if they don't spark joy you get rid of them, though she forgets what Marie Kondo says about storage, probably it's not ideal but you can make some allowances for your particular situation. Tidying is supposed to be personal. Lydia smiles back. It feels good to smile with another person. Jane, practically a child, has nothing real to organize or get rid of and does not even know it. Tonight Lydia may as well pretend it's the same for her. The boxes of things in storage are nothing but a few old shirts and towels and not her real life which is supposed to still be happening. Soon she can't remember the last time she stayed up so late and says so, and Jane says she can't either, and Lydia says, What, what are you again, 23, and Jane says, 21.

21?

I skipped a couple of years in school, so.

Oh, so you're a genius.

No, no, no. Jane bites her lip.

Aren't you up late all the time at your age?

I had a misspent youth, Jane says.

Oh really, Lydia says. Tom, the ex I mentioned, his son also had some problems.

Jane blinks.

With drugs, Lydia says. But he's better now. He seems to be. Also depression, though, he has depression. It's a medical problem. But also separately, or I guess because of that, I don't know, anyway he got into drugs, I think he had some friends that were not great for him.

Oh no, says Jane, misspent like I didn't do anything like that. I never even went out in college, never.

Oh, so you mean misspent because you didn't.

Yeah.

Jane tells Lydia about high school classics club, honor society, PSATs, SATs, a production of *Oklahoma!*, college debate.

Who were you? Lydia asks. In *Oklahoma!*.

I was just in the chorus. I wanted to try something different, I had never sung before, but I was terrible.

It must have been fun.

No, you don't understand, I was terrible.

All I remember from that play is when they go *OOO-kla-homa*. I wish I'd done something like that when I was a kid.

Lydia tries to imagine her mother in the back of some school theater. The tipsy darkness of the kitchen makes the spotlight and its dream almost possible. She takes a large gulp from her glass and the texture of the wine strikes her as oily. She drains the glass and puts it on the counter.

It was so embarrassing, Jane says, and then I ran back to honor society and never thought again about leaving.

So that's it, that's your misspent youth.

Exactly, says Jane. She finishes her own glass and gets the bottle out of the fridge.

You're still young. Your life now is youth.

Let's misspend my youth. She giggles and turns away to pour the wine.

I can't keep track, says Lydia.

Jane laughs harder.

Was that funny? Lydia asks. I'm not funny at all.

Jane puts the bottle down on the counter and slides down the front of the cabinetry, gasping. When she can speak again, she says, I don't know how, but she starts to laugh again before she can tell Lydia what it is that she doesn't know how to do. She catches her breath, stands, and pours more wine.

They drink in silence. Then Jane starts to sing. Her voice is reedy and faltering.

Don't throw bouquets at me.

What?

It's a song. It's from *OOO-klahoma!*.

Was that your song?

No, remember, I was in the chorus. We're misspending my youth, you're going to help me. *There's a bright golden haze on the meadow!*

The next morning Jane shields her eyes from the light and Lydia scrambles eggs in their kitchen.

Lydia and Tom were supposed to get a dog. They would have let Caleb name him. Or her. Whatever sex of dog.

It or she or he would have had red ears. It would have lain under her desk, curled up at her feet, as she worked. When she had to go to an appointment she would have carried it on the subway. Evenings it would have begged for dinner scraps. Tom would have loved it. That desk isn't hers anymore.

Now she works in her new bed or in the ugly orange armchair or hunched over at Jane's coffee table, because she wanted to be carefree, because she wanted to see what it was like to live without Tom, who thinks that she is so irrational it is not worth speaking to her. For the time being, he said, only for a while.

If they had gotten a dog when Caleb was younger and if she had let Caleb name the animal then and if it had been obvious that she loved him and it and all of them, their family, their evenings, Tom might not have left her. He might have loved her or felt guilty. But then she did not want pets.

Soon Lydia spends most of her evenings with Jane. Together they cook and drink wine.

Jane tells Lydia about the man who lived in her room until recently. He was a musician and bartender who called himself Capo, short for Christian. He took this name from the tension device for guitarists and was continually frustrated, Jane likes to say after a drink or two, by any unknowing delivery man who pronounced his name as if he were a figure in an organized crime syndicate or in a film inspired by the same. After another drink she would imitate his outrage.

Obviously it's Cay-po. Not Caaaapo. Caaaaaaaapo.

Jane's voice descends over the long A. Lydia feels a smile at the corners of her mouth and wants to allow it to spread.

Christian would pace the hallway as he went on at length about his indignation. Jane put on her earrings and repeated Mmhm.

It's just, she says, C A P O *does* spell Caaaapo, not to everyone but to a lot of people.

In the morning they drink coffee and Jane says she ought to clarify that Capo is very intelligent and hardworking and that it was not so bad when he and his girlfriend took over every surface in the tiny kitchen to make seitan. It takes a very long time to make seitan, says Jane, there is a lot of kneading. Things need to ferment.

After a month or two the girlfriend and Capo broke up. Jane was made aware of this development by the swift disappearance of seitan dough from the countertop and by the argument she heard through her bedroom wall late one night. The girlfriend, she gathers, asked Christian to Venmo her three hundred dollars to pay for his half of their abortion. Christian objected. The shouting was too much and without the girlfriend Christian sulked and snapped and Jane is lucky the lease is in her name. She refills their glasses.

It's funny, how you grow up with someone – like Christian – and you figure why not give living with them a shot, what's there to lose, and it's awful, and then you meet someone through a website and it's great. It's wonderful, living with you.

Grow up with someone? asks Lydia.

Jane drinks and says, His parents are friends with my parents.

Swipe for me, says Jane. Be me for a minute and swipe.

I don't know, says Lydia.

You know you should open a Tinder account. You should get out there. Why don't you?

Jane squeezes Lydia's hand.

Oh no, says Lydia, I don't think that . . .

Hail hits the windowpane. Lydia says that she's thinking of moving away from packaging and focusing only on logos.

Lydia wonders how or when or if Tom will make contact with her.

She used to greet his friends with kisses on the cheek. She reciprocated dinners, sent and received thoughtful gifts tied with bright ribbons. She had come to believe in the ribbons.

Now none of Tom's friends call or text. She wonders how he told them that it was no longer necessary to pretend they liked her. Evenings stretch out before her like unset tables, light slipping over dust and varnish and glossing no promise of company. Liz does not text either. Liz is busy.

Jane goes home to Westchester for the holidays. Lydia rings in the New Year alone in the apartment.

In February Jane will be twenty-two. Lydia says that they should have some of Jane's friends over to celebrate.

It means so much to me, says Jane, that you'd suggest that.

Two weeks before the party they go to a craft store to buy festive cushions made of imitation silk. If they put these on the floor they will have enough seating and can serve dinner at the coffee table. Everyone will be able to eat as long as they all mind their elbows.

Jane puts a cheap green cushion with yellow trim in their shopping cart and says she wants to decorate the room with white Christmas tree lights and baby's breath in jam jars.

At Tom's there is a long dining table and around it eight sleek chairs with tapered legs. There is a bedroom where another woman may by now sleep or Tom perhaps sleeps now in the bedroom of the woman in some other part of the city.

Lydia asks Jane if they should get all green cushions or green and purple or green and purple and blue or throw in orange and use all the color options provided by the manufacturer.

I say all green. This trim's coming off. I was wondering, should we use the armchair or will that be awkward? I mean if other people are on the floor.

Jane holds a yellow thread between two fingers.

You should sit in the armchair, says Lydia, it's your birthday. Put that one back in the pile and get another.

A cat says, HAPPY BIRTHDAY TO AN EXCEPTIONAL YOUNG LADY. A big-lipped striped bass says, Age is like beer. You're still here. Catch a great one!

Some of the cards are for family: TO MY WIFE, TO MY HUSBAND, TO MY DAUGHTER. Others abound with affectionate platitudes and depictions of cakes and champagne glasses. On some the black outlines of flowers sit over but do not meet blotches of weak floral color. Some cards are embossed in gold or bronze or copper or silver and some are blind embossed.

Lydia has been to CVS and Rite Aid and three small

stationery shops. She cannot find a card she likes. At least she's got Jane's present. And probably the cat card is good enough. She looks at the display of paper calendars and selects one for herself.

Caleb is working at a stationery store. She can't remember its name but she thinks it's somewhere in the East Village, or was it the West Village.

She'll buy the cat card just in case. She could keep trying for something better.

Before she leaves Paper Source Lydia takes out her phone, opens Safari, and searches for *village stationery store*, but the store where Caleb works is not Village Stationery, it's not Greenwich Letterpress, it has some witty name. She keeps scrolling down.

Contact Paper. That might be it. She tries to avoid slush on the subway steps and takes the F into the city.

At Contact Paper a woman slightly older than Lydia sits behind the register. She wears berry lipstick and has a single line tattooed around her wrist.

Let me know if you need any help.

Thanks, says Lydia, looking quickly at the cards and then around the room. She picks up and puts down pencils, turns over in her hands staplers shaped like whales. On a test piece of paper she tries out stamps that make letters and purple wreaths. She doesn't hear any movement in the back of the store.

There's no one else here.

I think I'm going to keep looking, Lydia says.

No worries, says the owner. Lydia puts her gloves on. A bell rings as she leaves.

She walks east for no particular reason. The days are short

now and the sun is almost down. Near Astor Place she sees a large silver Koons rabbit in the lobby of a plate-glass building. She keeps walking. The lights are off in one small shop but she can see cards in the window.

Dance Card, the sign reads.

Chapter Seven

At some point Caleb will have to go home to his father but for now he can sit at this bar and pretend Ellen is on her way to meet him. He still won't go to the real bar where she might be with Beau and Kenny but at this cleaner sleeker one he can imagine himself old and healthy enough to meet her like a normal person or to meet other new people or to have a drink after work. It's okay for him to be here as long as he doesn't order alcohol or talk to anyone. He's probably annoying the staff by ordering just his seltzer but as long as there are empty seats he's not taking a place that could have gone to someone spending more money.

He zips and unzips his hoodie. A staff member lowers the lights.

At a nearby table for two a young woman is beginning to cry, is saying to a young man I'm not the sort of person who. The young man is tapping the table with the long edge of a thin stack of cards, business or credit or membership. Caleb doesn't want to make the couple feel awkward or to feel awkward himself so on his phone he reads a post about the latest advances in prosthetic limbs. Soon a prosthetic hand will be able to tell the difference between soft and hard when, for example, it is squeezing between its thumb and other fingers a mattress or a sponge or a stone or a boiled egg.

A banner flashes up on his phone. Lydia says that she is sorry if it is not her place but she just saw him through the window in a bar. Is everything all right?

Yes, Caleb writes, everything is fine.

You're not drinking, are you?

Come see if you're so worried.

Caleb is reading about the strong chance of losing his retail job to AI although hopefully by the time that becomes likely he won't be working retail any longer but who knows and also the strong chance that no one will drive any longer because of AI. He wanted to learn someday so that he could drive if he and Ellen went on another road trip but now they don't speak although that's his own fault.

Hello.

Caleb looks up from his phone and sees his father's ex-girlfriend, or his ex-somewhat-stepmother, or his one-time-stepmotherish friend.

Oh, hi, he says. Look, obviously I'm not drinking, I'm underage.

She rolls her eyes and sits.

So no vodka in that, she says, pointing at his drink.

If you don't trust me then try it.

Of course I trust you, she says, but she pulls the glass toward herself across the square table.

As she is putting her lips to the straw he asks if she lives near here now.

I live in Brooklyn, don't you know.

Don't you know, she hears herself say. When have I ever said that before, never, who said that, listen to me. Listen to me.

I don't think of you as a Brooklyn person, says Caleb.

What does that mean?

I just don't. He shrugs.

She leans forward and says, Well, I guess that's fair. I guess I can see how that would happen. But nowadays, I mean, well, what's a Brooklyn person. I'm hungry, are you hungry?

She takes the menu from its place in the rack behind bottles of hot sauce and salt and pepper shakers. She opens it and lifts it slightly. She reads the list of salads. Is he looking at her forehead, is he inspecting the faint lines that run across it? She lowers the menu so he can see her whole face.

No, he says.

What?

I'm not hungry.

All right, she says, anyway I was picking up a birthday present and then I was looking for a card just now, for my roommate, but I didn't find anything. I think I'll have a burger.

Sounds good, says Caleb, clearing his throat.

Sure you don't want anything?

I'm sure, says Caleb. Lydia waves down the waiter and orders.

You'll have to have some of my fries. Anyway, my roommate asked for this candle, which was hard to find, but I found it, and now I can't find a good card.

The specific candle is said to smell like a specific kind of grass, a very exact and fragrant prairie. According to the blog that Jane showed to Lydia this scent is different from all other grasslike candle scents. Why is he so quiet. Below the table Lydia crosses her ankles and rubs one foot against the other.

You're still at home?

Yeah, he says. She waits for him to tell her about his father but instead he asks, Can I see it?

What?

The candle.

Lydia reaches down into her bag and takes out the white cardboard box. She holds it up in one hand.

Open it, says Caleb.

Lydia hesitates. I don't want to mess up the present.

Just open the top.

Lydia places the box on the table, with two fingers presses the small flap and draws it out. At the edges of the lid and of the flap itself and of the slot from which this small tongue emerges the brown interior layer of corrugation is visible. Lydia lifts the lid. She removes an ivory insert of shaped card and tilts the box. Now from above Caleb can see the O of the amber glass and the pale wax inside and the ready clean wick at the center.

I don't want to take it all the way out, says Lydia, I think it might mess up the box if I take it out and put it back.

Caleb smells the candle.

What's it supposed to be?

What does it smell like to you?

Grass.

It's a prairie, apparently, says Lydia, closing the box again. Some kind of special one.

Caleb runs one finger along the edge of their table. What kind?

Lydia checks the label.

Summer Prairie.

You know a summer prairie's not a kind of prairie, says Caleb, it's just a normal prairie in the summer.

You're making fun of me.

No!

But Lydia can see the corners of his mouth twitch. The waiter puts the burger and fries down in front of her.

That was fast, she says, pushing the fries toward Caleb. He takes two of them, puts them in his mouth, and eats. She watches. What do you know about prairies, anyway. Have you ever even seen a prairie?

I'm not sure.

I don't think you have, says Lydia. Anyway there are a lot of different extracts, in this candle, to get the scent right. Plant extracts. I read about it online. She picks up the burger and bites into it.

Mmhm.

Stop it! She wipes her mouth on a napkin.

Okay okay, he says. You know we have birthday cards where I work, why didn't you look there?

I didn't think of it.

Yeah, I work at this place called Dance Card.

I told you I forgot. Anyway, it was closed.

We close at six. Over Lydia's shoulder Caleb notices that the crying girl and her uncomfortable boyfriend are leaving the bar.

Early.

I'm just telling you the policy of the store. As a card professional.

Mmm. She chews and swallows, then asks, How's your father?

Fine, he says. He watches her jaw work and waits for her to ask more. She swallows again and takes another sip of his drink.

Finish it, he hears himself say, and then I can find you a card.

Don't you have friends to see or something?

Ouch, says Caleb. Seriously, let's go to a store, there's this place I know called Contact Paper if you don't mind a walk. I think it's open till eight.

I don't know that one, she says. Let's try it.

They don't talk much while Lydia finishes eating and pays for her food and their drinks. They stand up and put their coats on. He fumbles with his zipper and tells her not to help and pulls a flap of Gore-Tex away from the teeth with one hand until the closure works. She's watching. She pushes in her chair and he follows her out of the bar.

Together, quietly, they walk. Caleb has his hands in his pockets and Lydia grabs his shoulder when she starts to slip on black ice.

Lydia enters the shop first and hopes that the woman with the berry lipstick won't say, Hi again, or, You're back, or anything else that would tip Caleb off that she was here only a couple of hours ago.

The woman says, Oh, hi.

Oh hi doesn't mean anything, thinks Lydia. She turns to Caleb and asks, So how have you been, really, how's it going? The woman at the register looks down at her phone and pretends not to listen.

Caleb says he's fine, it's all going fine.

They look at cards with pugs on them, with frogs on them, with flowers and geometric designs, with sayings and blanks inside.

Caleb asks what Jane likes.

She's nice, Lydia says. And she can't sing.

Caleb throws his head back and smiles.

What, says Lydia, what's funny?

She's made him smile. She made him smile earlier too, with the information about the smell of prairies.

I mean, what does she like, like is she into music or interior decorating or . . .

Interior decorating?

Whatever, you know. He scratches his head. His hair is longer than it was the last time she saw him. She watches the movement of the new blond inches, watches how the locks fall when his hand leaves them.

I think really she likes people, says Lydia. Behind Caleb, at the back of the store, a man in a green parka picks out a pencil with pink feathers on its end and places it in a wire basket.

Caleb turns away from her and toward the card display. She looks at the back of his shoulders, looks up toward the back of his head.

And organization, she says helplessly, and strings of white lights, and flowers.

How quickly she spoke, and how slowly he turns back around.

How about this one, says Caleb. He shows her a card that has on the front several champagne glasses and the outlines of girls in dresses. She notices his fingers on the thin clear film packaging.

No.

Why not?

Isn't it a bit vapid.

It's a birthday card.

What's it say inside?

He turns the card over to read the back.

This says it says Happy Birthday.

I don't know. I don't think I like it.

It's not for you.

Caleb passes the card to Lydia, who runs her thumb over the plastic. She can see but cannot touch gold foil, can feel the indentations of white ruptures in the metallic gleam, indications of bubbles.

Later, in her room, Lydia takes Jane's birthday card out of her bag and sets it down flat on the dresser. She takes her earrings out, first the left, then the right, and puts them down next to it.

I feel better, he said.

As they left the store Caleb said, I'm glad you came and found me, I feel better, it was nice to have something to do.

A project, said Lydia, smiling up at him.

And then he got on the subway and went uptown, back to Tom, maybe to Tom and Diane.

Hello. I hope you and your father are doing well. Do you want to come to Jane's party? This Friday. I thought it might be good for you to meet some new people.

Lydia looks at what she has written. She deletes the part about his father. She adds that it was great to see him, adds the time of the party, deletes how great it was to see him. She presses send.

Chapter Eight

When Caleb was small Tom and Lydia ordered a vanilla cake for his birthday. It had strawberry icing. He liked it so much that the next year Lydia went back to the store and asked for the same cake again. In those days she wanted inexhaustibly for Tom to like her. He loved her. He smiled when she came home with the white cardboard box, when she untied its red-and-white string and lifted the lid. He looked in.

Caleb will love it, he said.

When it was time Lydia put the cake on a plate. She peeled the cardboard backing off of the clear plastic casing in which yellow and blue and pink and white candles lay. One by one she picked these up with two fingers, then pressed the blunt ends into the frosting. She felt the crumb give and pushed some candles further, pulled others back to make them the same height. She hoped that she had spaced them evenly. She lit them all. Caleb clapped. Tom sang off key.

Caleb grew older and decided he liked neither vanilla nor strawberry. They repeated the performance with a chocolate cake from the same bakery. Each year that followed they got the same one.

Last year Caleb spent his birthday in the hospital. The staff may have given him a cupcake. Lydia can't remember if she asked. She must have asked. This year she was in Greece eating baklava and clapping for old dancing men and gagging. Diane carried a cake into her living room. Tom sang.

In Lydia's vision Diane's cake is homemade.

Lydia flips through cookbooks. Caleb will tell his father that everyone loved the cake she made. If he comes, in the end, to the party. He said he would try.

On the morning of the party Lydia wakes up afraid.

The pale hairs of his eyebrows caught the light when he turned his head or leaned forward, for example when he looked at the gift. The bar light caught these hairs, which were golden. Then he leaned back again in his chair.

Violently she sees what a mistake she has made in inviting him. Her eyes tear up. She cannot take it back.

How unfair that he will come see her in her tiny apartment, with peeling paint and her beautiful roommate. Later he'll tell his father about the cushions on the floor, about her bad cake, which will be raw in the center or too dry.

She texts Liz and invites her and apologizes for the late notice. Now she regrets two invitations and so she breathes easier. Caleb can tell his father about the chocolate cake she'll buy this morning. He can raise his eyebrows when she cuts that.

By six-thirty the jars of baby's breath are out on the windowsill and the coffee table. One arrangement sits alone on the kitchen counter. Dips are in small bowls in the refrigerator, and on the shelf above is the cake in its box. Jane has pushed the armchair up to the head of the table. The cheerful cushions are stacked nearby.

When it is almost time for guests to arrive Jane plugs the strands of lights in and Lydia flips the switch to turn the ceiling lights off. Small points of radiance dot the walls and make constellations of the furniture.

We might need a lamp on, says Lydia.

They wait in the glow of the lamp in the corner and of the

tiny bulbs taped everywhere. Before long the doorbell rings and Jane runs to the intercom.

Just coming, she says, and then over her shoulder, It's Dustin and Maria. She rushes out of the apartment and into the stairwell. Lydia opens the fridge and retrieves hummus, tzatziki, and sliced vegetables in cold bowls, which she arranges on the coffee table. Soon she hears a knock on the door and Jane's voice from the other side says, I've locked myself out.

Lydia opens the apartment door.

There is Jane with white flowers in her hair.

Behind her Maria and Dustin, then two men Lydia does not know.

Lydia pours Jane's prosecco first, then five other glasses. She wipes up the spill on the counter and tries not to look at the door. Someone has been promoted and Lydia hears congratulations. People begin to eat carrot sticks.

By now Tom's got new bowls, new glasses, vases, new chairs maybe.

When the buzzer sounds again she says to herself clearly and silently and surgically it is Liz. It is perhaps Liz who has come, although Liz said she was unlikely to make it, tough to get a sitter on such short notice.

Jane returns and introduces Zoe to Dustin and Ryan.

Wait, another Dustin, says Zoe. She pushes her braids away from her face and takes off her parka to reveal a coral blouse with a metallic sheen, then waves across the room to Maria.

Yep, two Dustins, says Dustin of Dustin and Ryan.

The bowl of small tomatoes is empty. Lydia will fill the bowl of small tomatoes.

Zoe knows Connor Favignano from high school, and Ryan knows him from English 205.

Romantic English Lit. He tapped his pencil on the armrest constantly, that's what I remember.

I can't believe he even took that. I didn't think he read.

I mean, constantly, when I say constantly I really mean constantly.

Lydia salts the red vegetables and sees on the microwave clock that it is eight p.m.

Jane says, Your friend's here.

Liz has found a sitter, that must be it.

Will you go let him in?

Oh, says Lydia. Sure.

Slowly, carefully, Lydia walks down the stairs. At the last landing she leans forward.

Caleb is resting his hand on the door. As she approaches she sees his open palm through the plexiglass. She turns the lock. With the door open she does not know what to say.

He says that he likes her shirt.

She says that she also likes his shirt and that she's glad he could make it, she was not sure if his father would allow him to come.

I didn't say exactly where I was going, he says. Besides honestly he can't do anything, he's given up. Also I wasn't sure if I was supposed to bring a present so I got these.

In his left hand he's holding a bunch of orange daylilies.

That's very kind of you, says Lydia.

They should go upstairs. They start up. Lydia is aware of her hand trailing on the bannister and of his steps behind her.

Over her shoulder she says, Sorry about the walk-up.

Sure.

She stops and turns around. You know, I'm actually, uh, I want to take off my shoes for a minute.

All right.

She holds onto the bannister to keep herself steady. He watches her heel come out of the shoe, the arch next. Her toenails are painted jet black. One foot touches the floor and the other starts to lift out of its leather enclosure.

Is he looking at the places where the shoe pinched, the red worn skin.

I can go up faster like this, she says.

Okay.

Just a second.

Sure.

She picks the shoes up. Soon they begin to walk again.

Your feet are getting dirty.

Don't tell anyone.

Before they enter the apartment she leans against the wall to put the shoes back on. As she is sliding the second shoe on she looks up and instantly he looks away.

He's trying not to smile at her, she thinks.

When they enter the apartment Jane is dressing the salad. If Caleb thinks it strange that Lydia introduces him as her friend he does not show it. Later Lydia will explain that she simply didn't want to get into everything at the party, she simply doesn't want to bother explaining her personal life to these young people she doesn't know. How he is like her stepson but he is not. Someone like a stepson but not smiled at her in the stairwell as she leant against a wall. It's simpler not to mention it. It's best not to mention a breakup at a birthday party which is a celebration and anyway they are she supposes sort of like friends now.

Jane introduces herself. Welcome, she says. Caleb says, Happy birthday, and walks across the room to give her the flowers. She puts her nose down into the throat of one lily.

Lydia watches her sniff and raise her head.

Thank you, Jane says.

Caleb says he hopes they do not have a cat.

No, says Jane. There's no cat.

Caleb looks down and scratches his head.

Should we eat? says Lydia.

Jane is still standing at the head of the low coffee table holding the orange lilies.

Let me just put these in water first.

No one speaks as Jane walks to the kitchen. Now Lydia can't see her and can't know if she's shoving her face into orange. Is she shoving her face into petals and sweet scent.

The buzzer rings again. Capo has arrived. Jane invited him earlier in a fit of last-minute compassion but said that she did not expect him to come.

Lydia, can you go, do you mind.

Let me take my shoes off, otherwise I'm so slow on the stairs.

I can go, says Ryan.

Thanks so much, says Lydia, that's so kind of you.

Now Lydia sees the cutting board on the countertop, then green stems on top. Jane's hands press the knife down to cut. The door closes. Someone on the futon says, You'll never guess.

What, says another voice.

I want to show you something on TikTok.

Across the room Caleb is looking closely at the way the lights are taped to the wall.

I did that, says Jane. She brings the vase of flowers out and finds room for it on the windowsill. One bright lily is tucked behind her ear.

Over dinner they talk about the school shooting. Jane looks to the side and says little and twitches with exasperation each time someone adds a new detail.

But they should have known, says Zoe, the shooter posted about it on YouTube last year.

I heard some of these kids died shielding each other, says Capo. With their bodies.

Jane looks plaintively at Lydia and asks her to explain the Tetra Pak thing.

What's Tetra Pak, someone says.

It's a kind of packaging, says Jane, drinks come in it. And they market it as recyclable but apparently it's really not. Lydia, why don't you tell. Tetra Pak is everywhere these days.

I wonder why he picked Valentine's Day, says Ryan to Maria. She hushes him and asks what's happening. Jane says Lydia's going to tell them about Tetra Pak and explains again what it is.

I know what Tetra Pak is, says Maria, and resumes eating.

Her husband covers his smile with one hand, then looks at his watch.

You wear a watch? Caleb asks, incredulous. Dustin looks up coolly. Caleb looks down and away, leans forward in the armchair with his elbows on his knees, cracks his knuckles.

Shhh, says Jane, you all want to hear this. She claps her hands.

Wait, says Zoe, scrolling, I want to make sure I was right about how many people died.

Please don't do that right now, says Jane, and Zoe shrugs and puts her phone in her pocket.

Lydia looks around the low table. The faces of Jane's friends wear expressions of polite and skeptical attention. Caleb looks back at her. Maybe it's all the tiny lights that make his pupils look so big, his skin so radiant. These are unusual lighting conditions.

Well, she says, crossing her legs, Tetra Pak is made of three layers: paperboard, aluminum, and plastic.

Dustin shakes the wrist with the watch on it as if to relieve a cramp or get rid of something.

To remove the paper you have to heat the whole thing in a huge tank of water. But it takes a tremendous amount of resources, you need the water and also a lot of energy to heat it up. It has to get pretty hot. And most places don't even have the facilities to do this, which is why even if the consumer puts Tetra Pak in recycling it normally gets sent to landfill.

Across the room a strand of lights goes out. Jane excuses herself to go fix it.

Then you have this problem that you have a plastic layer and a metal layer. And they can't be separated at all, which is a shame because aluminum and plastic can each be recycled into many different products. But in this case you have to find uses where someone wants a polymer, metal and plastic together, even though there's not a lot of demand for that.

Lydia can hear Jane fumbling with the plug and wires.

Only cement, and some housing materials. Anyway, that's the gist of it.

Caleb puts his fork down and leans forward in the armchair.

Why is no one speaking, she wonders.

She wipes the palms of her hands on her jeans and wishes they could talk about something else, anything that would make Caleb pick his fork back up and eat and look away. She starts to speak quickly.

And those products you can make them into, the products that are made from polymer, are generally not recyclable. It's what we call downcycling, you recycle something into a product that will go to landfill, unlike glass packaging or some plastics which are more sustainable. Glass is the best. But Tetra Pak has, the company has very successfully made a big PR thing about the idea that it's recyclable, and so it spreads and spreads, and also because it's easy to ship, it can be shipped flat.

The small lights in the corner come back on.

So it's not recyclable at all in the end, says Maria.

It is theoretically completely recyclable, Jane replies. Caleb looks up at her as she passes. Would anyone like more wine, she says. Or soda? She looks at Caleb. He shifts in his seat.

Glass is the best, what an inane thing to say.

Theoretical, says Maria, see how much oxygen we get from the theoretical Amazon, or how many polar bears can live in the theoretical Arctic.

Yes, Lydia says, I would like some more.

Ryan says that he thinks that the milk that they buy comes in Tetra Pak.

Recycling's a myth anyway, says Capo. So is this really so different.

I think I met you before, Zoe says to him, but you had a beard. Is that possible?

It's not a myth, says Jane.

I haven't had a beard for a few years, actually I'm thinking of growing it back.

But is this packaging really worse or not, says Dustin of Dustin and Ryan, when you consider that you are saving, right, on the fuel emissions from shipping it flat, because you can fit more other things on the boat or truck or whatever. I mean, we like our oat milk.

We love it, says Ryan, and it's also better for the environment. So it just seems like there are trade-offs.

It's a lie, says Lydia. The whole thing's a lie. She can't say why she's been so stupid all her life. She can't say how she wound up in this cut-rate planetarium, being looked at and looked away from and thinking about glass.

It's such a shame, Maria says.

It *is* a shame, says Zoe. She looks up and leans back.

Oh gosh. Jane clasps her hands. Oh please don't rehash the primary again, please not on my birthday.

What? Ryan lets go of Dustin's hand and sits up.

They have this ongoing argument, says Maria's Dustin, about Bernie Sanders. I stay out of it.

He throws his hands up.

It's just, says Zoe, if you don't actually want progress then why are you even upset, if you continue to vote for this situation.

I didn't vote for this.

It's a shame, Ryan says, that people aren't more forward-thinking, but that's the truth, they just aren't.

Exactly, Maria says, Bernie would have lost. He would have.

Ryan raises his eyebrows.

Why isn't it called Tri Pak? asks Caleb. Paper, plastic, metal.

His eyes are bright and curious. When he was sick they were so dull. Lydia is proud of herself for inviting him, and then she feels as if she wants to shudder but can't, not in front of everyone.

It's six layers total, actually, she says, if you count the adhesives, and the coating. Excuse me. She stands up and reaches for a dirty plate.

I'll clear, says Maria. Seeing as I'm sure you've got other things to attend to.

What do you mean, says Lydia slowly. Then Jane gives a

coy smile and hunkers down in her seat, and Lydia says, Just kidding, and heads to the kitchen. She takes the white cake box out of the fridge and unties the blue-and-white cotton string. She can hear Jane say that six is still not four. Maria puts the dishes in the sink. Together she and Lydia put the cake on a plate, arrange the yellow candles and light them. Caleb and Jane are debating the name Hex Pak.

By the way, says Zoe, looking at her phone, it's seventeen, the number of people who died in the shooting.

Shhh, Lydia says. Maria walks across the room and turns off the lamp in the corner.

The next morning Lydia has almost finished breakfast when Jane walks into the living room and smells the lilies again.

Do you think Caleb had a nice time?

Lydia has almost finished her breakfast. She says he seemed to enjoy himself.

I'm so glad you invited him.

Sure, Lydia says, bringing her plate over to the sink. She turns on the faucet and begins to rinse off the undercooked jellylike bit of egg white she could not bring herself to eat.

Thank you so much for my party, says Jane. Thank you so much.

She wraps her arms around her roommate with startling enthusiasm. Lydia holds the plate too high and at the wrong angle and water sprays both women.

Sorry I couldn't make it, Liz texts later. When Lydia doesn't respond she calls, and Lydia answers and says it's no big deal. Liz doesn't know Jane so none of this is a big deal.

Was it nice?

Yes.

Who came?

A bunch of Jane's college friends. Nice kids.

By the way, Liz said, remember the kid I told you about? The kid with no teeth. In Phoebe's class.

Yes?

Liz tells Lydia that the boy with no teeth choked to death.

Apparently, she says, he put a battery into his mouth to feel the cold metal. That's what they think, anyway.

That's bad luck, says Lydia.

Yeah but you don't leave batteries lying around. If you have small kids. Any small children, let alone with a health issue like that. Utterly preventable.

A tragedy, says Lydia. Across the street a man is standing on top of a house. So basically, Lydia continues, watching the man take large steps up the roof's slope and past the chimney, the teeth didn't matter anyway. The fact that he had no teeth, it didn't actually matter.

Chapter Nine

Jane comes into Lydia's room and sits on the bed. Her eyes are bashful and animated.

Caleb's followed me on Instagram, she says. And Snapchat.

All right, says Lydia.

Her phone is on the night table. The phone, facedown, seems to pull her nerves toward it, demands constant attention to the silence in which Tom does not text, does not call, does not say that he heard that the party was wonderful, that Caleb had such a nice time. Once in a while the phone does make a noise, or her mind or some nearby quiet friction makes her think the phone might have vibrated. Then all of the nerves of her skin seem to wriggle, to want to burrow further into her body, to hide in the solar plexus and knot themselves together in perfect darkness. She tells herself she does not truly want to hear from Tom, and then she checks the phone. It is never him. She tells herself she did not want to hear.

By now she is used to the quick sad tinge and to the words she repeats to herself.

In the week since the party a new disappointment scares her. She does not want Caleb to text either, she says to herself.

How awful that he sat so close to her, how awful that Jane told him to take the armchair. She insisted on it. Lydia should not have invited him.

What is Jane still waiting for, lounging on Lydia's mattress. How vile she is.

But I, you know, I have no way to see him, he hasn't made plans and I don't want to ask.

You should ask, says Lydia. Why does he need to be the one who asks.

The line of visitors proceeds slowly up the gray stone steps. Caleb passes the brass doors and tells the security guards he has no bag to open on their plastic table.

In the lobby eager museumgoers shove past one another. Tourists stand at the foot of the giant dark stone pharaoh with the broken face. There was no real reason to say no when Jane suggested coming here, he likes texting with her and for a week or so they had a Snapstreak going, but now he wants to hide behind the group of frustrated tourists reading maps near a statue of a helmeted woman. He scratches the back of his neck and walks around the lobby. He sees the entrance to the Egyptian section where he went as a child and where he brought Ellen last year. If he gets better enough to talk to her and if he can handle the embarrassment of getting in touch after so long he'll remind her of the day they spent squeezing past children in a transported stone temple and maybe she'll accept his apology.

Under a gaggle of hot pink blossoms there's brown hair on the back of a head angled down. On his way over he elbows someone by accident and turns back to say sorry. Someone behind him and to the right speaks quickly in a language he does not understand.

Jane looks up when he comes close. She asks if he got the message that she'd be under the flowers, says that she wasn't sure he'd find her, realized that of course there are four vases of flowers, which should have been obvious, two carved into the stone wall of the lobby on either side of its entrance, two flanking the opening onto the staircase opposite, so which would she be at, how was he to know. She thought of texting again. Then again she wasn't sure she should say she'd be at the information desk. It has so many sides.

He shoves his hands in his pockets and says, Well, I found you.

She blushes and looks away. Caleb wishes he understood what he's done.

Jane reaches into her pocket and pulls out two white slips of paper.

I got our tickets.

She peels a square sticker off of one ticket and presses it onto his chest. Her eyes avoid his.

Thank you.

She puts her own sticker on quickly and says how about European painting to start. There's something she wants to show him.

Okay, he says.

This painting is one of the most important in the collection, apparently, says Jane. I read that it shows the beginning of the Renaissance style, which is more naturalistic, so in this case it means more affection. As opposed to the medieval style which is more formal and static and wouldn't show them in this kind of intimate moment. In the middle of an interaction.

Caleb's father taught him about this painting and he said the same thing. The virgin looks down at the child, the child reaches up to tug on her veil. This shows a new way of thinking about pictures or religion or time. There's gold behind the figures. Mary's cheeks are pink but her eyes look empty to him.

Do you think she looks bored?

No, says Jane, no, bored? She loves her baby, it's a loving gaze.

His father has always said the same thing. It's a calm, loving portrayal, Caleb. He bets if he brings Ellen to see this painting she'll say, Mary looks fucking miserable.

It's beautiful, he says, without looking at Jane.

And it is, though he can't explain why. The woman's eyes are beautiful, even if she's bored. And he does like Jane, generally. Nothing should be wrong but he does not know what to do.

Look at the thumb, he says, because she's waiting, she's clearly waiting for him to say or do something, I think it's the thumb, where the baby grabs the fabric you can see one big finger.

Somehow he's pleased her much more than he meant to. He studies the painting carefully. He keeps his face blank. The air around their faces is humid with her tenderness. Somehow he feels he's lied, although he only said, Look at the thumb.

He coughs and says, Let's keep walking.

Later, near a painting of a woman in a gold dress, Jane says, That's great, isn't it, and reaches out her hand to grab his. She does not reach far enough and grasps just the knuckles of his middle and index fingers between her thumb and forefinger.

He lets his hand fall out of hers. She touches her face. Together they look at the little paper plaque on the wall.

The woman in the painting is Salome. They step back and look at her. She has a leopard-skin rug at her feet and a large round metal platter on her lap.

Do you think that platter is for the head of John the Baptist? asks Jane.

Caleb can see Salome's inner thigh through flimsy gold fabric. I guess so, he says.

I can't tell, Jane says that evening, I can't tell how it went. Do you think.

What? Lydia asks.

Do you think maybe he's a bit young for me?

I mean. No. No, I wouldn't say so.

He's. How old is he again?

Um, I think he's twenty.

Lydia knows he is nineteen.

Right, says Jane, that's what I thought. I don't know, he just seems like he's not very assertive.

He's shy.

Maybe he just doesn't like me.

A hushing joy opens to light and just as quick closes itself. Lydia will not look there.

I'm sure he likes you, and she hears herself sound loud and strained, I'm sure he likes you. I think you should ask him again.

No!

Because he's younger, because he's younger you have to take control. You have to realize he's younger.

The week passes quickly. Lydia makes mistakes at work and needs to redo things.

She opens Illustrator, closes the window, breathes in. She goes for a walk. Is this a form of grief? Her clothing's tight. She wants a drink of water.

Jane says, You seem tense. Why so tense?

Lydia downloads Tinder, Bumble, OkCupid, makes profiles and swipes, answers questions. Jane sees her on her phone and says, I think it's great that you're doing this.

She wonders if she'd see him on any of these apps if she expanded the age limits.

Tom's never used any of these. Tom's never had to.

Slowly she's getting over Tom.

On Sunday morning he gets up early to go jogging. He counts his breaths and matches them to his steps and loses track of the numbers. When he starts to feel a stitch he has to go back to walking. After a few minutes he speeds up again and tries to figure out which part of his foot hits the ground first. He promises himself that he'll jog every day and that if he does he'll get better. He watches other runners pass him and sees how easy their pace is.

When he stops to rest he has a text from Kenny, who says to call him. Caleb does not want to talk to him and no one calls anyone anymore. He is running again when the phone rings and then the phone rings again. Caleb stops and answers. Kenny says someone has found Ellen dead in the park.

There was nothing anyone could do, says Kenny. She came over to Kimmie's late last night and went into the bedroom by herself without anyone exactly noticing. When he went to check on her she was slumped over in the corner. He wiped vomit from the side of her face. She was not breathing.

Wait, says Caleb, wait, I don't get it, you said they found her in the park?

Kenny says that they took her pulse and listened so many times and there was nothing, and that wouldn't have changed if they'd left her for Kimmie's parents to find. Still with her head lolling Ellen might almost have been asleep when he picked her up, and with only the moonlight he could barely see she was blue when they laid her out flat at the foot of a leafless tree. Then they went back to get the spoon and the shoelace and everything.

So you left her in the park, no one found her in the park, or you don't know if anyone did. Caleb wipes his face with the back of his hand. You lied just now, you lied to me.

No, says Kenny, we didn't, I mean, we haven't heard, but we figured that at some point . . . We didn't hide her. We wanted her to be found. Maybe it looks like she froze to death by now.

Caleb doesn't speak. Someone in a windbreaker jogs past him and he listens to the steps.

Kenny gives a slight cough. The thing is, what if there were security cameras somewhere along the way and maybe they can't quite tell it's me and then the next day I go back, like to check on her, but I give them a better look at me and she's dead anyway.

Caleb asks for the exact location and Kenny gives him the general area as best he recollects. Then Caleb says, Thanks. He hangs up and heads south and wishes he hadn't thanked Kenny and feels sick the closer he gets to the place where Ellen's body might not yet have been noticed by anyone.

From a distance he can see yellow caution tape between the dark tree trunks. Nearby an ambulance has stopped and its back door is open. Someone in uniform, an EMT maybe, is seated on the steel step at the bottom of the ambulance and he seems to be waiting for something.

He's difficult to read. Difficult to get to know. Even for me.

I just don't want to ask again, I asked the first time. And I think if he wanted to see me again he'd ask.

Even I find it tough to know what he's thinking, and I've

known him forever. I mean, I know him pretty well.

Jane's eyes get big.

What if you organized something? If you invited him to something, and we all hung out together, and then you could see if he seems interested. Would you mind?

Not at all, says Lydia.

In the days that follow Caleb is irritated and can't trust his eyes, which don't hide sadness fast enough and give his father a reason to ask what's wrong. He stays out late. His father sets an eight o'clock curfew. The next evening Caleb turns his phone off and goes by himself to the movie theater and buys a ticket for the next thing that's starting. He walks out half-way through but has nowhere to go and no one to go there with. He walks up and down Eighth Avenue until he thinks it's late enough to come home but he's wrong and his father is awake. His father is overjoyed to see him home safe. Caleb feels heavy and rotten to think how little his father understands. There is no punishment.

Other days he does not want to leave his room but his father says Diane has made dinner. She smiles too kindly and asks him to pass the salad. He does. He has trouble looking his father and Diane in the face. He has nothing to say and when they talk to him he has to think too much before he says anything back. They work around his presence with concerned and ginger glances. He hates them for examining him and for pretending they are not. More than anything he hates the honest slow body of grief.

After five days his father sits him down and asks what's wrong. Caleb explains about Ellen. His father's eyes, just now oppressive with love, lose their gleam.

I'm very sorry, he says. You know I did not like her, you

know how I felt about that girl, but I can appreciate it must be upsetting for you.

Each spring for over ten years Tom and Lydia drove out of the city and to a town near Rye, where a buffet lunch was set out across many gingham-covered card tables and women in block-heeled shoes crossed the lawn in search of their small children, who liked to go into the woods. These women were around Lydia's age and were the daughters and daughters-in-law of the Delaneys and their friends. The children liked to come up to Lydia and tug at her skirt or trouser leg. The grandparents watched the grandchildren and discussed their own children and businesses and where they would live in retirement. They avoided politics, having differing positions on taxation and the minimum wage. Lydia dressed well and brought something good to the buffet. She smiled and nodded where it seemed appropriate to her and hoped that she was correct in her smiling decisions and clung to Tom's arm. Tom told everyone that Caleb was fine and pivoted to new research on Dada and the digital. Someone ate the last of the pasta salad. Tom and Lydia and the Delaneys and their other guests drank margaritas and gin-and-tonics in blue whorled blown-glass tumblers all afternoon and into the evening light.

In mid-March Lydia opens an email from Kathleen Delaney. Please join us again, she's written, to welcome the spring. Lydia is surprised she's invited.

She might find in a well-tended eyebrow or knotted scarf or coat thrown elegantly over one shoulder the reason why Tom left her.

Lydia writes back that she would love to come.

Chapter Ten

The next weekend Lydia, Caleb, and Jane stand behind families and groups of young men until it is their turn to order popcorn. An orange-shirted saleswoman asks if they want butter on top. Lydia says yes. Jane asks for a packet of Twizzlers and Caleb would like a box of Junior Mints. Lydia gives the woman her credit card and tries to wipe other people's crushed popcorn off of the bottom of her shoes without anyone noticing.

I never go to the movies anymore, says Jane, it's great to go.

Lydia sees how she looks at Caleb. He must sense it too. He jams his hands into his pockets with straight arms, his shoulders high and tense. Jane looks toward Lydia as if for consultation. Lydia takes her card back from the saleswoman.

In the dark theater she sits between Caleb and Jane and passes the Twizzlers and Junior Mints across her lap between them. She offers popcorn. Jane doesn't eat much. On the big screen a sad man is dealing cards with practiced movements. Nearby a young woman in a cocktail dress is sitting on a stool, watching the game. She wears large pearl earrings. The shot sometimes widens to show the green semicircular felt horizon of the table, rimmed with dark wood, and resting hands or elbows on it or leaning on it the other players: a young bespectacled man, a fat woman with a loud voice and a thin husband, a bald man with a purple shirt and a snake around his neck. The fat woman wins the game and she and

93

her husband go off to celebrate. Other players crowd in. To Lydia's left Caleb fidgets.

The man in the purple shirt begins to tell the young woman about his pet alligator Herbie, whom he does not like to leave alone. Herbie is still small and lives in the bathtub. Unfortunately he does not fit on the man's shoulders as well as Janice does. That's the great thing about snakes, they keep you company. For now the two of them get along fine provided they both get enough mice but it's possible that will change at some point and then it will be tough. The purple-shirted man shows the young woman Polaroids of Herbie smiling, of Herbie in the half-full bathtub balancing an orange ball on his long nose, of Herbie's gentle cream-green belly and little feet.

How does he manage when you're not at home? the woman asks.

Oh, he's fine, the door is locked.

Lydia takes a Junior Mint and passes the box to Jane, who, she notices, is not looking at the screen but to the left, squinting, face pale and green in the projected light from the underside of the alligator.

The light goes red and emerald. Lydia hears the woman ask if she can join the game.

You've got to get on the list, says the dealer, there's a waiting list.

Here's his tongue, says the man in the purple shirt, and holds up a blurred pink square framed by white borders.

The first credits appear in white capital letters on the black screen. Lydia slides her arms back into her coat sleeves, reaches down to grab her bag and is ready to stand when she sees that on either side of her Jane and Caleb are still. She looks from left to right. Names throw light and recede. Tom always watched the credits too. Other moviegoers step over them and whisper and make their way out of the theater.

Once the large individuated names have all been shown and the list has scrolled into smaller and smaller lettering, Caleb starts to shift and Jane takes her cue from him.

Lydia collects their candy wrappers and stuffs them in her empty popcorn bag and throws it in the trash can in the dark hallway. Behind her Jane is saying, I loved that. Caleb, didn't you love that? Lydia would like to shush her but they're almost the last people out.

She pushes open the heavy double door and walks into the lobby. Caleb follows her, and when she looks over her shoulder she sees him hold the door for Jane.

His father taught him to hold the door for everyone. His father did teach him to be nice to anyone and everyone, hold the door for any girl but really anyone. She's glad he's such a nice boy.

My shoes are very uncomfortable, says Lydia.

I didn't know alligators could move so fast, says Jane. And I thought, um. I liked the chase scenes. And the special effects, the CGI was really impressive, I thought.

Caleb is looking down. Lydia follows his gaze but sees only pink rectangles, yellow triangles, blue circles in the scuffed worn black of the carpet.

Very impressive, Jane says again, and Caleb's mouth twists with a brittle slant that Lydia recalls from waiting rooms and hospitals and arguments, and she knows that something is wrong.

Shall we go? Lydia buttons her coat.

I was hoping we could get a drink, Jane says, if it's not too late? There's so much to talk about with this movie.

I'm sure Caleb wants to get home.

No I don't. He looks up and at Lydia. His eyes are big and immeasurably sad. I can get a soda or something.

Great, says Jane, great. She excuses herself to use the bathroom, and soon her slim form is lost in the crowd and then the back of her head is a dark dot on the other side of the lobby. Should Lydia turn back to Caleb, should she ask what's going on. He's not speaking.

Around their silence the chatter seems louder, young people in puffy jackets on their way into the theater, couples holding each other's cold or sweaty hands, checking tickets, Are we in number six or number seven, I kind of want to get some Good & Plenty, Are you sure you don't want anything. Around their silence the chatter is almost intolerable.

Do you really want to go out? says Lydia.

Caleb turns away from her. He's reading an advertisement. She says his name. The advertisement shows small wet-skinned and lumpish creatures at the periphery of a twinkling lavender nebula. She puts her hand on Caleb's arm. He says, That movie looks terrible, I don't get science fiction. Ellen died. I found out last week. And I'm arguing with my father, at home we always have chicken, each day, I'm sick of it.

Oh my goodness, what happened?

He doesn't answer. She should have said something different. Oh my goodness, what was that, she doesn't know where that came from. She looks at the misshapen animals on the poster, at their bulbous eyes. What happens if one of them dies in the movie? It looks like the kind of movie where at least one of them dies. He's turning toward her and she needs to know what to say.

Because he embraces her she can't see his face.

His breath sounds childish, watery and heavy and irregular.

If only she'd learned to be a mother she would know what to do. She never learned. Tom never taught her and she never wanted him to.

Lydia whispers Caleb's name when she sees Jane emerge from the corridor that leads to the bathroom. He coughs and raises his head from her shoulder and Lydia reaches, gently, one hand to his face. He shuts his eyes. She runs the first joint of her thumb over his undereye skin in a careful half circle. The thumb tip ruffles the closed lashes and the flat of the thumb peels a tear off the skin, and then she reaches up and touches with four fingers the upper curved edge of his ear. She runs one finger along and behind it and notices the tension of its cartilage. Jane is nearing them. Lydia lifts her hand. By now Caleb has opened his eyes and the tear has dropped and must be somewhere on the carpet with blue dots and yellow triangles and pink rectangles.

Lydia puts her hand in her pocket.

Is there anywhere you've been wanting to go? says Jane.

Nowhere in particular.

Caleb's quiet. Jane either does not notice or pretends not to notice that his eyes have a heavy wet cast, that he coughs loudly to hide a sniffle. Jane has a suggestion and no one objects. They head out into the night.

Who's making chicken? Lydia says as they round the corner.

What? says Jane.

The place Jane wants to try has a long bar with high navy chairs. On the host desk lies a lamp in the shape of a candle, its black cord and plug wrapped around its fake wax base. Lydia looks more closely at it. Caleb follows and looks with her. A weak ring of silver filament takes the place of the wick in a pointed orange bulb. Lydia watches Caleb's hand trace the false cascade of wax down the candle stem.

We think that one's broken, a man from the bar calls out, and he and his friend burst into drunken laughter.

The short-haired agreeable hostess says she has room for three. Lydia thinks they should not be here and Caleb should stop touching the candle. Jane is taking her coat off, Jane is following the hostess toward the low square tables at the back of the restaurant and the same candle lamps, these ones plugged in. They cast warm light onto the faces of patrons in low seats. Caleb shouldn't sit in any of those chairs. Lydia turns back toward him.

When is your father expecting you home?

Fuck what my father expects.

He tenses up when he says *fuck*. She wonders who he wants to notice his gruff tone. As they eat she remembers how he said the word, how anxious and angry he sounded, and looks all the more closely at his soft boyish brow and at the way his eyes ask for her permission and approval. Jane speaks quickly and Lydia tells herself to focus on the conversation. Caleb says he did not find the movie very funny although maybe he is missing something. He cuts his steak assiduously. Lydia feels his leg shake under the table.

I don't think it was supposed to be funny, says Jane.

The plates have been taken away and there are a few small stains on the tablecloth from meat juices and errant salad leaves. Jane has been laughing too loudly and at the wrong time, Jane has been drinking and each time Caleb glances at her she twitches and flushes with awareness of his attention. Jane has been glorious and awkward and blind to her own shivering want. Lydia is embarrassed by her or for her, cannot tell which but she does not like the feeling. She is thinking about how much she dislikes it when she realizes Jane has just asked if people would like to stay out. She was thinking maybe of a nightclub.

The waiter collects the signed check from Lydia and thanks her.

Lydia does not want to go to a nightclub and she does not want Caleb and Jane to go to a nightclub without her but she does not want Caleb to go home.

He's not old enough, she says. We could have a last drink at our place, she says, or mint tea or some ice cream or something.

We don't have mint tea, says Jane. Or ice cream.

I am old enough, says Caleb, anyone can get into these places.

We can pick up some ice cream on the way home, whatever flavor you like, says Lydia. It'll be much nicer than going out to some loud club. You can even stay over if it's easier.

She says the last part as nonchalantly as she can. She's already put her coat on. In Manhattan Tom's ears are pricking up for the sound of the lock unlocking, the door swinging open, beloved footsteps.

Caleb, says Jane, what's your favorite flavor of ice cream?

In the morning Lydia has texts and calls from Tom but does not answer. Jane corners her in the hallway and asks what she thinks Caleb's thinking about her and then says that it shouldn't matter, she shouldn't be so worried about it.

He's still asleep, says Lydia, let's talk about it another time. Because he's asleep on the futon.

Jane says all right and slips into the shower. Lydia tries to be very quiet as she passes Caleb, who breathes steadily.

When she got up in the middle of the night it was snowing

and he was awake and saw her. He said, Thanks for being so nice, and for, you know, not saying anything to Jane about –

Sure, she said.

They were very quiet.

And I meant to say thanks also for getting my cake. At the birthday party, I mean, the cake was like we usually have for my –

Sure.

My father didn't know where to get it this year, he said.

Lydia makes coffee and looks out the window. How many times should she let Tom get in touch before she tells him Caleb is all right?

It took only ten minutes for the boy hitchhiker to confess that his name was not Augustus. Ellen said she'd known all along. Your face, she said, your sweet little face. Augustus. Please.

Caleb felt himself flush red. Ellen asked if he wanted to stop at McDonalds. He didn't.

You let me know when you need to piss, Gus, said Ellen. She tapped the wheel.

What were you going to do then, she said, if I didn't come along.

Wander, said Caleb.

Are you crazy, she said, the sky's about to open.

She nodded toward the tall clouds at the horizon. In his loneliness he hadn't noticed their dark bellies.

What was your last name going to be? Augustus indeed.

He didn't tell her. Before long they pulled over to the side of the road.

What would your name be? asked Caleb.

How old are you? asked Ellen. I'll have to think about my name. You're shaking. Here. What's your real name, anyway?

He told her and slept better that night than he had the whole time he'd been at Las Palmas-Bridges.

Now blue Ellen has been stripped and photographed and cut, her organs weighed for reasons. The examiner will have found the stick-and-poke leaf on her forearm and probably overlooked the zigzag in the stem where Gus laughed too hard and got distracted and then went over his error again and again, wild and proud and sure of his own lucidity. The crook of the leaf must appear in governmental photographs of distinguishing marks. No one living knows who Gus is. He's heard they use a handsaw to cut through the breastbone, they line you with cotton before they put you back together for viewing.

Chapter Eleven

When did it start?

In a hallway, with orange lilies?

The bouquet was wrapped in white paper that rustled when he moved his hands, and the purple outlines of ideal flowers, evenly spaced, jumped.

They might as well see what's possible. Jane and Caleb might as well see. He would prefer Jane, who is younger and kinder and never lived with his father. Lived with, what a phrase. When Jane asks how Lydia thinks the evening went she doesn't have much to say.

Very insightful, Jane says, and sulks for the next few days, after which she says she isn't going to think about it anymore. About him, that is.

Good, says Lydia. Her phone vibrates. Caleb wants to know if she is free to talk.

She texts back, Yes, then turns to Jane and says, I think you have so much else going on.

Lydia and Caleb are the only customers in the café save one man with glasses, who stares at them over the top of his laptop and looks away when he thinks they notice. She guesses he's still listening. He wants to know why Caleb's been crying, why his eyes are red and he keeps looking down and tugging the sleeve of his sweatshirt.

Caleb speaks haltingly and Lydia tries not to seem frustrated. She says that there's nothing he could have done, obviously, from what he said. He wasn't even there.

I could have been in touch more, says Caleb.

How would that have helped?

I didn't even know she was shooting up, he says.

Lydia takes his hand and then lets it go.

It's my fault, says Caleb, and Lydia says, No, no, no, it's just very bad luck.

She takes his hand again between both of hers. He tells her no one else knew him and now he's alone and then he blows his nose on a napkin. The man at the laptop has stopped typing and is looking at them. The man working the counter has gone back into the silvery kitchen.

Here, Lydia says, and moves from her chair to the bench next to Caleb, who puts his head on her shoulder. She hears him breathe in. Unsparingly she meets the gaze of the man at the laptop, who looks away and starts typing again.

Later Caleb texts, I don't know what was wrong with me.

She writes back, Don't mention it.

Over the next week Lydia texts Liz six times and Liz texts back three. They plan to meet for coffee on April 3rd. On the 2nd Liz cancels and Lydia is relieved. She was worried she would blush and invite shameful questions.

The room is quiet when he enters. The light from the window falls on his father's rumpled white sheets. Caleb likes the house best when his father is not in it. The door clicks shut behind him and his feet in their socks slip slightly on the floorboards. He catches himself. Near the edge of the blue rug he sees one long pale hair.

The framed pictures his father keeps on his dresser are still in their same places. First there's his mother in a black dress with sequins, joyful in the light of the flash. Next he sees the same woman older and thinner. He's a baby in her arms, his mouth open, and Caleb is embarrassed, he was like that baby in the cafe with Lydia yesterday, opening his mouth for no good reason. It feels good to tell the truth but you always regret it. In the next image Lydia's young in her cap and gown, and her short uncomfortable mother looks skeptically into the lens. There's toddler Caleb in a tiny red sunhat, then Caleb and Lydia at the science fair, tunnels for ants at the edge of the frame.

He wanted their pictures to be dusty or missing, stuffed away in some drawer or nowhere to be found. He wanted to hate his father for forgetting them all. But his mother and his old self and Lydia are looking at him through clean glass.

Only a few inches to the right there are now two pictures of Diane.

In one she stands with his father in their kitchen, Caleb's kitchen, Diane's arm around his father's waist. The other image is creased and faded. Diane is six or so and shoves her face into the neck of a stuffed tiger. The orange-and-black fake fur of the animal hides most of her face but he can see one brown open eye. His father must have said, I love that tiger picture, can I have it.

He puts the pictures of Diane in his school backpack and goes out of the house. When the backpack is empty he stops in a bodega and buys mango Juul. He goes back to his father's room, lies down in the bed, and vapes. His father said they would be home at five. At four-thirty Caleb starts to get nervous and goes back to his own bed, where he reads Reddit on his phone. Before long, his father knocks on the door and says, Did you vape in my room? What were you doing in my room, vaping?

I wasn't there.

What are you smiling about?

But by morning he feels bad about the pictures. He's eating breakfast when his father says he's noticed they are gone. Caleb says he knows nothing. His father keeps asking and Caleb sticks to his story no matter how uncomfortable he gets. His father says, This isn't funny.

Caleb can't tell him that he would have fished out the pictures himself, arm up to the shoulder in gum wrappers, tobacco, fish guts, juice boxes, spit. He even got up early this morning and went back outside to the corner. But the trash can was empty, the black bag was new and the sanitation truck was driving away. He watched it pull out of sight.

On the day of the Delaneys' party Lydia Zipcars out to Rye. For most of the drive she is stuck in traffic behind a large blue truck but eventually it leaves the highway and she is stuck behind a pickup with an NRA bumper sticker. She takes an exit and the pickup keeps going north.

She finds a place to park around the corner from the house, turns off the ignition, and checks her makeup in the rearview mirror. She could get out of the car now and walk over to join the party. Alternatively she could go buy flowers first or alternatively she could go back to New York City or alternatively now a gray Saab just like Tom's is passing her. On the passenger side there's a woman with a blonde bob and a crucifix around her neck and past her Lydia can see him in profile, Lydia can see Tom in the driver's seat. The car rounds the next corner, headed for the party.

Only some crucifix blonde, looking for a parking space.

She doesn't look fifty-four.

Did her crucifix have a little metal body on it or not in which case it is a cross and not a crucifix. Lydia did not see because she was too far away. The woman's coral lipstick was perfectly applied. Her sweater was blue and her right hand lay casually over the top of the half-lowered glass of the open window.

Lydia gets out of the car and takes the pasta salad from the backseat. She shuts the door firmly and presses the lock button on the black fob and hears an electronic beep.

Tom will offer to drop the blonde off at the party before he looks for a place to park. Right now she is opening the car door outside the Delaneys' house, and Tom is saying, Really, it's no trouble. Tell them I'll be right there.

Lydia walks in the opposite direction. She takes a left and steps over a discarded electric bike. She takes another left and another. She wonders what voice a crucifix has or rather a crucifix-wearing woman and whether or not Tom knows she's coming. She should have said she could not come. She enters the party through the open gate. This year the tables are covered not in red gingham but in blue.

Is the crucifix real gold. Is she religious. She must be religious.

Lydia is about to enter the wooded area where the children go.

She turns back and walks over to the nearest table, puts the dish of salad down and takes the plastic wrap off.

I'll take that, says a voice from behind her.

Lydia turns to see Kathleen Delaney and a red-faced woman in chunky sandals. Kathleen says how nice it is to see her and yes the garden's great, later she'll take her on a tour. The pink roses are out early, it's a mystery. She says she'll just throw the plastic out and then she'll be right back.

The red-faced woman looks at Lydia expectantly and may be about to say something. Lydia steps a few paces off. On the lawn women in light dresses move toward and away from one another and rings and pendants flicker like captive fireflies. A dark-haired child in pink shorts sits on the grass and stands back up.

The red-faced woman is tenacious. And how do you know Kathy and Jim?

Oh, we've known each other for years. Mutual friends. And you, how do you know them?

The woman has worked with Jim. She is a psychology researcher.

Oh really, says Lydia, what are you working on?

The woman is working on a study of women aging, or more specifically a study about how women feel about the aging process. The beginning of the aging process specifically. Previous studies have focused on middle-aged women but no one has studied how women feel when they begin to realize they are losing their attractiveness.

Oh.

Their sexual attractiveness.

Oh, says Lydia, really. So there's a gap in the research.

Exactly.

And how does the study work, how are you, are you, collecting the data?

I interview women. Mostly in their late twenties but a few in their early thirties. I'm looking for people if you know anyone in that age bracket ideally anyone articulate. Basically they'd just have to talk to me about how they feel about wrinkles, seeing volume start to go, you know, in the forehead, the whole deal.

Painful, says Lydia. Don't you think it's cold out?

The woman hesitates. On the lawn nearby a child falls out of a cartwheel.

I'm sure you'd be a great interview subject but I can't use people I've met socially and besides, I think you might be a year or two outside, um, outside of the bracket we've set. So if you know anyone.

When Lydia saw herself in the mirror this morning she liked how she looked in this dress. Now she is cold and wonders if her palms have left dirt or sweat stains on the skirt. It is too early in the year for white cotton dresses and parties on lawns. She could go back to the car for her sweater and look at her crow's feet in the rearview. The woman with the crucifix or cross or gold body or no body in small cast gold or bronze must have crow's feet, must have lost volume, and yet has something outside all possible study. I fell in love, said Tom. Outside of the bracket.

That's fascinating, she says to the red-faced woman, I'll think, I'll certainly think about it, yeah, if I know anyone. Excuse me, I need to get my sweater. It's in the car. I'm freezing.

Lydia tries to walk casually. She is almost to the exit when she hears a voice say, Hello. She turns around.

It's so nice to see you again, a woman with curly hair and oval glasses is saying. We met at Molly Coolidge's a few months ago.

Across the lawn, over the shoulder of the woman she does not recognize, Lydia sees the blonde in the blue sweater, a glint of gold at her neck, near Tom's tall gray-haired form. He's wearing that ill-fitting seersucker suit still.

I think you're mistaken, says Lydia, and the faraway glint of cross light and the body that carries it and the ill-fitting suit on the kind lost man make their way toward someone. The glint of the cross disappears in a friendly hug. Something on the left hand catches light and Bob pulls back to look at the hand, the hand sparkles near the pinkie but not quite at the pinkie, Diane laughs and Tom is right that she is very beautiful.

How can you be sure of what it is that is catching the light? A beetle, a body, a promise, a demon.

But I remember you so clearly, says the woman in oval glasses, frowning. We talked about the new Paul Auster novel.

Lydia says she doesn't know a Molly Coolidge or read Paul Auster and she is sorry to be rude but she is cold, she has to go get her sweater.

They are still talking over there. The nod of a head, blonde bangs sweep left, seersucker scans the assembled anxieties. Individuals. So he does wonder if she's here or has someone already told him she is, evermore at some edge of something somewhere. Or he is just looking at the scene. He's going to marry her. Faraway Bob turns his head and Lydia envisions spit suspended by its own tension across the tops of new-cut grassblades.

Lydia locks herself in the car.

Is it possible she has right mixed up with left. Make a diagram in your head where there's Diane, where there's Bob. Where is Tom. Lydia's nowhere. It was the left hand.

There were moreover no rings on the fingers of the hand that rested carelessly over the rolled-down windowglass.

Is it possible that there are other left-hand rings worn for other reasons.

Someone has left a green packet of tissues in the glovebox but Lydia tells herself she will not need them. She could call Liz and ask if Liz has heard anything. She could venture back onto the slippery lawn and seize and inspect all hands. Her hands are shaking. She could drive away.

Lydia picks up her phone and calls Tom. He answers and asks if she's there.

I thought I saw you, he says, I would have said hi.

I am saying hi now, she says. Hi.

Lydia hears herself say Hi. How to say hi. How to say hello, are you getting married. Hello, do I hallucinate points of light on the hands of strange women, bright punctures. Hello, did I hallucinate years of companionship and pillow spittle tolerance. Lydia never minded not being married to Tom until someone else would be.

He hasn't asked because I don't want him to and he knows it, Lydia said at twenty-five and twenty-six and at thirty-two and more, I don't want him to and he knows it.

Did I hallucinate not wanting him to ask. Did I hallucinate points of not wanting.

Are you coming back to the party?

I don't know, I don't. She hears herself babble. It is coming to twilight and deer may be crossing the road.

Lydia, are you all right? I'm sorry things got so heated. I've been thinking a lot about my role in all of this, not just recently but also the past few years. I've been doing a lot of reflection.

Lydia pulls a Kleenex from the green package. She's wiping her eyes when she hears a tap, then another. She takes the tissue away and sees that a young man with a dark goatee is knocking on the passenger side window.

I have to go, Tom.

She hangs up the phone and rolls the window down.

Capo, she says, I almost didn't recognize you with that beard.

They agree they should get out of here. Capo sits in the passenger seat and tells her how much he hates his parents. There are no deer on the road. They find a diner and Lydia pulls in.

Is this okay?

This is okay, says Capo, smiling. He runs his fingers through his hair.

All right then, says Lydia. She presses a button and the car turns off.

He's young. How young is he? She could ask but she won't ask.

The overhead light reflects in the tabletop.

They just want to, I don't know, make me say hi to everyone from their dumb garden club, show me off to all their friends or some shit.

Parents like to do that, says Lydia. She touches the handle of the flat butter knife and moves it slightly to the left.

Yeah, but I just. He shifts his weight and leans back into the corner of the diner booth, reaches one arm along the top of the red vinyl upholstery. How did you end up at that thing anyway?

Oh I've been going for a long time. I go every year.

Old friends?

Not really, says Lydia.

Is something wrong? You look a little upset.

Nothing's wrong.

You can tell me, I just told you. Capo leans forward. Lydia notices that his eyebrows are very bushy.

Lydia looks him in the eye. Nothing's wrong. He's leaning back in the seat again. Lydia looks for a waitress.

Do you want to split a French toast?

The light in the diner is very bright.

See something's wrong, says Capo, laughing, I can tell. You think I can't but I see you.

I just want French toast, says Lydia, there's no problem.

Where's the waitress. Or do you actually want an egg?

French toast is cool, says Capo. Here, come round to this side of the booth, I wanna show you something. He pulls his phone out from his jacket pocket.

Slide over, he says.

Should she?

He's got one hand out and Tom is getting married. A child fell out of a cartwheel and someone spat on grass. She could sit next to Capo and let him show her.

Lydia spent sixteen years of her life with someone who does not tell her he's engaged. Caleb must know and has not told her. They'll make dinner plans together, Tom and Diane, Caleb and Jane. Cheers. No waitress is coming. Capo's got a lot of hair on the backs of his hands and arms. She can see where the cuffs of his shirt force it flat and black ends shove their way out.

Slide over. She could so easily and maybe it would resolve.

How could he not have told her?

I want to go home, she hears herself say. They're taking forever and I don't need French toast. I want to go.

Capo puts his phone back in his pocket. He blinks and says it's fine. He only wanted to show her the artwork for his new album cover. She's struck by how shy and weak he seems all of a sudden.

You can play me some of your music on the ride back to the city, she says, how's that.

To Lydia's surprise the album is beautiful, full of lush textures, unnerving rhythms and spare sad melodies. She cannot quite believe the voice is Capo's but when he speaks again to tell her where to drop him off she realizes it is the same person.

Chapter Twelve

Lydia leaves Capo at his brother's apartment on York and 78th, then drives off again. A few blocks away she pulls over and parks. All along the street in their neat dark plots the pear trees have come into bloom.

Does Liz know that Tom is getting married? She could call or text to ask.

Lydia gets out of the car and walks to the next corner, where a man sells pretzels from a metal cart. She buys one. Tourists walk past brokerage firms. She chews.

Liz will tell him she asked.

Lydia imagines another party.

Liz is sitting at the head of a long mahogany table. Tom sits nearby and Diane across from him. Married guests Lydia does not recognize fill the other seats. The women keep their elbows close in to their sides and the men wear good suit jackets. Diane is wearing her cross. In the back of this unknown room there is a glass-fronted cupboard full of cut crystal glasses and some of these are also on the table, filled with an inch or two of red wine. Liz takes a sip of hers and as she is drinking holds up a finger as if in recollection. As she puts the glass down on the table she says, Oh, Tom, Lydia asked about you.

Oh, says Tom, that's nice. Say hello for me.

He smiles and changes the subject.

Caleb is at the fridge getting himself a glass of orange juice when he feels his phone vibrate and hears the familiar ping.

He touches the home button and touches the screen and swipes to see a message from Lydia.

Are you home? she asks.

He writes back, Yes.

Can I come over?

He presses his glass into the ice dispenser in the fridge door. Ice clatters into it. His hand is cold. He pours juice and puts the carton back in the fridge and texts Lydia to say she should come over.

He buzzes her into the building, then waits for her at the apartment door. When she comes out of the elevator her dark hair is messy and her coat is open.

I like your dress, he says.

She smiles gently and lets the smile fade. Her eyes are bright and lively. He smiles back. She purses her pink lips and looks down as if to stop some pleasure from making itself undeniable at the twitching corners of her mouth. She blushes and he realizes that he has answered a question whose terms he cannot make clear in his mind.

They're not home yet, I assume, she says.

I, my dad, um, no, not till later, I think.

He must sound like a child. How is he like a child all of a sudden?

He blushes too. He tells Lydia to come in. She asks what he's been up to. He has to think about it. It's strange to see her in this apartment again. She walks into the living room and he hears the jangle and rustle when she throws her bag and coat on the sofa. She returns and stands in the doorframe, one hand on her hip, waiting. He thinks that he knows what is going to happen. He thinks that he's been waiting for this for a while.

Did you know your father's getting married?

What?

Your father and Diane.

No he's not.

Yes he is, I saw. She walks over and kisses him. His mouth isn't moving. Is her mouth moving? When she pulls away he looks nothing like his father to her.

He grabs her hand and leads her to his room. As he lies down on the bed he knocks over the half-full glass of juice on the nightstand.

Sorry, he says, I forgot about that.

The single bed is narrow. His movements are awkward and endearing. When they are tired he sleeps. She gets up to switch off the overhead light and notices there's no blind on the window in this room. How bright it must be in this room when the sun comes up, she never thought of it. She returns and slides under the covers and wonders if she should leave in a few minutes or wait until she hears Tom's footsteps. When will she hear Tom's footsteps. In the end she decides to sneak out while she still can.

At home Jane offers her grapes, cold and sweet. Jane had Dustin and Ryan over earlier and they brought the grapes and some cheese and some chocolate but the cheese and the chocolate are all gone. The wine is almost all gone and Jane speaks a bit too loudly. When she says something that she thinks is funny she looks over her shoulder at Lydia, who sits on the futon with her legs crossed. There's a slight swing and recovery in the twist of Jane's neck, as if she does not expect her head to be so heavy, as if she just catches herself.

She dries wine glasses and asks Lydia if she should take the LSATs this coming year or wait one or two more. She asked Dustin and Ryan this question but she is interested to get Lydia's perspective.

I don't know, says Lydia, looking at the orange armchair.

I mean on the one hand there's the fact that if I know I want to go, maybe I might as well just go, but then again –

A glass hits the floor with a hard splintered noise, and Jane curses.

Lydia doesn't look but tells Jane to go put shoes on. Be careful, she says, until you've got your shoes on.

I am careful, says Jane. What's so funny?

On the other side of the city Tom is probably home by now. Lydia wonders if she has done something wrong. Jane is wearing slippers when she comes back into the room, grabs the broom and dustpan from the corner.

What else were you saying about the LSATs? Lydia asks.

Jane says that the reason to wait is that maybe she needs to just enjoy life a bit, and besides, people go to law school later all the time, it's not as if there's some kind of rush.

True, says Lydia, there's no rush.

So what side do you come down on, says Jane. She throws the broken glass from the dustpan into the garbage.

I don't know, says Lydia, looking at her own knees. She knows Jane is glancing sidelong at her, is wondering if she's okay. Is she seeing Jane with her peripheral vision or just feeling the questioning glances. She doesn't know what she's done, does she, Jane can't possibly know what she's just done. Caleb looked at her face.

Lydia says, I don't know anything.

Jane sits next to her on the futon. Look, she says, you seem a bit upset, or frazzled, or something.

She's blinking, she's breathing in slowly, she's eager to say something. She places her hand on Lydia's wrist with a conspiratorial air.

I have, um, do you want a Xanax?

Lydia says no, she's all right.

I'm not supposed to share them, says Jane, I mean I have a prescription, I'm supposed to take them, I'm not supposed to share them. I just thought.

Lydia wipes her eyes and places one hand on Jane's thigh just above the knee.

It's very kind, says Lydia, I appreciate it. I do.

It must be tough to end a relationship after so many years. It must be really painful. I thought you seemed better recently, but it would make sense for it to take a while.

Yes, says Lydia, looking for flies on the ceiling.

You can't bury things, says Jane, you can't keep things inside.

Yes, says Lydia. There are no flies but the paint is chipping.

That's what I learned, says Jane, you're going to have to deal with pain sooner or later.

Jane tells Lydia about the mathematics tutor who between questions 26 and 29 in the preparatory materials for the PSAT began to slide his hand up her skirt such that by the end of the Calculator portion of the test two fingers were inside her, at which time he rolled her onto her back on her parents' kitchen table and she tried to solve question 33. When it was over she told the tutor her answer. She was wrong. It was B. She put on her underwear and they solved the rest of the questions and the tutor left and Jane took a shower. Her PSAT results were excellent. She did not think much about the encounter until at college she could not sleep and talked to a psychiatrist and got a prescription for Xanax.

I'm very sorry, says Lydia.

Jane waits for more.

Anyway, I'm sorry that happened, Lydia repeats, without looking up. Near where her field of vision ends an elbow moves and Jane might have tucked her hair behind her ear. She speaks tentatively.

That's, I mean in part, one of the reasons I like Caleb so much is that he's been through something too, so I think. I think he'd understand. I feel like I'd be able to talk to him about it.

Lydia doesn't want to look up. You're so smart, she says, and so beautiful, and interesting, and young, with everything ahead of you. I don't think you should worry so much about men.

But do you think he'd understand?

Look, says Lydia, running a hand through her hair, anyone ought to understand. I don't know that he's more likely to understand than anyone else.

But he's really suffered, he understands pain. He brought flowers to my birthday.

Those were just flowers, says Lydia. They're dead now. We threw them in the garbage and took the garbage out.

For a few seconds Jane is silent. Then she says, I want to go to bed.

When Caleb wakes alone and hears his father's step and his father's voice saying, And Gene told me, actually, that apparently if you die in debt there it used to be that your family wouldn't even bury you, so they just have a totally different approach to these things than the Greeks, when Caleb hears this and knows it is Diane on the other end of the line, almost surely Diane who is learning about not being buried if you are in debt in some place, he thinks with satisfaction of Lydia's body and of his sweat on it.

He picks up his phone and sends her a message. It reads, Where did you go?

In the middle of the night Lydia goes downstairs and opens the door for Caleb. In the street behind him she sees a white van pass and thinks its driver makes an effort to look her in the eye. As they walk past Jane's bedroom door Lydia hopes that the whir of the white noise machine will hide the sound of a second set of footsteps.

Do you think this is weird, she whispers to him.

No, he says.

Are you sure –

Yes.

She takes him at his word. In the morning she elbows him before the sun comes up and tells him to get home before his father notices he's missing.

Over breakfast Jane clarifies that she really shouldn't share her Xanax, it was a bad idea and she can't offer it again in the future, it's a prescription medicine.

Chapter Thirteen

Your father would be very upset.

I don't have a problem with that.

He's lying on his side. She can see the shape of his face clearly against the pink wall behind him. His cheek rises as his face breaks into a boyish smile. She traces it with one finger.

It's funny that they call this an apple, she says.

They do?

This part. She taps the rosy skin over his cheekbone. They call this part the apple of your cheek.

Why?

They just do. She moves her hand to his throat. And they call this an apple too. Isn't it funny?

They are lucky that most days Jane gets up early. They stay as quiet as they can until they hear the front door shut and can be sure that she has left the house. He tells his father he's sleeping later and later these days and hopes he doesn't open his bedroom door.

As quiet as little mice, Lydia mouths one morning.

What? Caleb mouths back. The light falls through the top sheet and into the tent they've made of it. She moves closer to him.

Mice, she whispers into his beautiful ear.

Mice, he whispers back.

Is that it?

Hm?

Am I, am I in the right. Uh.

When Lydia was a child she would go grocery shopping with her mother at the big Stop & Shop outside of town. They would buy burger meat, canned corn, ketchup, Cheerios, Cheetos, canned tuna, sometimes sugar if they were out of it, sometimes flour and baking soda and things like that if they were out, eggs, Kraft Mac and Cheese, Kraft American Cheese, apples, bananas, peanut butter, toilet paper, sometimes bacon, paper towels, Brillo, frozen peas, Dole canned pineapple.

In the summer, after they put the groceries in the hot car, Lydia's mother would on occasion ask if she wanted ice cream. Lydia always did. They would leave the car in the supermarket parking lot and walk across the road to the place that sold soft serve. Lydia's mother would flatten the bills out before she handed them over. Then they would sit at the table outside and Lydia would lick rainbow sprinkles and creamy cold vanilla underneath.

Sometimes Lydia's mother would tell her about the railway accident in which her own father who did not speak English had lost his right hand and most of that arm. This far up, she would say, tapping above her elbow. As they were sitting outside a family with a German Shepherd would sometimes walk by and often the eager dog would try to shove its face between Lydia's legs and she would flush red. Usually the mother or father or oldest girl of the family would hold the dog back and say sorry but once the youngest boy had the leash and he was not strong enough so that the dog did shove its long snout there and Lydia dropped her ice cream in embarrassment. The mother grabbed the leash and pulled the dog back quickly. She apologized and offered to buy Lydia another ice cream. Lydia could feel herself getting redder and redder and said no and the woman said, Are you sure? and Lydia said that she was sure because she wanted the woman to go away, the child to go away, dog to go away, all of it away, vanilla and rainbow splattered and melting on the pavement. The woman apologized again and the family and the dog walked on. Just as Lydia could breathe again her mother said, If you washed better that wouldn't happen.

Sound of Caleb's elbow on the mattress.

Here, says Lydia, let me show you.

His chest is still bony. She can feel the rib under the edge of the brown mark where that bone branches off from his sternum and the hollow next to it. She runs her nail around the edge of the dark spot, then places one finger on top and presses lightly. She wants to flick it but doesn't. About two fingers' distance from the mole she finds a round pale scar.

What's this from?

Remember, when I had the chicken pox.

That's from that?

Yeah. He touches the mark with one finger. You were there. You couldn't stop scratching.

You brought me soup.

I did. She rolls onto her stomach and kisses the fleshy area where his shoulder becomes his armpit.

He pulls the blanket up over their bodies. They hear the rush of water from the kitchen faucet and the burbling of the coffeepot. Jane is getting ready for work.

Oh shit! whispers Caleb. Lydia wriggles her nose into the flesh of his armpit and muffles her laughter with his skin.

This week Caleb has been running faster. He tries to go every day after work. He likes when he comes home and his father sees him still sweating, red-cheeked and near gasping. His father says, Good run?

Yes, he says, and he is telling the truth.

Once his father and Diane are asleep he leaves for Lydia's.

In the morning he stops at a bodega on his way to the subway and buys coffee and Jolly Ranchers. He likes making eye contact with the guy behind the counter and putting the change in his jeans pocket. The sour apple Jolly Ranchers are the best. If Caleb's father knew about him and Lydia he'd say, I can't look at you.

At work a girl with blue eyeliner asks if they sell maps. They don't. She buys thank-you notes. He rings her up. It's easy. Being around other people is so simple now, like sliding a packet of thank-you notes into a slim blue paper bag and folding the top edge over, sealing it with the usual round white sticker. Is it possible that it was really this easy all along, all those years when he felt weird when anyone looked at him, all those months when he fumbled sticking circles over openings and thought everyone knew his hands were clumsy and too slow? If his father found out he would say, I don't know what's wrong with you, and Caleb would understand why. Caleb hands the blue bag to the girl and tells her to have a nice day. You too, she says.

Ellen would be happy for him. It hurts that he can't tell her. He puts a Jolly Rancher in his mouth, remembers the shape of Lydia's legs, and wishes she could be with him all the time.

Before long his father sits him down and apologizes for opening the door to his room that morning.

I know I invaded your privacy, but I need to know where you were.

Caleb doesn't know where to put his hands. He tells his father he was at his girlfriend's.

Oh, says his father.

Caleb makes himself look up and at his father's face.

He says that if he hadn't had so many problems he wouldn't live at home anymore and then his father wouldn't even know if he came home at night or not.

I wouldn't want you to miss out on a normal part of life, says his father, looking at the corner of his room and adjusting his glasses awkwardly, a normal part of life just because of the hard time you've had. But at the same time . . . It would make me feel more comfortable if I could meet her.

Maybe someday. Caleb flexes his fingers.

Well, who is she? What's this girl like?

Caleb tells his father a story about a fictional young woman. Her name is Jenny. She wants to be a designer.

Well, his father says. By the way, have you seen those pictures I asked you about? I know you said you didn't take them, but have you seen them?

No, says Caleb. The next time he goes over to Lydia's apartment he posts a close-up of the corner of her pillowcase on Instagram while she's out of the room. No one who sees it will even know what they're looking at, it's only creases and seams, and anyway he barely has any followers. Still he feels guilty when she comes back.

Do you like living here? he asks her. His hand is on her shoulder and he can feel a tingle in his arm where her shoulder blades and weight are cutting off his circulation but he does not want to move, not yet. Do you like it better than living with us?

She is not sure what to say. If she had only understood last year what she knew when she was very young, what she knew at twenty-one in Professor Montgomery's office: that you have to take what you can get, that you then have to keep it. On the professor's desk, amid his papers, this was clear, and then somehow over the years she forgot.

We had some good times together, she says. He nods. I like it here now, with you here. She sits up and moves. He can feel his arm wake up.

You like it with me better than with my dad, he says, grasping her hands, pressing his fingers between hers.

She's kneeling on top of him now. Yes, she says.

Yes what, he says, almost shyly.

When he leaves her loneliness is new and delicious, nothing like the loneliness she felt before. When she is supposed to be working she pauses frequently to recollect his mouth and fingers. Tom's the one who behaved badly. What's wrong is how Tom behaved.

On Sunday morning Lydia leaves Caleb in her room. In the kitchen Jane is cutting a red pepper into strips. Lydia grabs a filter from the drawer and asks if Jane wants coffee.

I've already had some, says Jane.

Lydia takes the glass pitcher from the Mr. Coffee and fills it with water to the eight cup mark. Jane puts her kitchen knife down on the cutting board and watches Lydia flick out the black plastic drawer and put the filter in.

Did you sleep badly?

Yeah, says Lydia, counting out spoonfuls of coffee grounds. Any plans for today?

Jane puts a handful of red pepper slices into a tupperware

container and says she might go for a run in the park.

Hmm, says Lydia. You've got so much energy.

Doesn't Caleb run? I was thinking I might ask sometime if he wants to come with me.

No idea.

Jane rinses another pepper. He hasn't messaged me since we all saw that movie together. So maybe I shouldn't.

When the coffee is done Lydia fills a cup. As she walks to her room she hears behind her the rhythm of the knife on the hard board.

Caleb is sitting cross-legged in her bed. She hands him the coffee and moves her lips to say, silently, Careful. She points at the cup with her free hand and mouths, It's very full.

Okay, Caleb mouths back, but when he takes the cup in both hands he spills the hot liquid on the bed.

Shush shush shush. Lydia places one finger at her lips. Shh-hhhhhh.

She sits next to the spill and wonders if Jane heard the noise that Caleb made before she could quiet him. He sits on the floor while she changes the sheets. Before long the front door shuts and they begin to talk at full voice.

I don't see why she can't just know, Caleb says.

He gets back into the clean bed.

Let me get more coffee, Lydia says, we can get two cups now.

When she reenters the room she says, You know she likes you.

He shrugs and shifts his weight and cracks his knuckles. Lydia hands him his coffee and he takes a sip.

She wonders when he started drinking coffee. She ought to remember but doesn't. Maybe it started during one of the times when he was in the hospital or maybe she just forgot. She wonders if they serve coffee in the hospital in the first place or if she just wasn't paying attention when he started drinking it.

I just, I mean she'll have to know eventually. His voice is tentative and hopeful.

Eventually?

Lydia is surprised by the word. Eventually. She listens to herself say it aloud. She sounds the word out again in her head.

Yeah, says Caleb, I mean.

Look, she says, let's not talk about eventually.

Why not?

Lydia lies back on the bed. You've never had a girlfriend, she says.

Sure I have.

Well you never introduced one to us.

My father doesn't get to know everything.

Well, then, she says, making light circles on the skin of his forearm with her thumb, then you know that these things start and end. That you can't tell how long they're going to last. Look at me and your father. Especially given . . .

What, says Caleb.

Lydia doesn't say anything. His skin is very soft.

I almost told him the other day, says Caleb, and kisses the side of her face.

What.

I want him to know, he says, and moves his hand between her thighs.

The next evening Lydia is eating a burrito on the futon in the living room when Jane comes in, leans against the doorframe, and asks if she's got any news. Lydia chews and swallows and is careful to keep a straight face.

News?

That's what I said.

No, nothing.

Jane sits down next to her.

Really, really nothing?

Nope.

All right, says Jane. She crosses her arms and changes the subject.

While she loves him, and of course she does love him, of course, she finds herself irritated by the smell of vape and by his awkwardness. His father hesitated too, although not quite so much. And his father did not ask so many questions. Two days ago Caleb asked her what herbivorous meant.

A deer is herbivorous, she said. Caterpillars are herbivorous. Manatees are herbivorous, and so are horses.

She wanted him to guess what these animals had in common, but instead he said, What's a manatee?

It means they eat plants, she said, and rolled over, and he said, But what's a manatee?

On her side, facing the wall, she imagined that there was a man behind her who knew how to describe the eating of plants, knew when she needed to be comforted, could earn money, could talk about the political process and the need to retake the Senate. When she tries to talk about politics with Caleb he can only speak in fundamentals about right and wrong and will not strategize in any manner that seems to her to recognize America in its current state. The last time they talked about possible candidates for the next presidential election they did not see eye to eye at all, although they both acknowledged the urgency of the situation. She said, But it's politics, you're not talking about politics, you're not thinking politically.

We've got real responsibilities toward the future, he said gravely, one hand reaching for her breast. She batted the hand away.

But the next day Caleb texted her a video of a pigeon eating a pizza crust by the curb, and Lydia texted back, And?

Caleb wrote, Look at the way he moves his neck.

Chapter Fourteen

In early May Lydia shields her eyes and says, See, this is how the world's going to end.

Caleb says, In the sun?

In the sand at Coney Island there are Bounty wrappers and cans of 7-Up. Yes, says Lydia.

At least the water's still cold, says Caleb. They are holding hands.

Isn't your generation supposed to be the ones who are serious about this? Gen Z kids. I thought you were all climate warriors. Lydia smiles past him and toward the sea.

Aren't I a Millennial?

I'm pretty sure you're Gen Z.

Well, almost a Millennial.

They came out here because they thought no one would be here.

Last night she stayed at the apartment on the Upper West Side because Tom was away for the weekend. Caleb wanted them to sleep in his father's bed but she said, It's too risky, he'll notice. Caleb said, No he won't, and anyway if he does he won't know it was you. She said, What if he starts asking questions?

As a compromise Lydia took spare sheets and made up the bed she used to sleep in with his father. She slept badly. In the morning she drank coffee alone in the living room and listened to the street outside. She put her feet on the furniture. Caleb got up and told her to come back to bed. One second, she said, and went to put her cup in the dishwasher. On her way past the fridge she saw on the whiteboard calendar looping handwriting that had to be Diane's.

Around noon Caleb said, Let's go out for lunch. She said, Where? He said, I don't know, anywhere, just in the neighborhood. She said, Are you crazy?

No, he said, I don't think so.

I mean we might run into someone and people will –

Lydia stopped speaking. She did not know what people would do or how to tell him. Recently she thinks he does not understand anything about other people, about how they talk and judge and point and watch. She tasted salt at the back of her mouth, but she had not eaten anything salty. She covered her mouth with her hand and coughed to get rid of the taste.

We're not going to run into anyone, he said, and besides people have seen us together a million times. So basically we just stayed in touch.

He scratched the back of his neck and as he did so his bent arm made two sides of a triangle that outlined the white of the wall behind him. The curve of his shoulder and his neck completed the edge of the shape. She thought that she could see in his forearm, backlit in the clear light from the window, the working of the little muscles that made his hand move behind his head. The half-gloss finish of the white shape threw daylight through his movement and recalled to her the interior of a shell left behind on some pellucid beach and never displaced.

I'm worried, she said. Move, I need to put your father's sheets back on.

As a compromise Lydia and Caleb took the F all the way out. Now four teenage girls lie on bright towels uneven with the undulation of the sand and a family sits in deck chairs.

Who do you think they think we are? asks Lydia.

He shrugs. A man walking a sheepdog smiles at them as he goes by. Lydia wonders what Caleb thinks about the girls on the towels. What Tom might think about Caleb thinking of them. What Tom might think about Caleb thinking about her or about her thinking about Caleb. Twice she almost asks Caleb if it's too weird, what they're doing, but she lets each moment pass and they stop to eat hot dogs and she gets mustard on her shirt and they feed part of the bun to a gull.

I haven't been so happy in years.

She did not expect him to say anything so serious. Again and again the gull bites quickly.

Well you've had a difficult few years.

Caleb kicks sand.

Soon the sun is going down. A young man dances on each step as he makes his way toward the F platform, and Lydia and Caleb are stuck behind him, waiting, as he takes a wide step and brings the second foot to join the first, snaps his fingers, takes a wide step back to the left, joins, snaps, finally takes the next step up, snaps, keeps dancing. At first Lydia rolls her eyes in annoyance but then Caleb squeezes her hand and she realizes that there is no rush. The young man is having a good time and his movements are catlike and precise and full of rhythm. Lydia finds herself smiling. They almost miss the train but they make it.

Over the next month they go to every beach they can think of. They go back to Coney Island and over to Brighton Beach, once to Manhattan Beach, then Orchard Beach, Riis Park. They go out to Rockaway. She lets him hold her hand and lets people watch. She drives them out to Gunnison, where they are completely alone, and one day to Wolfe's Pond, where a family glares at them. She tells herself that it's too early in the year to go to the beach, that no one they know goes anyway, that at the beach they are not themselves but others and so cannot be recognized. Maybe they met on an app, or in a bookstore.

Lydia makes the occasional conjecture about the ring that she saw from across the lawn.

Maybe they're going to tell you soon and they're just not ready.

I told you he would have told me by now.

I saw it, says Lydia. Are you saying that I didn't see what I saw?

It's too cold to swim but Caleb dives in once anyway, at Riis, and then never again.

I told you it's not the Bahamas, Lydia says, shaking with laughter as he swears and shivers.

Eight million people, he says. Eight million people doing whatever, going wherever, fucking whoever (whomever, she tells him, whomever, and he says no one says that) and that's not counting the commuters, the Westchester people and the Holland Tunnel people all buying things and walking down the street and checking their phones and eating sandwiches and buying coffee so they can use the bathroom and getting parking tickets and flu shots and any of the other things that happen in a usual or relatively usual day, not to mention the things that happen on big days, people's mothers dying or siblings getting hit by cars or being rejected from jobs or colleges or by potential girlfriends or boyfriends, being admitted to the hospital, losing your house, getting food poisoning, not having a text returned. See that lady, he says (Caleb don't point, Lydia whispers in his ear), fine, sitting across from us and to the left, with the knitting.

The train screeches as it speeds up. Yes, says Lydia.

Well she's not looking at us, she's thinking about what to make for dinner tonight or whether to go to nursing school or whether her husband is fucking her sister or whomever, he says, see, and he kisses her neck. The woman Lydia told Caleb not to point at looks to the side and then down at her knitting. The needles click. She puts one into the end loop on the other, she makes a new loop and it slides and again and it slides. Eventually Lydia agrees that she and Caleb can go out to dinner together.

At a restaurant, he says, a normal restaurant.

At a restaurant.

You'll see, no one will care. I don't even think that my father would care.

The knitting lady puts the needles and the scarf in her bag and the magnetized clasp clicks closed.

My father wants me to be happy. We could even tell him.

Lydia makes the reservation. She wears a black dress and black heels and sheer black tights. Caleb wanted them to get to the restaurant separately like real separate people, actual people dating or an actual real couple with two lives that make a shared one over dinners, breakfasts, illnesses, anniversaries, arguments. Lydia said yes to that insofar as it pertained to this reservation.

The G is largely empty. Lydia sits in the short bench at the end of the car. Above her ads for headphones and Brooklinen and erectile dysfunction treatment line the curved area where the wall meets the ceiling save for one unused advertising space on which a tall slip of paper blocks electric interior light. It is too far away to read but Lydia can tell from the shape and placement of the paper and from the triangle on it that it's an ad for Keano the psychic. From this distance she cannot see the eye in the triangle.

The train pulls into Hoyt-Schermerhorn and a woman sits down next to Lydia. She balances on her knee a device with a dull small screen and a large black keyboard and begins intently to type, pressing letters one by one with her outstretched pointer finger. When Lydia glances over at the screen it reads WHAT IS MOST IMPORTANT TO PATIENT NOW and underneath the woman has entered TO BE PAIN FR and then she sees Lydia watching.

Lydia arrives at the restaurant first and takes the table. She orders a glass of white wine and looks at the sycamores outside and then at the other diners, at the people, who, she thinks, shortly will be watching her.

She told Caleb no, they should not tell his father. She can't forget how young he is and how poorly he understands other people. The young are idiots. She must remember that. He's got no idea what his father likes or wants, but she does. And soon all of these people drinking wine and eating fried olives and caprese salads and pasta and veal, they'll all know what she wants and likes once he comes in, once he sits down, once he takes his coat off and kisses her, they'll know, unless they think she's his mother. All of these people.

Lydia looks down at the neatly folded white napkin, the gleaming heavy-handled cutlery. At the edge of her vision a loose rhinestone bracelet scrapes the tablecloth as a bony wrist moves a hand and a silver knife butters bread. Nearby another hand puts a napkin in a lap. Lydia does that too and then she looks up. A forkful of meat passes thin lips in a woman's drawn face.

Soon Caleb arrives. He takes his coat off and puts it on the back of the chair. They are all going to watch.

He says hello. She only half stands up so that he has to lean over as they kiss. He holds her face awkwardly with his thumb at the corner of her eye and when he sits down in his own seat Lydia thinks that they have caught the notice of the bony-wristed woman in navy. The waiter seems anxious. Caleb orders sparkling water. She tears off a piece of bread and butters it. When she puts the small knife down he grabs her hand and holds it on the table and smiles broadly. Lydia can feel the eyes of the thin-lipped woman in the corner and wonders if she recognizes her from somewhere.

Who cares about them, says Caleb. When her pasta comes she has to ask for the hand back. His steak hasn't come yet so she waits with her hands in her lap until he asks if she's ashamed of him.

Don't be silly, she says.

When the waiter puts Caleb's plate down in front of him he cuts into the meat without speaking.

The people at the next table are trying loudly to decide if Jim will for sure want a scotch or if they'd better wait until he gets here, trouble on the G. Someone says it was fine half an hour ago although it's like that nowadays, so unreliable, and someone is saying the MTA is going to bring in or has brought in a new transit expert who is the city's last and only hope when Lydia says, quietly, I love you, and Caleb softens. He doesn't speak right away. Then slowly and with gentle disbelief and pleasure on his face he tells her about this time he was waiting for the 1 with Beau and his friend Colleen Someone. Colleen dropped a plaid scarf onto the tracks, and then as soon as the train pulled out of the station it stopped in the dark tunnel and they couldn't stop laughing because they thought the problem might have been Colleen's scarf.

But also we felt bad, he says, still pink-cheeked.

Hmm, says Lydia. She asks about his father and Diane. He says they seem fine. Diane's been making good fish.

Your father hates fish.

When they ask for the check the waiter puts it on her side of the table.

Later she will recall that they were at Riis or Coney or Brighton Beach looking out to the ocean when the sea was rough and she observed that it was too bad that there was no lighthouse.

Why?

Can you imagine the view from a lighthouse on a day like this?

There's a lighthouse in Montauk.

His final K is especially careful. Montauk. She repeats it in her mind.

My father goes out to Montauk. He picks up a gray stone and pockets it. Or used to with my mother, before I was born, but I've never been.

Tom never told her that. She's never been out there. On the sand nearby a white bird arches its neck and makes a long call.

Let's go to Montauk sometime, she says, and see the lighthouse.

In Montauk they'll be like any other couple, like his parents, like couples who wear striped shirts and rest on the beach. In Montauk, in fact, they'll be not like any other couple but only like his parents and couples like them, and Lydia will wear the right shoes, will take off the right shoes to walk on the beach where they'll pose for the photograph which, she says to herself now, should not be taken, no photograph of her with Caleb should be taken because they are like no other couple and not like his parents.

That night she is alone. She Googles *what to do in montauk long island* and finds an article about a sporting boat accident. The captain recalls the passengers scrambling off. Bobbing orange spots. Lydia searches, Lydia clicks. There is the view from the lighthouse. There is an article about house prices and rooftop pools. She finds a site dedicated to the Montauk Monster. Readers have sent in snapshots of decomposing animal forms, often white-bellied, sometimes red-backed, skin sloughing off. The animal is large and has a strange face. At first, writes one reader, I thought it was a dog, but then I got closer. The limbs are large and their joints to the body are webbed like a frog's foot but only in certain images. The site creator promises she will get to the bottom of this and in the meantime a sidebar links to a form for those who would like to advertise with Montauk Monster and below this link is a list of drugs in plain blue lettering: Accutane, Adderall, Amoxil, Caverta, Cialis, Celexa, clomiphene, clonazepam, diazepam, doxycyline, Elavil, Fioricet. Lydia scans down to Zovirax and back up the list and down again through Lamictal and Neurontin and Soma and Tramadol. If she scrolls down further, recent comments tout cheap clit vibes, tickets to basketball games.

Chapter Fifteen

She tries not to ask about the thing she saw sparkle on Diane's hand in April but one Saturday morning she wakes up anxious and too early. She goes into the kitchen, makes a piece of toast, and eats it with butter and some marmalade that Jane must have bought. When she climbs back into bed Caleb rolls over and comes close to her. She can feel the skin of his face on the side of her neck.

I smell oranges, he says. She cannot help herself.

She whispers, Can you ask him?

Caleb looks up.

What?

Can you ask him why Diane was wearing a ring at the party.

Why would I ask him that.

It doesn't make sense and I want to know.

You're obsessed with him.

I'm not, she says.

He sits on the edge of her bed and pulls his boxers on. She says his name. He asks what it's supposed to be like out today. She says, Caleb, come on. Soon he is almost dressed and she says his name again, louder than she meant to. He is pulling a sock onto his exquisite foot and she kneels on the ground and kisses its arch, its heel, its ankle.

Stop it, he says, laughing.

Shh, she says, Jane's asleep.

In the kitchen or the hallway something clatters to the floor. She reaches for the button of his jeans.

When they wake up again he asks, Will you give me a stick-and-poke?

Lydia sits up and checks her phone.

Are you listening? he asks.

I thought we might have overslept.

I don't have work today. Will you give me a stick-and-poke?

She turns to face him.

What, like a tattoo?

Yes, says Caleb. Will you give me a stick-and-poke tattoo?

Once, while searching for more beaches online, she found an article published in 1997 under the headline IF WE'D ONLY KNOWN BREEZY POINT WAS SUCH AN AWFUL PLACE.

What if we went to Montauk after all?

Caleb kicks her foot lightly, playfully, under the sheets. First give me a tattoo, he says.

I don't know how.

I'll show you how.

Right now I want coffee.

Lydia walks down the hallway and listens for movement in Jane's room, then walks back and into the kitchen. She can't find anything out of place. Earlier she must have imagined the noise of something falling, or maybe when Jane got up she found whatever it was and put it right before she went out. Lydia washes dishes while the coffee brews.

They scrounge freely around the apartment. There is thread. There is a sewing needle. There is a pot and water they can boil to sterilize the needle. Lydia thinks she has some India ink but cannot find it so Caleb says, Let me run around the corner and get it while you draw. That way when I come back it'll be a surprise.

What should I draw?

Draw me a ghost, he says.

When he gets back she says her ghosts look bad, they look like weird lumps like sheets with black dot eyes, they are ridiculous.

I like them. Do that one.

He points to a curved outline with a ragged lower edge, little round holes for eyes and a dark surprised O of a mouth.

What's the thread do?

Here.

With the pad of his right thumb he holds the needle against the pencil near where the yellow paint ends and the wood begins to narrow toward the tip. He takes the thread and starts to wrap it around, binding the needle onto the pencil. Lydia can see the beginnings of a sharp tool. Then his hand slips.

Sssst. He flinches and shakes his hand. The pencil drops onto the ground and the thread falls on the kitchen floor next to it. The needle is a silver shot nearby.

What happened?

I stabbed myself.

She has the thought to tell him that that's what the whole thing is for, that that's what tattoos are, that's what they're making with the pencil and the thread and the sterilized needle. Instead she kisses his thumb. A red pearl of his blood breaks on her mouth.

We should boil the needle again, she says, now it's been on the floor.

They shave the thin light hairs from a spot on his back just to the left of his spine, about halfway up. Then they sterilize everything again and he sits sideways on the futon. She kneels behind him and starts.

I'm not sure I'm doing this right.

You put the needle in at kind of an angle. I think you've. Yeah.

And so I make dots first –

Yeah so you make dots around the edge and you go over it to fill in the lines.

And what if I fuck it up?

Fuck it up like how?

She wipes the blood from his skin.

I don't know if I'm putting the needle in far enough.

Then it'll just fade, you can touch it up later. If it fades it's more like a real ghost anyway.

A real ghost. Really.

After the ghost is finished they cover it with gauze. He puts his shirt on and says that now they should go out. She's about to say she changed her mind, what if they run into someone, but he looks at her and she knows he'll say she promised. Anyway she recalls what he's said about eight million people and watches the T-shirt move where no one else knows a bloody ghost is settling into his body and she is overcome with happiness. She takes his hand. At the diner they order pie and she asks him to go to Montauk with her the next day. He says it's only eleven, why not go now.

On the train out she puts her head on his shoulder and they are travelers like any others as Long Island rolls past the window. There is a field, there is a school. There is a boarded-up business. There is a golden retriever and holding its pink leash a happy child. Faraway somewhere, she thinks, Tom and Diane hold hands, but her ghost mark is on his son and he has no idea. There are tracks in need of repair and ripped plastic bags that float in the breeze and settle alongside newspapers bottles wrappers and old floss and there is probably some concern among distant managerial parties that the tracks may catch fire but it appears no action has been taken. Caleb naps. When he wakes the tracks are cleaner. Before long there are shimmering ponds, there is a swan, the girl in the row in front of them is overjoyed at its neck and says it's beautiful. Her father says it is but swans are actually violent so you have to be careful. They are territorial, he says. Caleb and Lydia hear the little girl ask why. Meanwhile out the window there is a balloon, there are perfect houses of slatted white clapboard, octagonal boathouses even, there are cattails and gliding ducks, there are gray rushes.

They go up to the lighthouse first. The land just below them is covered in green, and soon it slopes down to the ocean. Near the shore there are rocks and seconds of frothy disturbance that vanish as fast as the wind brings them. Far away the sea meets the other sharp blue of the sky. Lydia takes a picture of Caleb leaning against the plate plexiglass.

The woman at the exit says, You're lucky you got such a clear day.

Where next? asks Lydia.

Halfway through their walk along the beach he stops to show her something.

What are we looking at? she says, amused.

If you squat down and put your face right near the sand it looks like Mars.

As each wave after lapping the shoreline draws back into the sea tiny punctures appear in wet sand and close, pop up elsewhere, close up, in quick-changing constellations of air.

I don't really think it looks that much like Mars, says Lydia.

It looks like another planet, then. Put your face closer so it's big.

She does.

Don't fall in the water, it's freezing.

I won't. Don't you fall in, either.

He puts his hand on her hip to steady himself or her or both of them, slides the hand under her shirt. She touches the beach with both hands, leans onto them for better balance.

How long do you want to watch this for?

His palm is warm and she is looking at the tan sand just in front of her, at the small holes in it disappearing, when the next wave comes and then keeps coming, closer than she thought was possible. Cold water covers her hands, and she flinches and lifts them and feels Caleb grab her. Then she lands on her side. The sand is hard against her hip and water shocks her skin. The wave draws back into the ocean. Caleb's fallen sideways too. She gets up and helps him stand.

Oh my god, she says, laughing. Wow, that's cold.

Ow, it stings, he says.

Caleb rips the salt-drenched gauze off of his new tattoo and throws it in a public trash can. His shirt is wet too and so he takes it off and holds it in one hand, shivering.

At the nearby kiosk — if you can really call it a kiosk, thinks Lydia, someone could live in there, it's probably winterized — glittering snowglobes and pewter swans sit in neat rows near rotating displays of nametag keychains and piles of soft gray sweatshirts that say MONTAUK on the front. She buys two of them, one larger than the other, and two pairs of sweatpants. He puts the sweatshirt on.

They walk down the road and find a restaurant. The man behind the bar is in his forties. He wears a faded red shirt with the top button done up so that his neck looks painfully constricted. Lydia wonders if his gaze lingers on Caleb's hand, Caleb's thumb, resting on the exposed skin of her lower back where her wet shirt has ridden up as she leans on the bar, or if his gaze is lingering on her lower back itself, or if he's looking at something nearby on the wood floor behind them, a mouse perhaps, and he does not want to say anything, or if she has made all of it up. She tells the man that they want to sit at the bar but they're going to change first, they slipped and they're wet so they'll just use the bathrooms and change. He says Fine in a curt tone and wipes a glass with a dishcloth and puts it away.

What's veritable mean? Caleb wants to know.

What?

Veritable.

You know that.

I don't think so, he says, and kisses her.

She pulls away and looks into the bag from the kiosk, reads the glossy white labels at the waistbands of the sweatpants.

Here, she says, and hands him the pair in his size. And you should wash your tattoo off too. Doesn't it still hurt?

Not as much anymore.

It's going to get infected. We should have stopped to get Neosporin. We should go to a drugstore.

It's not my first one, you know. I know what to do.

Just wash it carefully. Do you want me to come help you?

No, he says, I can do it.

I'll meet you back here, she says, and heads off down the hall.

The floor of the bathroom is made of brown tile. Lydia shuts the door and slides the pin into the lock, which hangs from the doorframe on tiny screws that have loosened with use. When she has changed into the gray sweatpants and sweatshirt she looks at herself in the mirror and sees her smudged makeup and is pleased. Lydia in Montauk is not who she thought she might be. She is not from here, has never been here before and has the sweatshirt to prove her enthusiasm. With a paper towel she wipes off as much makeup as possible and goes to order a drink from the tight-collared man. As she sits at the bar she notices a woman with white hair and dark eyes who seems to look at her over the shoulder of her friend, past the gestures of her friend's active hands. No, Lydia thinks, the woman is probably not looking.

She feels a hand on her shoulder. Caleb has come back from the bathroom in his matching sweats.

Hey, MONTAUK, he says, pointing at the letters on her chest.

Hey, MONTAUK, she says back. I ordered you a seltzer, do you want anything else?

Fries.

He smacks his lips and laughs.

She looks at him sidelong as she orders the fries. The tips of his fingers drum the wood bar top. She feels his other hand slide under the back hem of her sweatshirt.

What made you think of veritable?

What?

Veritable.

He points behind the barman at the exposed brick wall on which once-bright painted tin advertisements hang. One shows a duck. One shows a sailboat. An ad that shows a yellow-haired girl might be made of plastic because it's less reflective than the others, but Lydia is not sure. Caleb's thumb draws shapes on the small of her back.

A veritable ale, he reads.

Veritable is slow and she cannot understand why it is so funny.

It means real, she says, you know that.

Lydia's eyes meet the white-haired woman's. She wonders if something is wrong at the bar behind her, if one of the neon signs will soon fall off the wall and throw blue sparks everywhere. She turns to check and cannot see anything wrong.

The fries, when they come, are pretty good. Lydia points to his ankles and says the sweatpants are short on him.

Yup, he says.

Suddenly she says she wishes they could go on a trip to another beach further away, maybe a different coast or different ocean altogether.

Maybe we could.

She leans close, puts a hand on his arm, and says, Do you know why they're staring at us? Everyone's staring at us.

No they're not.

Okay, not everyone, but that lady is staring at us.

Lydia points her out. He stands up. He looks again and sits down and looks away. He hides his face with one hand.

Lydia is saying, What is it, what is it?

He's aware that he must look strange because Lydia is staring at him too. Lydia and Diane are both staring at him. He breathes more and more quickly. He looks away and down at the grain of the counter. Someone is saying his name.

A strange noise slips over the room like light on an oil slick. He doesn't know how far he is from everyone's eyes, from swirls and eddies and the jagged sound that slips and sticks and shifts and hacks and catches in the body where he must be empty, he must be what coughs and cannot breathe, and then he feels a hand on his back.

You're laughing, Lydia is saying, it's all right, you're just laughing.

He tells her to pay and she pays quickly. They knock the fries over and he steps in them. The man behind the bar leans forward and looks at the mess on the floor. The white-haired woman is standing up now, is looking at Caleb with alarm.

Sorry, sorry, Lydia says to the bartender, and then over her shoulder to Caleb, What's wrong, I don't understand.

Let's go, let's go.

As Caleb pulls her through the restaurant door she hears a woman's voice call out his name.

How does she know you? Lydia asks. He hurries down the wooden steps. On the way to the train he tells her and she does not believe him.

Let's get you a bottle of water.

That's Diane, he says, you don't understand, that's Diane.

But it isn't, she says. After a minute she asks him who she saw at the party. He doesn't answer and won't let her touch him. On the way home he drinks water in small sips. His father is calling and calling again.

See, Caleb says, she's told him.

But I'm not even wearing any makeup, she says, and this ugly sweatshirt.

Caleb does not pick up his phone and eventually turns it off. Lydia puts hers on silent. He says he wants to stay with her tonight. It's dark and the few birds fly low.

When they are about halfway home Lydia looks at her phone and puts it away quickly.

What, he says.

Nothing.

She keeps her face still.

What, Caleb says again. Is my father calling?

She tries to look out the window but it's dark enough now that she can only see her own face and the cushions of the train car and strangers playing with their phones in seats across the aisle. He leans forward so she can see his face too. She looks down.

What's my father saying, you know I can take it.

Lydia turns her head to look directly at Caleb. She tells him that Jane knows about them and wants her to move out as soon as possible. She watches his face make small movements and wonders what he's deciding not to say.

Can she do that?

Sure she can do that.

Let me see her text.

No.

Why not.

Because it's my phone.

I still want to come home with you, or wherever . . . wherever you're going.

Lydia stares at the brown vinyl back of the headrest in front of her. After a minute she grabs her phone and asks Caleb to stand and let her out. He does. She walks to the end of the trian car. Behind her he is saying, Where are you going? She doesn't stop.

Lydia leans against a door and rereads Jane's message. I know you're sleeping with Caleb. He's been stealing my Xanax and I need you to move out.

Lydia texts, I don't know where you got this idea. I can't tell you how shocked I am. I would never do that. What makes you think he's been stealing your Xanax? When did you notice it missing?

Lydia stands and waits. After a couple of minutes she has an answer.

I heard you this morning, you said his name.

I'm on my way back, she types, we can talk when I get back to the apartment.

Don't try to argue with me, Jane writes, Zoe and I have been talking this over all day and I can't live with someone who has some guy over who steals from me. I'm at her place now and I'm going to stay here for a few more days. By the time I get back I want you out.

But you misheard me, Lydia writes. Also, what happened with the Xanax?

In the window in the train car door a man's reflection opens the *New York Post*. After a few minutes Lydia walks back and sits next to Caleb, who says, Where did you go?

Go to sleep, she says, I'll wake you up when we're almost at Penn Station.

Chapter Sixteen

When Caleb's breath is deep and steady Lydia gets out of bed as quietly as she can. She takes small steps and feels in the dark for the jeans he threw on the floor when he got undressed. He makes a faint moan in his sleep. She takes his clothing down the hallway and into the living room and turns on the light.

In his pocket she finds fourteen dollars, his phone, and his housekeys.

Jane was lying. Jane was angry, so she lied.

Back in her room Lydia slips into bed and is relieved when Caleb does not stir. A gleam from streetlights or the moon enters through the window. His face is relaxed. His mouth is gently open. There's no one to hide from anymore.

In the morning Lydia tells Caleb to call his father back and when he refuses she sends him out for bubble wrap and cardboard boxes. She's folding her clothes when her phone rings.

Where is he? says Tom.

I think he's at CVS.

Don't do that, don't joke with me.

I'm not. I gave him cash and sent him to pick up a couple of things and I think he probably went to CVS. Unless they don't have cardboard boxes. Do you know if they have cardboard boxes at CVS?

After Tom hangs up Lydia texts Jane.

I would appreciate more information about your suspicions

regarding the Xanax. You might be upset but this is his health we're talking about.

Soon Caleb comes back with the boxes and helps her pack. Lydia finds a man with a van on Google, books a slot for Tuesday afternoon but asks if they can give him the destination address the day of.

They take Jane's quilt off her bed and nap under it. They eat off Jane's plates. They use her forks and bowls. In the evening Lydia convinces Caleb to call his father.

Okay but I want you there, he says.

Yes.

He lies down on her bed and she follows him. They pull the pink quilt over themselves and she rests her head on his chest. She hears the phone ring as they wait for Tom to pick up.

Even with the drawers shut the dresser across the room looks different now that she knows it's empty. The iron handles seem to stare at her. She hears Tom beg and plead. He tells Caleb he doesn't know what he's doing. Caleb insists he does know. Lydia hears his heart beat. His father tells him he's still a child and Caleb makes Lydia move so he can sit up, then leaves the bedroom and takes the rest of the call in the living room. When she goes after him he motions for her to stay away. She goes back to her bed and searches on her phone for rooms in shared apartments that will accept couples. Only one place in her price range is available immediately. She sets up a viewing for tomorrow. Caleb will be working at the greeting card store but she can go take a look.

The available room turns out to be dingy and small. Next to the bed there's an old lamp with a scuffed shade and daisies painted by hand on the square ceramic body. The man who shows the room to her is friendly.

Look, he says, I gotta meet your boyfriend before I say. I hear you when you say you're in a tight spot and I would love to help you out but still.

She calls Caleb, who leaves work to come. Lydia waits at a coffee shop around the corner. This could be her new place. She could come here in the mornings or for a break or if the coffeepot in the apartment broke. They sell cannoli. In theory she could meet friends here.

When the man meets Caleb, he says, Nothing personal, but I don't want to live with a kid. Good luck.

On the way back Caleb tells her he's quit the job at the card store. When he got to work this morning the owner told him he needed to be more careful. She said he'd been shelving sympathy cards on the thank-you shelf and that was not the only mistake he'd made in recent weeks. He said he'd improve but was frustrated and quiet as he restocked rubber stamps. Then he got Lydia's message and said he had to leave early to check out an apartment, and the boss said, You can't do that, not at such short notice. Lydia sighs and says it doesn't matter.

Later she searches again but still can't find anywhere else that will take couples and that is available now and that she can afford. She could see if she can find a room for herself and then Caleb could stay there secretly but they're so tired.

Leave your keys on the kitchen counter, Jane texts back.

You can't stay, Liz says. I've already got houseguests.

Lydia says she and her friend will find somewhere and that she's got to go. After she hangs up she stands in the kitchen for a while.

Liz did not ask which friend and did not say who her houseguests are. There are no houseguests and Tom has told her already. She was alternately flustered and acerbic but in each word clearly disappointed. Lydia wishes she had texted. Then she would not have heard Liz say, I cannot believe you called me, when she picked up the phone.

Lydia walks over to the futon and sits next to Caleb and asks if he has any ideas. He promises to ask Beau if he knows anyone they can stay with. They order pizza. When he's finishing his second slice he says, You know I need to get into my father's house somehow, because I have to get my meds and some clothes.

His medication. She had completely forgotten.

What have you been doing for the past couple of days?

I skipped them, he says.

You can't do that, she says, you need to be careful with prescriptions.

I guess I can get them tomorrow while he's teaching.

But you should have gone to get them the first day. You need to go now. You just can't play fast and loose with things like this.

I know what I'm doing, you don't think I know?

Lydia doesn't respond but calls Tom and asks if he and Diane will meet her and Caleb for dinner at Chez Napoleon. Shouldn't they go somewhere bigger, Tom says, somewhere where they won't be overheard. But I want to go to Chez Napoleon, she says, it has to be Chez Napoleon. Fine, says Tom, Jesus, under the circumstances, whatever you like.

Why does it have to be Chez Napoleon, Caleb asks after she hangs up. Behind her the light from the window is very bright and it makes her look small.

We're not going, so why shouldn't it be Chez Napoleon?

At seven o'clock he goes into his father's empty apartment. He packs his pills and as much clothing as he can fit in his duffel bag. Only a few days ago he lived here. He thought he would be brave when his father found out but here he is walking quietly around the apartment even though there is no reason not to make noise. He drinks juice and leaves the used glass on the counter. Here he is sneaking in and sneaking back out. He almost turns back to wash the glass and put it away but he makes himself leave it. He gets back on the subway.

When he gets home, or back to Jane's, Lydia is pacing the living room and talking with his father on the phone. She says it was all a big mistake, they meant some other night, and if Tom's so upset then they should just not do it at all.

He can hear his father shouting that he and Diane waited at Chez Napoleon for twenty minutes before they figured it out, waited for another hour just in case, would have waited all night because what is she doing to his child.

What did you order? Lydia asks his father. Caleb loves how her eyes get bright when she is excited. He wishes he could fight with his father like that. He slides his hand up her skirt. Oh no, she tells his father, you should have gotten the escargot.

The next day the man with the van comes. They take the boxes to Lydia's storage unit in Red Hook. Beau texts back and says this is all wild, really fucked up, and his roommate says no but they can stay with his parents. Should we see if they'll let us come over now, says Caleb.

No, Lydia tells him, Jane won't be back until tomorrow, just say thank you and ask if we can please stay tomorrow.

That night Caleb is unusually affectionate, kissing, rubbing, nudging Lydia until she tells him she has got to sleep. In the morning they gather the last of their belongings. Lydia moves slowly. She'll miss the blue walls of the living room and will most likely never see Jane again.

We should go, Caleb says.

Let's have a coffee first.

When the coffee is ready they sit on the futon. Caleb observes that it looks beautiful outside, and Lydia says yes but doesn't add anything. He asks how long she thinks they'll stay at Beau's parents' and what they'll do after, and she says she has no idea. She drinks slowly. From time to time she looks at the door.

Why did it take you so long to get back the other night?

What?

From your father's, why did it take you so long.

That's how long it takes, he says, it takes at least an hour. You know that.

Maybe.

Why are you looking at me like that, he asks. She looks at him like his father used to. We should go, he adds, we should get out of here before Jane gets back.

I guess we should.

They finish the coffee and wash the mugs by hand. Lydia remakes Jane's bed.

They take the F to the R and head out to Bay Ridge. Beau's parents live in a cream-colored house with a peaked roof. Lydia and Caleb walk up the steps to the porch and ring the doorbell. Beau's mother answers the door and says hello and that they should both call her Cindy.

Lovely to meet you, says Lydia.

Cindy loses the curve of her smile and nods and recovers and says she thinks they've met, and Lydia stands up straight to bat back the hot spreading feeling she won't call shame.

Beau's parents offer dinner. Lydia says they don't want to trouble them and Caleb sits there as if he can't understand how awkward this is for her. Cindy and Alvin insist.

We've learned a new way to roast chicken, Cindy says. It's almost done.

When the chicken is ready the mother cuts it into pieces and they eat it with vegetables and rice. No one talks. Caleb notices the feeling of the drumstick bone, hard and slippery, between his lips, and then gives up and moves on to his breast piece.

Alvin asks Lydia if they've met before. I think at some school night or something. Or did you ever drop him off here?

Once or twice, says Lydia. And then he got older and stopped needing it, and then his father left me.

Right, says Cindy, and picks up the white paper napkin from her lap. She folds the open rectangle back into a square and the square diagonally again into a triangle, blots her lips and looks sideways at Alvin. He asks if anyone wants more rice.

I was joking, says Lydia, but also, that is what happened.

I'd have more rice, says Caleb.

Actually, if there's any more wine, says Lydia, and she watches Caleb's face as Beau's father says of course there is and pours her another glass. She takes a big sip.

So what's going on, Alvin begins, pouring a large glass for himself. Cindy says, Darling.

They eat and drink in silence. A few times Lydia wonders if she should say something, almost breathes in to say it, realizes she doesn't know what she'd say and exhales and drinks.

It's nice that you've stayed close with Caleb since the split, Cindy ventures after a while. Not everyone does.

Alvin puts his fork down and claps slowly.

After dinner Lydia helps clean up. Cindy tells them Caleb will be in Beau's old room and for Lydia they've fixed up the sofabed in the den. It's a very nice sofabed, she says.

I'm sure it is, says Lydia, just as Caleb is saying, But we –

and Lydia says loudly that she's sure it'll all be perfect. She's sure it'll all be perfect. They're very grateful.

Lydia washes her face quickly, brushes her teeth, lies down on the sofabed and listens. She can hear Alvin and Cindy upstairs but can't make out the words, at least not most of the time. She does hear the phrase *call them on it*. When she wakes up again it's past midnight and Caleb is in the bed with her. Upstairs the parents raise their voices. The argument is not about Lydia and Caleb anymore. Last year Alvin was in a snit the whole damn time they were in Tucson, and he says it's because he was worried about work but he's always like that with her family, Cindy says, especially with her sister but always with her whole family.

Do you think they know we can hear them, Caleb says into the back of Lydia's neck.

I don't know. I expect so. She turns toward him and tugs at the hem of his shirt.

The next morning the parents are underslept and awkward and say that Caleb and Lydia will have to leave. As they're packing Cindy puts a hand on Caleb's arm and says, Call me if you need anything, really, even if you just need someone to talk to.

You know that's how this started, says Lydia. Cindy recoils as if burnt.

You really should go, she says, and Lydia says, Yes.

On the subway Caleb says he thought they'd be more relaxed.

They're not your friends, they're your friend's parents.

Where are we going?

The desk clerk has a thin black mustache and concerned blue eyes. She leans on his desk and fiddles with her credit card.

Why did she come here.

Next to her Caleb is doing something on his phone. She wonders if he's texting his father or buying drugs, though if he's only buying Xanax she doesn't know why she should care so much. But Jane was lying, she has to have been, otherwise the situation is intolerable, but also Lydia shouldn't care.

The man with the moustache tells her they're in room 429 and begins to tell her about breakfast.

She interrupts to ask if there's a different one, a different room, somewhere else in the hotel. He asks if there's anything in particular she's looking for and she says, I'm avoiding the fourth floor.

He raises his eyebrows and says, Okay. Let me see what I can do.

She knows he thinks she's unreasonable. She thinks she's unreasonable. Caleb looks over at her. The face of the man with the mustache relaxes into careful professionalism.

How's 318, he says.

Is that at the same price point.

Yes.

As they head to the elevator Caleb says, What's wrong with the fourth floor?

Room 318 has the same blond chest of drawers as the one she stayed in months ago but not in the same place. In the first room it was just inside the door and in this room it is past the bed against the far wall. In this room the carpet is blue. In the room where the man with the red ties was staying she thinks the carpet was beige and the chest of drawers was between the windows.

Caleb puts his bag down and says, Why didn't we get a room in an Airbnb?

In an Airbnb you have to talk to the host.

She takes a quick shower and then he does the same and lies down on the bed and takes a nap before heading off to see Dr. Antonelli. When she's alone she calls Tom and leaves a message saying she just wanted him to know they're well and they're thinking of him and they hope that he's well too.

Liz calls again.

I am hoping that you and Caleb are free for dinner in the next few days.

The voice maintains studied control. Years ago Lydia helped Liz practice breaking up with the boyfriend before Liz met Marty. Gerald I think you're really wonderful, they rehearsed, Gerald I respect your commitment to your work. Stay calm, Lydia said then. Now Liz sounds like she's talking to Gerald, but she's asking Lydia and Caleb to dinner and Liz hasn't had time for Lydia in months.

You've been so busy, says Lydia, I've missed you.

Horns honk in the street outside the hotel.

Liz clears her throat. Tom's very worried, she says.

We'd love to have dinner, says Lydia. We'd be delighted. We'd absolutely love to. Let's hash out the details over email.

It's urgent, says Liz. Tomorrow.

Fine.

After they hang up Lydia goes out and buys needles, black ink, a lighter, pencils, a notepad, a razor, hair ties, bobby pins.

So, asks Dr. Antonelli. What's been going on?

Not much.

The doctor waits. His eyes are patient.

Actually, Caleb says, there's something I haven't told you. I met someone.

The doctor makes a note and looks back up at him.

Actually, Caleb continues, it's someone I already knew. But we've fallen in love.

Where did you know her from?

She used to date my father.

Caleb thought the doctor's face would change but it doesn't. He repeats himself but the face still wears the same expression of detached and infuriating calm. Caleb tells Antonelli that he's in love with Lydia.

The doctor does not flinch.

Tell me how this started.

Caleb explains and says his father knows and seems upset. Or sad.

Did you have an expectation as to how he might react?

Caleb does not speak. He remembers how he once thought he would sit his father down on the sofa in the living room. He would be sitting in the armchair when he said, I have something to tell you. His father would go pale. His father would wait patiently. Caleb would speak slowly and his voice would be full of dignity and promise and power. He would say, I've been seeing Lydia.

Seeing?

Once his father got his head around what Caleb meant he would most likely cry and would ask questions. Caleb would say, That's personal. His father would say, It's horrible, and Caleb would say, I understand that's your opinion. Then the real argument would begin.

Antonelli is still looking at Caleb, waiting for an answer.

Not really, says Caleb, I didn't really think about it specifically.

Look, says the doctor, I find this relationship very concerning.

Caleb doesn't say anything.

Why do you think I find it concerning? If you had to guess.

I don't know why you think what you think.

What do you talk about, when you're with her?

All kinds of things, he says. He scratches his ear.

Do you talk about your father?

Sometimes, he says, I mean as I said, we talk about all kinds of things.

I don't think you're in love at all. I think you're angry.

Caleb notices on a shelf behind the doctor a glass globe containing, on a sand or false sand ground, a little cactus or cactuslike object and a tiny antelope skull. From this far away he can't tell if the skull is porcelain or plastic or if the cactus and the sand are real. No one could tell from this distance. He wonders if you turn the small false desert upside down and put it back right side up does sand like snow fall over the green and spiny succulent and into the eyeholes of the make-believe skull. Or will the cactus and the skull fall with the sand into the globe's curved bottom so that when you put it right again everything's mixed together, earth and succulent and fabricated animal remains all awash as one artificial landslide. Or is the sand or what looks like sand glued down.

Why, he says to the doctor, why do people fall in love? Why don't you explain. And then I'll know what's normal.

What makes you ask what I think about that?

I'm going to leave, Caleb says, you're not helping, why don't you ever help?

He waits. The doctor makes a note.

Is that new, says Caleb, that snowglobe thing.

When he opens the door of the hotel room she gets up.

I want a ghost like yours on the back of my neck.

He closes the door behind him.

What?

First of all how was your session, she says, taking his hands in hers.

All right. What did you say you want?

She explains again.

I don't know how to copy the one you did on me unless you trace it.

No, you draw one for me, a new one, but make it sort of like the one I did for you.

He bites his lip as he draws. When he's finished he shows her the image and she says she loves it. He helps her pin her dark hair up and out of the way. She sits on the floor at the edge of the bed and hangs her head so he can shave the back of her neck.

Stay still, he says.

Wait, wait. I changed my mind, I don't think I want to.

Chapter Seventeen

The next evening Lydia and Caleb get to the restaurant first. Its walls are covered in carved wood paneling and the waiters are young. The man who asks if they'd like still or sparkling is bearded and wears a button-down shirt with a subtle grid pattern.

Tap, says Lydia. And a scotch for me.

Soon Lydia spots Liz across the room. She carries a large black handbag and walks quickly between the tables toward them. Behind her Marty gives a halfhearted wave. When they sit down Lydia notices they both look old and tired. Liz's blonde hair is pulled back in a tight ponytail and Lydia wonders if that's why her face looks so strange and her eyes have so much distance in them. From Liz's expression Lydia would think it's her own face that has gone wrong somehow but maybe it's the tension of the hairstyle or perhaps in the months since they've seen each other the two old friends have forgotten each other's faces.

Well, here we are, Liz says. Hi, Caleb.

Marty adjusts his glasses. His hair has much more gray in it than Lydia remembers, and he's grown his beard out.

Yes, here we are, so nice to see you, says Lydia. How's Tom?

Not very well, says Liz.

That's too bad.

Fucking angry's what he is. Marty looks Lydia square in the face.

Marty, says Liz.

That's really too bad, says Lydia.

Caleb reads the menu.

The waiter returns and places a glass of scotch in front of Lydia. He takes drink orders from Liz and Marty.

Lydia says, And a sparkling water too, for him. With lime.

When the waiter leaves Caleb says, I was fine with tap. He tries to make eye contact with Marty, who looks at the menu and says, I had the schnitzel last time. I liked the schnitzel.

You're ordering an appetizer too, I hope, says Lydia.

Liz raises her eyebrows. I don't think we –

Oh, but we haven't seen each other in such a long time.

All around them are voices and clipped sounds of silverware being placed down on china and the sawing and scraping of knives cutting meat as agreeably as possible.

How is their bibb lettuce salad? says Lydia.

Liz says that the bibb lettuce is excellent.

Well, how's things, Caleb, says Marty. He pushes his chair out an inch or two from the table and says again pointedly, How's things.

Marty, says Liz, we talked about how to handle this –

– and we had no real plan, Lizzie, we couldn't come up with anything.

No one reacts when Caleb says he's fine so he has to repeat himself. I'm fine, he says, I'm good actually.

Look, Liz says, your father is very worried. Very upset.

You can tell him I'm happy.

The waiter brings Liz and Marty's drinks and pulls out a notepad. Liz orders the bibb lettuce and the guinea hen, and Lydia says she'll have the bibb lettuce and the steak frites, and Caleb says the same. Marty wants the wedge salad and the schnitzel.

I'll have a glass of the sauvignon blanc as well, says Lydia.

Right away, says the waiter.

You're really setting a bad example, says Marty, what with everything he's, you know.

A very bad example, says Liz.

You're just finding problems.

You shouldn't drink in front of him.

Tom does.

Not in front of him, says Liz.

You're making things up, of course he does, he always has. You're just upset. Anyway Caleb knows what he needs. He's not a child.

You've developed this self-serving –

Well, tell me what you really think, Lydia says, and smiles.

I don't need an example, Caleb says. His voice is measured, slow, and loud. He likes the way it sounds and is surprised.

Liz and Marty seem especially uncomfortable and Lydia thinks of the way she'll kiss Caleb when the hotel room door is closed behind them. I was so proud of you, she'll say. She uncrosses her legs and crosses them the opposite way.

I'm very concerned, she says, leaning forward, about the melting of Antarctica. It's really speeding up. A huge chunk of the ice shelf might just fall off, smack in the water, and then of course that raises the sea levels. There's already a big fracture, it's only a matter of time.

Marty, drinking water, begins to laugh and then to cough. Liz asks quietly if he is all right and he says that he is. Lydia looks at them.

How's Phoebe?

Fine, says Liz, just fine. She leans forward. Caleb, really, how are you? You can tell us.

I'm really happy, he says, nodding. Lydia grabs his hand under the table.

Because this is weird, it's really very weird, the two of you. Very, very weird. It's not all right, it's not healthy for –

It's incest, Marty interjects.

That word makes people look, says Liz, Marty, don't say that word in the restaurant.

The woman at the next table turns back to her friend.

It's not, says Caleb, while Marty continues, That's what it is, I'm going to call it what it is.

It's not, says Caleb again. She's not my mother, she's not my stepmother, I'm an adult.

No, says Liz, you're not. Listen to me. You are not an adult.

Actually, he is, legally, says Lydia.

The salads arrive. No one speaks while the waiter places each plate on the table, saying, Bibb lettuce. Bibb lettuce. Bibb lettuce. Excuse my reach. Iceberg. And here's that sauvignon blanc.

Thank you, says Lydia. I hear the pretzels here are fabulous, can we get a pretzel for the table? Actually, make it two. She turns back to Liz and Marty. Anyway, the ice shelf. Apparently all of these bacteria, there are prehistoric, you know, ancient bacteria – she takes a bite of salad – that have been frozen in glaciers for millennia, well, they're going to come back to life when the ice they're in melts. And none of us have any immunity to any of these diseases.

Lydia puts down her knife and fork and takes a sip of wine.

This is ridiculous, says Marty.

The second coming of the microbes. And what's more, also, the Bikini Atoll and all these other bomb test sites are going to be underwater, because we picked little islands because we thought no one important was there, even though of course people were there, these were their homes, and they had to leave because we made these places totally radioactive.

167

I don't know what you're talking about, says Caleb.

Nuclear testing, says Liz, for World War Two, but –

Actually, says Marty, it was the Cold War.

Liz looks at him, then cuts a bite of lettuce with extreme care.

Right, says Lydia, we were trying to develop the best nuclear weapons, sounds awful but that's what we were doing. We wanted to test them. So we picked, the US picked, this island called Bikini Atoll in the Marshall Islands –

Where?

In the Pacific. So we made the Indigenous people there relocate so we could test bombs there. We told them it was temporary but the atoll is radioactive now and the people who are from there can never go back.

That's horrible.

I know, says Lydia. It is. But also on top of that, on top of how horrible it is for the people whose island we stole and destroyed, which is of course awful, the thing is that Bikini and the other islands we used as test sites are unsafe for the next 50,000 years or something like that, and they're about to be overwhelmed by seawater. So the radioactive material will be everywhere, the whole ocean, and who's going to do anything about that?

Listen, says Liz. She puts her fork down and clasps her hands and puts them on the edge of the table. Listen, we're here because we love you, and we're very concerned, and Tom's very, very concerned –

Oh but tell us about you, says Lydia. What have you been up to? How have you been?

Fine, says Liz, but what Diane saw, in Montauk –

How is she?

Very worried and upset, like we all are.

How's Phoebe.

You asked that already. She's fine. Look –

You've been seeing a lot of Tom and Diane, then, recently, says Lydia. These past few months.

We've all been friends for years, so, yes, we've tried to, to, keep up the friendship.

You haven't had time for me, says Lydia.

The pretzels show up. Lydia excuses herself and goes to find the restroom. Caleb turns his head and looks over his shoulder until she is no longer visible. Then he turns back to Liz and Marty and says, Did you see what Trump tweeted?

Caleb, look at me, says Liz. Look at me. I'm glad we have a moment alone with you. This is insane.

Completely, said Marty.

Caleb looks at their faces as they wait for him to speak. Liz nods repeatedly in what she must think is encouragement and her wide eyes keep widening further in small pleas that annoy him. He pushes his glass away. Marty puts his head in his hand.

Marty, says Liz, as if she wants him to intervene somehow.

I'm disappointed in you both, says Caleb.

They both look at him in surprise. When he does not say more, they say that he can't possibly know what he wants, he is being abused, and when he cuts in to say he's not they say that of course that's what Lydia has convinced him of but he isn't in a position to make any real choices after what he's been through, the mental health and whatnot, especially considering how young he is.

You have to remember how much you've been through, Liz says.

I do, says Caleb. I do remember. He leans back.

Well then, continues Marty, basically, it's like in recovery, you have to take care of yourself, you have to really think about your choices, your motivations –

You're doing this because you want us to think you're a grown-up, says Liz. You don't love her. You don't even know what a relationship is, a real grown-up relationship, what it entails, you can't imagine.

Marty looks at Liz and then at the table, blinking.

Caleb stands up and announces that he's going outside to vape. Liz runs her fingers over her hair and pulls a few strands near her temple out of the ponytail. As he walks away he hears Marty's voice behind him saying, Let him go.

Outside he watches cars pass and wonders if there is a chance they are right, any small chance, because it's true that he wants to be an adult but then again he is. He is and he wants to be. And he is and wants to be in love with Lydia. And an adult. Across the street a man pushes an open metal canister on a metal trolley. It spews white gas. Caleb can barely make out that the label on the front says NITROGEN. He takes another drag of the vape. He would have thought they would recognize him for what he is.

When he gets back to the table Lydia is seated again and Liz is saying, It's so obvious, it's just so obvious.

I don't know what you mean, says Lydia, and Liz says, I mean, have you lost your fucking mind.

The waiter comes back with the schnitzel and the guinea hen and places the plates in front of Liz and Marty. I'll be right back with those steaks, he says, and leaves.

Caleb reaches under the table and grabs Lydia's hand. She blushes, blinks, glances over at Liz, blushes redder, and puts their joined hands on the table, running her thumb over Caleb's skin.

Liz looks at their hands.

I can't be here, I can't. This is disgusting. Marty, Marty did you bring cash like I told you. I want to go now. Marty, just put some cash on the table, enough, whatever. I'll meet you outside.

Liz grabs her bag and walks out of the restaurant without looking back. Marty places twenties on the table in a slight green stack, thinks, adds another twenty, pats the money.

I don't know what you think you're doing, he says to Lydia, and leaves.

The waiter comes back, a plate in each hand, and watches them go.

Is something wrong? Is everything satisfactory?

Lydia breathes in and out again. She picks up the cash and counts it.

Everything's great, she says to the waiter, we're excited for the steaks.

The waiter puts the plates of meat in front of Caleb and Lydia. Caleb picks up his knife and fork and begins to cut. Lydia puts the cash in her purse, then calls the waiter back and says, Actually, I'll have another glass of wine and if you could pack those up to go. This hen thing and the schnitzel.

And the steaks? the waiter asks.

We'll eat the steaks. We're eating them.

The steaks are well-seared on the outside, juicy in the red interior. The fries are crunchy, salty, perfect. Caleb and Lydia eat quietly. The waiter brings them a brown paper bag with the guinea hen and schnitzel inside in cardboard boxes. For dessert they order a creamy vanilla flan and share it.

Liz and Marty's cash covers the check and tip with some left over. Caleb and Lydia walk past a church called Mary Star of the Sea and under the overpass of the BQE. Before long there are no more brownstones and the purple-black evening seems to open around the calm large forms of industrial buildings.

This is right near my storage unit, says Lydia.

Back in the hotel's large gray-blanketed bed she finds to her surprise that she does not want to have sex. In the morning they decide to leave New York.

Chapter Eighteen

Lydia signals and looks over her shoulder but the blue Honda will not let her into the left lane.

It's not even itself anymore, she's saying, no one can be in New York. No one can live in old New York, real New York, because it doesn't exist, it's been priced out of itself, it's all chains and empty storefronts. We should have left already.

Up ahead the UN building comes into view like a fact. Caleb watches it get close. Soon they go into a long underpass, a half-tunnel open to the river on their right.

I guess.

They are about to pass the quarantine ruin on Roosevelt Island. At first he can see blue sky through the holes that were once doors and windows, and then gray buildings on the far side of the river, their windows sparkling, flit across the apertures. The interior of the old hospital must have collapsed a long time ago. He's always wanted to go walk around there but is not sure if you are allowed.

He feels the car slow. Lydia honks.

The ruin thing we just passed, the one where they quarantined people, do you remember what they were quarantined for? What the disease was.

Typhoid or smallpox or something.

They get on I-95 North.

Where are we going? he asks.

Halifax.

What?

Halifax, Nova Scotia. It's in Canada.

I know where Halifax is. Why are we going there.

Because that's where we're supposed to drop off the rental car.

Why are we supposed to drop off the car there.

She knows he's staring at her. She's glad she's driving so she has an excuse to not look at his face.

That's the option I selected on the rental car website.

In the pale summer evening they walk by the water in Newburyport and read plaques about the old shipyard. They eat cheese sandwiches in the damp breeze that comes off the ocean and walk past brick buildings in search of ice cream. Caleb seems to enjoy his cone of mint chocolate chip so Lydia is sure everything's fine. But before long he gets distracted and twitchy. Lydia asks what he's thinking. He won't tell her. She uses Expedia to find a Motel 6 outside of town and they check in. The sky is beginning to darken. She tells him to call his father and tell him they've left the city while she goes for a short walk along the highway. Cars zoom past her. She feels small.

After ten minutes or so her phone rings and it's Tom.

I'm going to call the police, he says.

You can't, he's an adult. Or you can, but they won't help you.

She can hear him breathing. She could ask if in the past few months Caleb has seemed slow or dreamy or confused. She could ask if he would help her figure out whether or not the boy in her hotel room is about to get sick again.

How much, Tom asks.

What are you talking about?

How much do I need to pay you to leave my child alone?
She turns around and begins to walk back to the motel.
He's not your child, I mean he's not a child.
How much, name your price.
I don't know, Lydia says, and hangs up.

The next morning Lydia asks the man at the desk where she can get a coffee.
There's a machine in the lobby.
Yeah but if I wanted to go out. Get some fresh air.
He gives Lydia directions. Outside a pickup truck runs a red light. Across the street a terrier pisses on a sapling. This stretch of road looks different in the daytime.
At the coffee shop there's a line of people waiting to order. Directly in front of Lydia a woman in a pink dress chats to her friend on the phone.
I wish I could be an announcer, she says. Or a monologist.
Lydia listens and stares out the window. A green SUV drives in and parks.
Well if that's not a job, says the woman, it ought to be. Hang on a second. She orders a muffin from the waiter and fishes for bills in her wallet. Anyway, I thought about trying some stand-up but the thing is you can't just be funny, like be a funny person that likes to talk, no, you have to write the jokes, they really prepare, write them like plan them and get them to land, and part of that is the deliverance. Did you see the Tig Notaro Netflix special? Well, in the extras they let you see how she develops a joke. And you see. Yeah, she tries it out and it changes a lot.
Thank you, says the woman to the server, who hands her a blueberry muffin on a paper plate. Do you have any forks?
The forks are over there, says the server.

Thank you. Anyway they let you see how Tig gets it from being not funny to being funny. It's not just the joke itself but also the way she says it that changes. And you realize how often when comedy fails it's because their deliverance is just not on point.

Lydia buys coffees and muffins. When she gets back to the motel room Caleb is sitting up in bed. He looks toward her as soon as she opens the door.

Have you ever heard of Great Bay National Wildlife Refuge? he asks her.

His eyes are clear. He is honest and healthy and lucid and she is ashamed of herself.

Anyway, he says, it's on our way to Halifax. I just thought we could stop off, but if you don't want to it's not a big –

No, she says, sitting down on the bed. Let's go. Here, I brought you breakfast. She hands him his coffee and the paper bag of pastries.

Thanks so much, he says.

And if he were not healthy she would help him. She could love helping him. She is honest too. They eat together in bed and get crumbs in the sheets.

While he's in the shower she texts Tom, No amount of money.

They spend the morning at the beach and then get back in the car. Later in the day they wander around mud flats and small ponds. He swears he saw an eagle but she says it was a vulture.

It had that fat body, she tells him, and that tiny pink head.

That afternoon Lydia sees a used car dealership by the side of the road. She pulls over and calls Enterprise and asks if she can drop off the rental car anywhere close by and they say she can drop it off in Dover or Portsmouth no problem. She hasn't ever bought a car before, though she thinks she went with her mother once a long time ago and she did go with Tom to buy the gray Saab but she didn't really listen to him, she was looking at the sad planting of stupid red pansies near the curb and also at the beautiful husband who was about to test-drive a car that he was considering buying as a gift for his wife, whom he mentioned loudly and often. Alicia was the light of his life. The man had long fingers and wore a dove-gray suit. She has no idea how much the Saab cost and so can't say if Tom did a good job buying it, if he asked the right questions, whether he tried to negotiate.

Lydia buys an old white Toyota for $849. It's banged up but the salesman is kind. He says for that price it's a fabulous car and Enterprise has promised they'll refund her the extra days of the rental. They'll need a car because they are not going home. She tells the salesman she's just going to return the car they've been driving and then she'll come back to pick their new car up.

Sure thing, he says.

Caleb asks if she can drop him off somewhere on the way and then go give the rental car back and then pick up their new car and come get him. He says he wants to get out for a bit, stretch his legs, grab a soda or a coffee or go for a walk.

All right, she says, keep an eye out for a good place.

Soon they spot a red sign that reads LAURA'S COFFEE SHOP and she leaves him there. She returns the car on the outskirts of Dover and calls a local cab and barely wants it to come because it's so nice to be alone. But it arrives. Back at the dealership she gets into the white Toyota and onto the road just as she did in the rented Chevy with him beside her and as she sees the red sign in the distance she has the urge to drive past it. Tom would pick Caleb up and they'd both hate her. She'd be far away, making some hairpin turn or trying to stay awake in miles of monotonous and delectable straightaway through some sunburnt territory with no one else's music.

The next night they stay in a motel like the one they stayed in the night before. Caleb keeps saying, Why not an Airbnb?

Late at night Lydia asks Caleb if he misses his mother. He says he's not sure if he remembers her or not so doesn't really know what to say, what's missing someone, anyway, exactly. Do you have to remember someone to miss them?

I don't know, says Lydia. I don't think there's a rule.

The red tail light from some passing car traverses the frosted glass window and cuts pink across the pebbled texture of the cream ceiling. Caleb says to Lydia, You remember your mother, don't you?

Of course, says Lydia.

The pink light fades.

They cut west. They do not stop in Laconia or Keene or Marlboro or Readsboro. The car's air conditioning breaks. Caleb rolls down the window and smokes the cigarettes he bought at Laura's Coffee Shop. They spend one night near Troy. Each motel they stay in feels like their place. Theirs the slippery quilted blanket in pink or blue or tan. Theirs the shabby desk. Theirs its chipping varnish and the Bible in the drawer. Theirs the rough sheets and in the morning the checkout.

Past midnight in Erie, Pennsylvania Lydia hangs up the phone on Tom again, reaches into the desk drawer and feels for the book she knows will be there, opens it and tries to find the part about blessed are the peacemakers and the some-things, meek, she forgets what else but the earth-inheriting part. She cannot find it. A few of the crisp light pages have been torn out at the spine and maybe the part about inheriting the earth is on one of those transparent clean pages, gone now, or maybe she just does not know where it is. She does not like the book and has never liked it, but her mother once told her that her father liked it, although maybe that was one of the things her mother said about her father because he was not there to say that he did not read the Bible.

Someone probably tore the pages out to use as rolling papers. She glances toward the window.

Through the flimsy curtains she can see Caleb's shape, backlit in the glare from the lights in the parking area. She sees the brighter point of whatever he's smoking and sees it make a streak in air as if the ember has followed ash, she sees the shape of his hands. Is he is talking to his father on the phone? She hears the voice but cannot make out the words.

When he comes in she smells his hands, she smells his breath. He smells like tobacco. She goes outside and breathes in the air where he was standing. She wishes she knew what to do and breathes in and wishes that he'd been smoking marijuana.

Show me your pockets, she says when she comes back into the room.

What?

I want to see what's in your pockets.

There's nothing in them.

But I need to see, she says, I need to, and she starts to cry. He turns out his jeans pockets and shows her the cotton flaps inside, blue stitching, lint.

The next day he cannot bring himself to talk to her so he

looks out the window and counts Mobil stations and golden retrievers.

Each day the grass by the roadside seems more parched. Spring has become summer and he is in a car with Lydia and broken air conditioning. He browses Reddit on his phone and reads her facts from Today I Learned until he gets carsick. The car sound system doesn't work so he plays Spotify from his iPhone. He has no way of getting home. He counts Dunkin' Donuts or looks for the most green lawn or plays other games in his mind that he does not want to admit. Lydia drives fast and is careful to park in the shade. In the parking lot she leans against the front of the car and he leans against its trunk and smokes and drinks the lemonade she bought him at the gas station.

No, Caleb hears her say, I won't tell you where we are. I won't.

You told me to stay away and now I'm telling you.

I did listen. I ran into him completely by accident. At a bar. You had some woman stalk us on Long Island.

Fine, so you don't believe I ran into him by accident and I don't believe she saw us in Montauk by accident. No I don't. So we're even.

I told you we're not coming back.

You're just jealous, admit it.

When Caleb answers his phone his father won't fight with him but says he's sad and disappointed and worried. He wants to know how he can help. Caleb's responses are always stilted and leave him with a shifting muted rage that presses at the underside of his skin. He decides to stop answering. He prefers to smoke and drink lemonade and listen to his father and Lydia.

They drive past farms and apple trees and shopping centers, lottery advertisements on billboards and signs for local candidates on lawns. They don't stop in Cincinnati but spend a few days in a town called Downeyville. Caleb looks out the window and counts the dead squirrels and chipmunks that cars before theirs have flattened and reddened. They keep going. At gas stations she buys him water and Monsters and Snapple and lemonade, Ho Hos and Sno Balls and Donettes. For herself she gets Keebler Sandwich Crackers, either Cheese and Cheddar or Cheese and Peanut Butter or occasionally Lance crackers which are almost exactly the same as the Keebler ones.

In the passenger seat Caleb uses his phone to search for cheap places to stay. Most nights they wind up at Days Inn or Travelodge. Sometimes he suggests independent hotels but usually Lydia says no because the rates are higher. Once they stay somewhere called Country Hearth and later learn it's part of a chain. Tom calls frequently. Lydia starts to delete his voicemails without listening to them. Caleb doesn't ask her not to, tells himself he's not really disappointed.

In the mornings Lydia works on her laptop in their room while Caleb gets breakfast or goes for a walk. In the afternoon they drive. Soon they will have to stop somewhere because she can't afford this anymore. They have to stop somewhere but nowhere is right.

I like going on road trips with you, she tells him.

When Lydia and Caleb stay in air-conditioned rooms the vast heat presses in at them through every shut window and door and stifles them as soon as they leave. Other nights the eager weather enters hotly through the window and sometimes a slight breeze follows as consolation. They love thunderstorms.

One night he wakes up sweating. Earlier he saw an ice machine in the hallway so he gets out of bed quietly. He leaves the room and shuts the door behind him, finds the machine and lets the cubes clatter into the plastic cup.

Outside he sits on the curb near the empty parking lot and runs ice over his forehead, his cheeks, his wrists and up the insides of his arms. He watches the taillights of passing cars and is glad that no one's looking back at him. The color of lemons appears over the treetops and shows him the old black telephone wires. He stands up and walks across the lawn, pours the cold water on a patch of dirt where small plants look to be struggling.

When he gets back she's sitting up in bed.

Where were you?

Getting ice.

What do you mean getting ice.

They pass St. Cloud but stop short of Beardsley and head south to Cawker City, Kansas, to visit the world's largest ball of twine. They turn back east and take a detour through Man, West Virginia and head north through Snowshoe and Seven Springs and a town called Indiana. They pass a trailer park with a white sign at its entrance that reads Tally-Ho Estates.

They are only half an hour from the Shuteye Motor Inn when Lydia notices a small red barn with a tattered white sign that reads APARTMENT FOR RENT. She pulls over.

Do you think it's really a barn on the inside? asks Caleb.

Who said anything about living in a real barn, says Lydia, why don't we call.

I want to get out of the car, says Caleb, so they walk around the building and try to see inside through the curtained windows. From the trees nearby or from the yellow field opposite comes the buzzing of some insect whose name they might learn if they lived here.

Lydia calls the number on the sign. After a few tries a woman picks up and says hello. Lydia asks about the barn by the roadside. The woman says it's basically a studio. She can show them if they're interested.

They wait by the side of the road for an hour and a blue Ford Focus pulls into the driveway. The landlady is around fifty and has dyed blonde hair and friendly eyes. She unlocks the door and lets them go in first.

To the right of the door is a little alcove with a refrigerator, a sink, a tiny stovetop and an oven underneath it. The only furniture is a metal-frame bed in the back corner with a naked pink mattress on top and a tiny square window above it.

There are pots and pans in the drawers, says the landlady, if you want to check.

Lydia stands in the center of the main room and looks around her. Caleb is pacing the right side of the room, opening and closing the windows there.

See.

Lydia looks to her left to see that the landlady has opened a cupboard and is holding a small metal pot in her hands. She nods slowly. Sheepishly the landlady puts the pot on the unlit stove, then walks out of the kitchen area and opens a door on the long left wall.

I use this space for storage. You don't have your own furniture?

No, says Lydia.

Well, I guess I could loan you some while you get going. I thought whoever moved in here would have their own furniture.

Lydia nods again and turns, looking around the room. Maybe it's the proportions of the space that are so beautiful. She can't figure out what it is.

Sorry it's dusty, the landlady says. To be honest I did this place up last year, renovated it and everything myself, well, with my husband at the time, my ex-husband now, but barely anyone's been interested so I haven't been here much recently. I was actually starting to think of trying to sell but if you want to rent –

We do, says Lydia.

That afternoon the landlady gives them the keys and a big round white metal table along with three matching chairs.

This is really outdoor furniture, she says, but I don't know where the stuff I thought I had is. I guess Jerry took it.

We appreciate this, says Lydia. Caleb helps her move the table into the center of the room.

The landlady gives them also a set of wooden drawers that have been painted sage green. On top she places a lace doily and china figurines of a cat and a girl raising up her skirts to show a crinoline.

Later that day Caleb and Lydia drive to the mall for sheets and a few extra plates and four metal fans. Then they go to the Price Chopper for food. At home they unpack their things from the car and take cold showers. In the morning they drink coffee and look out across the road at the field.

It reminds me of Greece, says Lydia, and Caleb smiles.

In August they buy a round chintz tablecloth. Caleb begins to look into going back to school in the fall. He sees Antonelli via Skype and tells him how happy he is. It's true, he thinks, though sometimes he does take a few of the Benadryl he found in the bathroom when they moved in so that he can sleep the afternoon away and get the day over with. He tells Lydia he's feeling a little sick and she seems to believe him or at least to be unsure enough about whether to ask him that she doesn't. It doesn't matter anyway because he has no way to get more. Maybe in the fall he can fake allergies and then she'll buy him some.

One day Lydia says, Let's get a dog.

Okay, he says. They eat lunch outside in the shade of a tree. He wonders if whoever owns the field would let their dog run around there. In any case the dog could play on their small patchy lawn. He wipes sweat from his face.

That evening they sit on the bed and look online for nearby shelters. Caleb says since they're in the country they should get a big dog, a Great Dane or something.

But what if we move back, Lydia says. Not soon, I mean, someday. You can't have a Great Dane in the city. We should get something small.

Do you want to move back?

She types something. Then she says, How about Gambit? Look at Gambit.

It takes them an hour to find a mutt who looks like a good compromise. Lydia says she'll fill out the application. Caleb lies back on the bed and imagines tossing a tennis ball to Alfie, wonders if they should change his name or not. Two days later Lydia tells Caleb the shelter staff emailed to say they only give dogs to families that have secure fenced yards.

Oh, says Caleb. I guess we could get a fence.

They search online for prefabricated fences. On weekends they drive to a lake and jump in. She lets him drive them around graveyards. No one knows who they are or says hello. After a month he invites his father to visit.

I want to at least see him, says Lydia.

He doesn't want you here. He told me.

Can we turn the fan on any higher? She wipes her palms on her dress, walks over to the electric fan near their bed and bends down to fiddle with the knob on its base.

I turned it on high earlier.

Lydia turns the knob to Off and back up, down to Low and all the way back up, and the whirring stops and starts and grows slow and then loud again. Caleb says, That's as high as it goes. It's as high as it goes.

What about the other ones?

They all are. And anyway you're leaving. He'll be here soon.

She gets her bag and the car keys from the hook near the door.

I'm going to do my errands, she says, and then I'm coming back. You and your father can be talking at the table, and I'll come in with the groceries.

He doesn't want to see you. He told me so.

Lydia turns around. Her eyes are sharp. For a second Caleb thinks he does not recognize her. He knows she looks like Lydia or that she looks like Lydia looks or that she looks like the woman that Lydia looked like until an instant ago. She has the same dark hair lightly streaked with grays he does not mention and the same small nose. But her eyes were full of pleasure when she argued with his father on the phone. Maybe they would be sharp as they are now if she argued with his father in person. Maybe with his father she would make some expression Caleb alone would never get her to make. And his father would show some new face too.

Come back in an hour, he tells her, or maybe a little less.

Lydia wonders if she'll see the gray Saab in the oncoming lane. Or maybe it will be behind her. Maybe Tom is lost. Or maybe he'll be in a different car. She tries to find him in her mirrors and someone honks at her.

He might have Diane in the passenger seat. Lydia misses his glasses but is in love with Caleb. She passes the small white church and exhales and pulls into the school parking lot where a guard asks her who she is there to see.

No one.

You've got to move along, then.

I just want to sit for a minute.

Ma'am, you can't be here if you don't have business at the school.

Lydia drives out. Is Tom there yet. She brakes at a stop sign.

A girl crosses the road slowly, texting.

Lydia drives to the grocery store and buys apples, tomatoes, crackers, bananas, milk although they have milk but they could use more, green grapes, eggs, Triscuits, Cheerios, onions, peanut butter, Pop-Tarts for Caleb, chicken, corn on the cob, and a cabbage. She is not sure what they will do with the cabbage but they will think of something. She will think of something. They will use the extra quart of milk.

In the parking lot she repacks the groceries so that the Pop-Tarts are on top of one paper bag and the green grapes are on top of the other. The bags are almost too full. The green grapes almost spill out and the Pop-Tarts might fall onto the dry grass as she walks with one huge bag in each arm from the car to their front door. Her front door and Caleb's. She'll pick the Pop-Tarts up and balance the box again on the top of the bag in her left arm. It will all be very complicated. She will have to put the bag with the grapes on top down on the ground in order to pick the Pop-Tarts up and put them back in place and then to pick both bags back up without letting the Pop-Tarts fall again. The grapes might also fall.

She will make it to the door with her groceries and try to open the screen door with the scrambling hand of one encumbered arm. She will not be able to open the door all the way but just enough that as it swings back shut she can get her foot in and try to keep it open so she can wedge herself through and by then Caleb or Tom will be there to help. It will likely be Caleb who helps. She will put the groceries on the table and Tom will glare at her. She will put the grapes in the refrigerator first. She is imagining how she will not look at him, how she will put the grapes in the refrigerator and the Pop-Tarts in the cupboard just like anyone, anyone who wears a blue sundress and puts away grapes and processed goods adored by a teenage lover, and she is thinking of how he will notice the sundress and how she will look back from the fridge and see him noticing and show him her dismay at his attention when she hears the sirens and pulls over to the side of the road to let the fire truck pass. When it has gone she gets back on the road and keeps driving. At the edge of the yellow field she has to pull over again.

I dreamt I heard her say, Is there anything to put these in?

I did not dream the electric sound of my heart. I did not dream all the little pulls of sticky tabs and needles where I was now part of apparatus after apparatus after salt water in its heavy hanging bag. I am glad I did not let Diane come with me, because then she might be here too, hooked up to machines. I heard the sound of someone rummaging.

They're too tall for this, Lydia said. Do you think there's anything to cut the stems with?

I dreamt I heard her ask him to go ask the nurse. I heard or dreamt the sound of my child walking, my son's gentle pace which I had not heard since the spring. A long time ago he ran down the hallway barefoot, and she laughed when she saw his glee at the sound of his own little feet. He kept stamping them. His smile was wide.

I heard his steps grow louder again, and then something metallic scratching or trying to slide.

It won't cut, I heard him say.

They gave you craft scissors, said Lydia, for children.

PART TWO

Chapter Nineteen

So you have no idea how it started.

Look at the kid, someone said, he's in shock.

We'll need to ask you again tomorrow, the first officer said.

Caleb had watched tall slits of orange billow out from between the wood planks of the barn. The flames had not reached him because he was across the road.

They lived there or had lived there.

At some point her car had pulled up some yards away and then she had walked toward him along the edge of the field.

He hasn't been able to tell us much.

What happened?

Ma'am, he hasn't been able to say in detail.

Is he okay?

He's in shock.

What about the man in the ambulance?

Before the roof had caved in Caleb had run out and called 911 but had not known the address. He had told them to go to the barn that the people had been trying to rent for a while. There was a fire. They had asked how many stories the building was but that was later in the call. He said one. He said that his father was in there. That was earlier. Caleb had described the area to the dispatcher and luckily one of the firemen knew. One of the firemen drove past here every day on the way to the station. That was lucky, a paramedic said later, considering.

His father's face had been very red. Caleb had seen that.

He needs to be checked out at the hospital too. The young man. He should come with us in the ambulance.

No, Caleb said.

We'll follow you in the car, Lydia said, I'll bring him.

I'd really advise you to come in the ambulance.

No.

The man in the ambulance, said Lydia, is he okay?

I don't want to say too much just yet. What is your relation?

The driver of the ambulance shut the door.

We're the tenants, said Lydia.

Once Caleb had been examined and pronounced all right they sat on blue chairs in the waiting room. Eventually a doctor came and found them and said that they had dressed his father's burns and were continuing to give him oxygen. Caleb ate snacks from the vending machine. It got late. A red-haired nurse came out of Tom's room and told them that they might as well go get some rest. You can see him tomorrow, she said.

All right, said Lydia, but once the nurse had left neither of them made any move to get up. Lydia kept glancing at Caleb as if she wanted to ask something but he did not care what her question was.

They drank coffee and went back to the vending machine and got Skittles and sat down again. At the back of the room a woman in a black hijab held her baby and sang quietly to him. Other families came in and sat in the blue chairs and waited. After a while some of them left and the woman with the baby made a phone call and said, Can you come get him, he needs sleep and I really feel like I should stay in case something goes wrong. He's actually being amazing right now but I know soon he'll start screaming.

The redheaded nurse came up to Caleb and Lydia with a concerned look on her face and said, There's a sleeper chair in his room, like a cot. Should I set it up?

Caleb and Lydia looked at each other. Then Lydia looked away and wiped her face with the back of her hand.

That would be very nice, she said.

They followed the nurse into Tom's room. She flipped on the lights and said, Don't worry, he's pretty out of it, we won't wake him up. Caleb saw the plastic mask and tubing over his father's face and looked away. The nurse pushed and pulled the cushions of a tan vinyl armchair until they clicked into safety as one long flat surface.

Now there's one, she said, let me see what we can do for the second person.

We'll manage, said Lydia.

You sure?

Yeah sure, Caleb said, we can take turns.

He felt Lydia's eyes question him but heard her agree. He thought he heard his father moan but was sure he was wrong. When the nurse was gone Lydia asked if he really wanted to take turns.

No, he said.

She nodded slowly. He saw fear in her eyes like light on the surface of water. Behind it was some question she did not want to ask. He waited. She hesitated for a short while. Then she said, I don't know how we'll sleep after all that coffee.

He lay down on his right side first so that he faced away from his father and then turned onto his left with his eyes closed. Through their lids he felt the light turn off. Lydia crawled in behind him so that her body pressed against his back.

Can you move forward at all, she asked.

He wriggled an inch or so forward and then felt the arm-rest against his stomach.

I think that's as far as I can go.

He listened to the careful steady noise of the machines and to Lydia's breathing behind him. At some point he must have fallen asleep because when a slew of beeps erupted and the lights came on and three nurses ran into the room he did not know where he was.

Lydia and Caleb were sent outside. They sat in the blue chairs and waited while his father was intubated and placed on a ventilator. Soon they watched the nurses wheel the machine and the bed and the patient out of the room and down the hall.

A tired doctor with glasses and a dark ponytail came out to speak to them. She asked Caleb how long his father had been in the house after he had left and where in the house he had been.

I don't know, exactly.

You said he wouldn't leave because he was looking for something.

Yes. But I don't know what.

And then what happened?

I ran, said Caleb.

The doctor explained that it looked like the insulation or the pipes or the furniture or something else or all of these things had been made of some material that in burning had released chemical fumes. Because his father had inhaled too much of these gases a rush of inflammation now swept his airway. He was being moved to intensive care.

You really can never tell which ones will have this delayed reaction, unfortunately, said the doctor. Inhalation injuries are tricky.

When can we see him?

I'm hoping later today, but we have to wait and see. You really should get some rest now.

We'll be fine, said Lydia. We'll wait here.

The doctor nodded. Then she turned and went down the hallway and through the double doors.

From time to time the redheaded nurse walked through the waiting room. After a few hours she came over to Caleb and Lydia and said, Do you have anywhere to stay?

The internet told them that the Shuteye Motor Inn was not far from the hospital. Lydia was quiet as she drove. An automated female voice sometimes interrupted Caleb's thoughts to tell his girlfriend to make a left turn or a right turn after a certain distance.

They would have been driving this way last month if they hadn't stopped at the roadside and called the number on the sign to ask about the barn. They would have gone past the barn and kept going and passed the Walmart they were passing now, the Giant Eagle Food & Drug, the Staples, the Sweet N Low Coffee Shop, a garden center in whose parking lot shoppers carried wilted plants to their hot cars, now this green pasture where white-splotched cows stood and stared at him, chewing. The next field was full of horses with gray masks on their faces and flies crawling where their eyes should have been visible. Not long afterward they found the motel they were looking for and the voice from Lydia's phone told them that they had arrived.

The rooms at the Shuteye Motor Inn were clean and bright. Lydia pulled the blue curtains closed and lay down on the bed. He followed her. He brushed her hair away from her face.

She said, I'm so tired.

Me too, he said. She took a breath as if she was about to say something and then he saw her decide against it and close her mouth. Then she tried again.

I wonder, she said carefully, looking at the ceiling, what he was trying to find.

I told you I don't know, he said, because it would hurt her and because he did not want her to know that he was to blame.

They slid under the thin white blankets. The curtains were thin too and through his eyelids he could see red daylight. He was so tired. He was half asleep when he thought he heard her say, Were you smoking inside. He tried to say no but everything was heavy.

As they drove back to the hospital a few hours later he asked if the horses could see through the fabric on their faces and she said, It's just for the flies. He said That's not what I asked. She said I told you they can see through it.

Do you think you'll understand if I bring him flowers? Lydia asked the nurse.

Sorry?

I mean do you think he'll understand. Do you think he's aware. I was thinking I could run out and grab some or if there's a gift shop.

There are no flowers in the ICU. We don't allow them. But he's heavily sedated, to answer your question, so he's not aware of anything, which is probably for the best. Just imagine he's having wonderful dreams.

Lydia put her hand on Caleb's shoulder and said, Do you want me to get you a sandwich? Then she turned to the nurse and said, Will you stay with him while I get him a sandwich?

I'm sorry, I have to check on my other patients, but I'll look in again soon. Again, he's really very heavily sedated, so don't worry. He's not suffering.

Caleb sat with his father while Lydia went to the cafeteria. They had said they were going to keep the initial silver dressings on for 48 hours total so another 20 or 30 or so, he had no real idea how long was left, and then after that they would reassess and see what needed to be debrided. Assuming all goes well with the ventilator, the doctor had said, and Caleb did not ask her to explain. He did not ask her what debrided meant. He watched the machine work and looked at his father's crimsoned face and at the bandages on his arms and legs.

Not long after Lydia had gone out to get groceries, his father had arrived in a blue car he did not recognize. I want you to get in the car with me and leave before she gets back.

He had said no. He had said he had brought his father here to show him his new life, not to leave it.

This is not your life, his father had said. I love you so much.

His father had looked at him with pity on his face and asked how he was feeling overall. Fine, he said, and then again said he would not leave Lydia. His father ran his fingers across his forehead. Caleb saw him give up. He had not expected it to happen so soon.

Then his father said, Look, I came here to talk to you but also I want those pictures.

What pictures?

You know what pictures. The one of us together. And the one of her with the stuffed tiger, when she was a kid. It means a lot to her. Her father took it. There are no copies.

I don't have your fucking photos, said Caleb, who felt tears in his eyes and was angry and wanted to blow his nose.

His father said to tell the truth. Then he opened a kitchen cupboard and looked inside. Across the room Caleb noticed blue flickers coming out of the electric heating unit that ran along the baseboard.

Look, he said to his father, and pointed.

His father shut the cupboard, walked a few steps, and opened the door to the landlady's storage.

You're not looking, look.

What? His father turned around.

Fire, said Caleb, and pointed again. I'll get water.

No, don't get water. You can't pour water on an electrical fire.

What do I do?

Turn the power off. Where's the circuit breaker?

But already the flames were bright orange and growing fast. The wall was beginning to burn. The smoke smelled bitter.

I don't know where it is. I don't know.

There was a rushing noise, and then the sound of something creaking.

I'll get a blanket, said his father, walking toward the bed. We need to smother it. You tell me where those pictures are.

The room was very hot now. Fire leapt to the bottom of the rightmost curtain and began to climb it swiftly. A big spark flew into the air. Caleb coughed. The smoke hurt his throat.

Stop it, he said. We need to go now.

If you just tell me I can grab them and –

Caleb ran out into the road. Behind him there was a loud crack and when he turned around his father was not with him. He thought he would see his father at the door but he did not. He called 911. The windows were full of flame and the curtains burned away and still he did not see his father. He was too afraid to go back. He watched the fire from across the street and soon he heard the sirens. The paramedics took his father and put him in the ambulance. Around then Lydia arrived. His father was taken to the hospital and put on the ventilator. Lydia asked if she could bring flowers and went to get Caleb something to eat. She came back with a turkey sandwich and sometime after that his father died.

Afterward, Caleb wished he had peeled up one of the bandages and looked at what he had done though they said it was smoke inhalation that killed him and so whatever flesh or char or leg or jelly was under the bandage he would not have seen the wound by which he had killed his father. He would have had to look at the lung. The nurse had said his father was sedated.

Chapter Twenty

Diane's been calling, Caleb told Lydia.

It was morning. Tom had been dead for one night. A cat-bird made its noise outside their window.

Do you want to call her back? Lydia said.

I don't think I can.

I'll do it, said Lydia. But there was no answer. She left a message.

I don't know if she didn't pick up because she doesn't know who it was or because she does know who it is, said Lydia.

Caleb did not respond. He was propped up in bed, drawing a picture on a paper napkin spread across the top of his thigh. Lydia moved closer to him.

Let me see.

He covered the napkin with two fast hands and said no. Something was strange about how quickly he covered the napkin and also about the fact that he had not cried yet but the thought was horrible and her phone was ringing. She turned away and answered.

Hello, said a voice. This is Diane.

Her voice was not at all what Lydia had expected. It was flat, plain, and in no way musical. Lydia tried to remember what it had sounded like at Montauk and could not. As she spoke she wondered why a woman with this voice was hearing from her the news that Tom had died. Then Diane began to cry and she understood.

But why did you not tell me earlier, Diane said, when I could have said goodbye?

The next morning Lydia watched Caleb as he slept. It was good that he slept and that so far he was eating normally. Most likely he would soon become so unwell it would scare her. She would have to be with him all the time. Unless he was not grieving. But most likely he would soon show her that he was.

She drove to the nearest mall and bought T-shirts and shorts and underwear and socks and toothbrushes and toothpaste for both of them. When she got back she sat in the car a long time and wondered how he'd be when she went in. But he smiled when he saw her. He was playing a game on his phone. She washed their dirty clothes in the motel sink and hung them on the towel rack to dry.

Later that day they were eating pizza in bed when Lydia's cellphone began to vibrate on the desk across the room. She got up and answered it and sat down in the chair, hunched forward.

The fire investigator had determined that there had been rodent damage from a nest the previous winter. The animals had chewed through wires and once someone started using the building again it was a matter of time.

So it was rats, she said slowly.

Could be, said the low voice on the other end of the line, or could be squirrels.

She heard Caleb open the pizza box again. Then he came close, offering her a slice of pizza on a paper towel. She waved him away. She picked up a packet of sweetener and began to play with it.

But I didn't think squirrels did that, she said to the officer.

Sure they do, he said, they'll chew anything. All rodents. They're not eating, understand. People come to me and say, Why does a squirrel want to eat my house? It doesn't. Their teeth are growing all the time so they need to chew to shave them down, your house is just the loser in the bargain. Otherwise they can't even eat, those long teeth are gonna get in the way.

Oh, said Lydia.

Mouth full of teeth, said the officer. Anyway, next order of business, you might want to hire a lawyer, or your friend the son of the victim might.

But we don't need one, why would we need one?

The landlady might face charges. Best for you to get all the advice you need.

But I thought you said it was squirrels.

She could still be charged with negligent homicide, said the officer. There's also failure to provide a smoke alarm.

Oh don't do that, said Lydia. She heard the springs of the bed. Behind her Caleb was lying down. We hope you don't do that, she said, we don't want that at all. But can I ask, how sure are you? About the squirrels or the rats or whatever, do we know for sure?

The fire inspector is very confident, said the officer. Excellent fire inspector, too.

Oh, said Lydia. That's good.

She thanked the officer and he said no problem and it was time to end the call. She did and put the phone down slowly. She heard Caleb move and knew that he was looking at her, waiting. She was furious that he was sitting there, attentive and dependent and blameless and unavoidable. There was nothing to be done but to tell him about the rodents.

The next day the landlady called while Caleb was outside smoking.

The thing is, she said, I wanted to say how incredibly sorry I am about the death of your family member. I'm not even supposed to be calling you, but I wanted to say that. I am so sorry. My lawyer told me not to say that but I have to.

I won't tell anyone, said Lydia. I promise.

For lack of a better idea Caleb and Lydia stayed at the Shut-eye Motor Inn the next night and for two nights after that. Caleb lay in bed and Lydia went for long drives alone. She saw farmstands and billboards and horses in fields, empty bottles discarded by the roadside, Sunoco stations, small birds. When she returned she told him about the farmstands, the horses, the fields, the small birds. She invented purple flowers and added them to the story and hoped that her tone was encouraging.

What's your fastest turnaround, she said over the phone to the man at the crematorium.

A few days later she drove Caleb to pick up the ashes and said she did not want to come inside. All right, he said, and went alone. Rather than waiting there she retraced the route from the day before and found a farmstand that had been deserted the last time she drove by. Now young men sold summer squash and tomatoes and corn and wildflowers tied with rough twine. Her phone rang and she turned it off. She bought flowers and got back in the car and back on the road.

Tom's death had little to do with her. She drove through green woods. After half an hour or so she found herself on a narrow road that followed the curves of a river whose slow trickle and dry pitted banks showed a dearth of rain. In her mind she told Tom that she was allowed, that he had no right to be upset, no right, what with his son now an adult and Lydia now let go, let go by him, that if she wanted to love his child she was allowed and it was not for him to get himself set on fire and ruin everything. It was not for him to get himself set on fire or choked or inflamed by his own body or whatever had happened and so to never see her again. When she realized he would never hear her because his eardrums like the rest of him had been reduced to dust she caught her breath and counted the big branches in the beaver dam up ahead in the river. She had only counted four when she passed it. Then she did not know what to count and Tom had still left her and was still gone.

If Tom had only been able to understand what was important, but he couldn't, but he didn't get it, but his priorities were just all wrong and now what was she supposed to say to his son. Now what would he have said.

The road left the woods and straightened out. Tom would not know anything about whatever she did next, where she and Caleb went, whether he went back to the hospital or died or hated Lydia. Tom would not know what happened to them. In the fields hay had been gathered into big golden bundles. She sped up. On her right there was a ramshackle blue building with a sign that read WE'VE MOVED .8 MILES SOUTH ON THE LEFT.

Two hours later when she returned to the crematorium Caleb was not waiting outside with the box. She parked and checked her phone.

Where are you? said one message.

I'm going to walk back to the motel, he had written an hour and a half ago.

She found him walking along the dry roadside carrying

the white cardboard box. It was bigger than she had expected it to be. She slowed down and pulled over.

In the car he was impatient and tearful. He sat in the passenger seat with the box on his lap.

There's room for that in the backseat, said Lydia, blinking.

I'm keeping it here.

Suit yourself.

Caleb told Lydia that Diane had messaged to say she was out of the apartment and did they want to go back. She had said that she thought they might want to.

That's the first piece of good news we've had in a long time, said Lydia. Let me see.

Caleb showed her his phone. Diane wanted to know if he was all right. She said that Lydia had told her that he was doing okay under the circumstances but she wanted to hear it from him. Also she wanted to know if she could do anything and to tell him that she was out of the apartment now so he could come back and have it to himself.

Why doesn't she think I'd come back with you, said Lydia. I can't wait to go home.

The next day they put their bags and Tom's ashes in the back of the Toyota and checked out of the Shuteye. As Lydia was pulling onto the highway Caleb's phone pinged, and he said, Diane wants to know when the service is going to be.

We'll organize something wonderful, said Lydia, I promise. Tell her that.

When they got back to the apartment the gold clock on the mantel was gone. The sofa had been reupholstered in black and the green carpet taken away and replaced with burgundy. Lydia shut herself in Tom's room and wept.

Chapter Twenty-One

On Lydia and Caleb's first night back in New York they slept in his childhood bedroom. The single bed was uncomfortable.

On their second day back in the city Lydia drove downtown with Caleb in the passenger seat. When stoplights went green she did not put her foot on the gas soon enough and was honked at. Soon they would get into a freight elevator and walk down a long white hallway with gleaming oil-gray floors. A red metal door would retract one by one its thin segments into the ceiling. In the unit, still boxed, were her things from Jane's apartment and the belongings she had not touched since her life with Tom. Books she had read while he lay, unwanted, in bed next to her. Clothing she had not worn since she moved out.

And now who would unbox them all, the same woman, the one whose clothes were folded and stacked inside, the one who'd worn them in distaste and negligence, the one who'd worn everything out. She did not want to unfold them. She was not sure she could fit all the boxes in this junky car. She could not afford movers right now, but soon perhaps she would be able to, although she would not be moving again for a long time. She wondered when she could ask Caleb about Tom's money. The driver behind them honked at her again and when Caleb asked, Do you think it was our fault, she said, What. What.

That night Lydia looked at the closed door of Tom's bedroom. She suggested they sleep there.

No, said Caleb.

When she woke up in the middle of the night she wanted to shout at him for disturbing her, but he was sleeping peacefully. Her back hurt and his father was dead and he was sleeping.

In the morning she took Tom's clothes out of the drawers in his bedroom and left them in piles on the floor while she cut open the top of one of the cardboard boxes of clothing she had brought from storage. She put her things in the dresser where Tom's had been. She made sure to leave Caleb half the room. When each box was empty she filled it with Tom's stuff and sealed it with packing tape. She found the shirt he had been wearing when he broke up with her and threw it in the garbage. She cleared space in the closet. Caleb knocked on the door.

What are you doing?

I need your help, she said. They lifted the full cardboard boxes and carried them down the hall and stacked them on the rug in his room. They brought Caleb's clothes back down the hallway by the armload and put them in the drawers with Lydia's. After the last trip they shut the door behind them. From then on they slept in the master bedroom.

During the day Caleb lay in the large bed and slept or streamed shows on his laptop. Sometimes Lydia put her head on his shoulder and watched *The Sopranos* with him. He had been too young to watch it when it aired and still too young six or seven years ago when she had rewatched the series with his father. Together they watched Silvio ask Adriana why she was crying and tell her it was all going to be fine and then pull off the road into the woods. He got out of the car and went for the trunk. Adriana clung to the steering wheel. Silvio threw her on the ground and she crawled offscreen through autumn leaves and a shot rang out. Tom used to fast-forward through the violent parts. Caleb watched them straight through.

One day Lydia opened Tom's desk and threw his index cards and papers and post-its and bulldog clips in the garbage. She took his books from the shelf and moved them into Caleb's old room, except for his well-worn copy of *Middlemarch*, which she kept by her side of the bed.

Just organize some kind of service, Diane said, and then I'll be out of your hair. He should have something. Or I can organize it, I'm more than happy to do it myself.

No, said Lydia, I will.

I know he didn't go to church, said Diane, but please find a nice one. There are a lot of nice ones in Manhattan. Maybe somewhere right near home would be best. Or what about that big one where they bless the animals?

I'll find an excellent one, said Lydia.

After they hung up she went online and found a church in a small town about two hours outside of the city in the direction of the place where Tom had died. She asked Caleb if it was all right.

I don't know how I feel about it, he said. I guess it's okay.

It'll be better if the service is small, she said, it'll be easier for you.

On the day of the memorial the minister did his best although he knew little about Tom. There were no other speakers. Lydia didn't want Diane to speak and Diane didn't want Lydia to speak and Caleb did not feel he could.

Afterward, guests waited in a line to shake his hand. Many of them said, Your father was such a good man, or something like that. Others said, What a terrible accident. Caleb said,

Thank you. Thank you for coming. He had not thought so many people would come to the service, out here, in some town where his father had known no one. People had driven out from the city to tell Caleb how sorry they were and how sad it was. He wished they had not come because it hurt to shake their hands. He felt bad that the wrong thing hurt him, that the worst was having everyone come up to him and say, Your father was a wonderful person. The truth was he felt nothing about his father's death except when people wanted to make him talk about it. He could never tell anyone that. He kept his face still and again said, Thank you for coming.

Even now, said Bob Mackenzie, he and Caleb's father had last had dinner two weeks ago. He was very worried about you, Bob said, and Caleb said, Yes, and then, Thank you for coming. Bob nodded and left and Caleb felt bad and wished he would come back. But a blonde woman wearing a cross necklace had come to give her condolences.

He had thought that he understood death because in the past he had wanted it for himself. He shook the woman's hand. But his father had not wanted death so he was muddling everything. He was muddling his own death, which had not happened, with his father's, which had.

The woman was called Sandy. She said she was a new colleague of his father's and that he had helped her settle in to the department and she would always be grateful. His death was a great loss to scholarship.

And he was becoming a friend, I thought, a real friend. He was going to come to my wedding next month. I'm so sad he won't be there. I saw him at a faculty meeting a month ago and it's so strange to think that was the last time.

Caleb felt dizzy. He thanked her for coming. Two short men were next in line and then a dark-haired woman with delicate lines around her large eyes and heavy sagging cheeks.

You remember me, she said. Kathleen Delaney.

She gave him a hug and put her hands on his shoulder blades. Her fingers were tense and made him uncomfortable because he understood why they were tense. He thought he was beginning to understand now what he was.

Of course, he said.

I wish I were seeing you under different circumstances. I'm so sorry.

When the last mourners had moved on to the parish hall for coffee and mini-pastries Caleb sneaked out to the parking lot side of the church. There dense hedges and the side of the building made a dappled green-brown cloister. He slid in. He found a spot where a large sign would hide his legs all right and made himself small there and had just lit a cigarette when in the parking lot the voice of his father's cousin Edgar said, Want me to tell you something exciting?

Between the trunks of the hedge and over the top of the sign Caleb saw toddler feet in silver sandals jump over the white line that separated two parking spaces.

Bar bar bar bar bar, shouted the child. Caleb tried to stay very still.

I guess not, said Edgar, and some other grown-up giggled. Caleb ashed into the mulch and hoped they would drive off without saying goodbye.

Lydia had been leaning against the wall and wondering who would say hello to her when a woman with a blonde bob had come out of the sanctuary and joined the line of people on their way to tell Caleb how wonderful Tom had been. Lydia had watched her. She looked very different without the large smile Lydia remembered from the Delaneys' party. But Lydia recognized the bright eyes that even now seemed happy, the sharp nose, the necklace with the cross on it.

Lydia wanted to know who she was and to tell her that she had ruined everything with her ring and her cross and her smile. Tom had shown up with her and Lydia had thought that they were getting married. Lydia had come home from the party and gone to see Caleb. Now Tom was dead and she was responsible for him, Caleb, she was responsible for Caleb, which she would not have been if Tom had not driven that woman to the party.

Tom had had so many friends. And none of them had told Lydia how sorry they were. She had been standing alone at the edge of the room.

White-haired Diane had sat in the last pew and left immediately after the service. Lydia was disappointed. She had wanted to hear her voice again, to prove to herself that Diane and the woman who had seen them at Montauk and the woman who had cried for Tom over the phone were all real and were the same person.

After Caleb had finished his cigarette he waited until the voices were all gone to come out from behind the hedge. He put his hands in his pockets and tried to walk casually. Lydia was alone in the church except for the minister, who was in the sanctuary folding a piece of red cloth. She was standing in the middle of the aisle.

You were talking to a blonde woman, said Lydia, she came to talk to you in the line. She's short, she wears a cross.

What about it, said Caleb.

What's her name?

There were a lot of people. A lot. I don't know, Suzie or Sandra or some name like that.

Which one? Try harder.

I just met like a thousand people.

It was not a thousand.

A lot. Caleb kicked the side of the pew. I want to go home.

Anyway, said Lydia, where were you all this time?

Shaking hands, I told you.

After that. You disappeared.

Sandy, he said, I think it was Sandy.

Let's go. Your father would have thought this church was ugly.

When Caleb's father was alive the way he lived had organized the belongings in their home. He left books on the floor of the living room because he read there. He kept other books in his bedroom because he might read them in bed. The surface of his desk was littered with pens because he had just been writing and he sometimes left a sweater in the chair because he had taken it off when he got too warm. Now the desktop was bare. The water glass that used to sit on the coaster on his father's bedside table was back on the shelf in the kitchen cabinet with all of the other glasses like it. His sweaters were all packed together in boxes which Caleb himself had carried down the hall. And Caleb lay in his father's bed the whole day long.

All of his father's friends had told him they were sorry. He had thanked them.

In the mornings he put one forearm or a blanket over his eyes and waited for Lydia to get up and leave the room. When she left he looked at the dust on the windowsill and the desk where his father's pictures had once been. He remembered Ellen. He had killed her too.

Days kept coming. On breaks from work Lydia sat at the

edge of the bed. He heard her small movements, felt her concern, and hated her.

Your father would want you to be happy, she said, and he told her to stop it. He told her not to talk about his father. Their sex, when it happened, was tentative and shameful.

She brought him glasses of water and seemed encouraged when he accepted them. He could see her relief when he played Plague Inc on his phone.

Look at you, she said, you're sitting up.

I know I am, he thought, but he did not say it. He noticed he was much worse at Plague Inc than he had been before.

Occasionally, when he was alone, he got out of bed and went down the hall to his old room and took some of his father's books from the boxes in which Lydia had packed them. He sat on the floor cross-legged and tried to read. Short phrases slipped past one another and away from him and he understood nothing.

Chapter Twenty-Two

Caleb slept badly. He responded slowly when Lydia spoke to him. She begged him to talk to Dr. Antonelli.

I really don't know what to do. I don't know how to help. Neither does he.

Your father wouldn't have wanted this for you. He was such a caring person, he would want you to take care of yourself.

She sat on the bed next to him. He did not move.

Maybe, she said, we would all have been friends by now. Maybe everything would have calmed down a little. She ran her fingers through Caleb's hair, which needed to be cut soon, and tucked a lock behind his ear. I read in the *Times* there's this play on Broadway now about Sarah Bernhardt playing Hamlet. He would have liked that. Imagine if the four of us had gone to the theater together.

Caleb buried his face in the bedspread.

Do you want water, or a glass of juice maybe? Do you know who Sarah Bernhardt was?

When he did not respond she said, I just feel so helpless, I feel so helpless, it's awful. She started to cry. He sat up.

Eventually he agreed that she could talk to Dr. Antonelli. He said she could tell Antonelli he'd agreed to it, but Antonelli said he needed to hear it from Caleb himself. Caleb called and left a voicemail in which he informed Antonelli of his consent. Then Lydia and Dr. Antonelli scheduled a time to talk.

I don't want to know about your phone call, said Caleb, don't tell me anything about it.

For the next few days she cooked his favorite meals and stroked his head while he lay feverish with sadness on sheets she had just changed. She covered him with quilts and brought him hot chocolate. The therapist was going to ask her how he seemed. She would say, You don't understand, I'm very good to him, I am, I bring him warm drinks, without me he couldn't manage. We are in a difficult situation, an unusual situation – in her head she practiced calling the situation weird and discarded this option, she practiced calling it difficult, she practiced calling it unusual, she practiced calling it tough, she could not decide which was best – we are in a tough situation but he needs me. *And* he needs me. She would say *and* rather than *but*. It's just how things have turned out, we've had bad luck and he needs me, I make dinner.

When the doctor called Lydia thanked him for making the time.

I want to make clear that this isn't a session and you are not my patient, said Dr. Antonelli. I want to make that very clear.

Of course not, said Lydia. I just want to get a sense of how he is. I appreciate this so much.

Well, I haven't spoken to him, as you know. So I'm not really able to assess his condition.

I thought I could describe him to you, kind of tell you how he's been and then you could give your assessment based on that.

You can certainly talk to me about your concerns and observations. But I want to be clear that this is not ideal and certainly not the same as if I spoke to him myself.

Sure.

Lydia told Antonelli how Caleb slept, what he ate, and how she took care of him. She said that he was not leaving the house and did not seem to engage with friends much, though who knew what he was doing online, but she didn't believe that he was in touch with friends.

It sounds like grief, said Antonelli, and very possibly a worsening of his depression, which can happen when a parent dies, especially in patients with a history like Caleb's but really in any patient. It's really, I don't want to quite say it's what one would expect but it's not unheard of by any means.

We are in an unusual situation, Lydia said. There was silence on the other end of the line. She felt very stupid.

I really think he ought to have a session, said the doctor. It could be a phone session or a video session like we've done before, if he doesn't feel up to coming into the office. Will you let him know that?

I can try.

Please tell him. Really, to be frank, you're not well positioned to help him with this. He should talk to me.

You mean because of our difficult situation, Lydia said. She wanted to tell Antonelli about the macaroni and cheese she had made and the fact that she and Caleb were watching *The Sopranos* together and also about the sheets and pillowcases and quilts and towels she washed and his dreamless if paltry slumber. At least he said he had no dreams during the sleep he got. Lydia could not find the words to tell Dr. Antonelli about any of this.

At the risk of overstepping, I believe your involvement with Caleb has been deeply unhealthy for him. I've told him this. And I usually don't, I usually wouldn't give direct advice, certainly I try to support my patients in making their own decisions and I don't tell them what to do, but you're not my patient and under the circumstances I would feel remiss if I weren't frank. This relationship is very bad for him.

Is that your opinion.

Yes. And to be blunt – I don't relish being blunt but I believe I need to under the circumstances, there's no other way I can help – frankly, you seem dismissive of your impact. Of the impact of your sexual involvement with him. Let's not mince words. You cannot help him grieve given your sexual involvement and your prior relationship with his father. You are essentially his stepmother.

I think it's possible that he stole some prescription medication from a friend of mine around three months ago. Xanax. Does that worry you?

On the other end of the line the doctor sighed.

Under the circumstances it's really not a major concern.

I mean I'm not *sure* he did, but if it's true wouldn't you say that –

Given that it's been a few months, and that during that time his father died and he likely feels he bears some responsibility, honestly, Xanax is nowhere near the first thing I'd worry about. I don't think you have a good grasp of the stakes of the situation. I would be much more concerned about his coping skills and his support system now. And as I said, you are not well positioned –

Do you expect me to leave him, then. Would that help.

Probably not immediately. I don't know that he needs more disruption right now even if it's for the best in the long term.

He can't even wash his own sheets.

On Dr. Antonelli's advice Lydia made Caleb a schedule. He was to rise at eight in the morning, get adequate exercise, journal, take his medications carefully, and go to bed on time. He was to make sure to get out of the house every day. She told the doctor she would make sure that Caleb followed the plan. If she were not there, she reflected, he would have no hope.

It rained often that fall. He listened to it.

When it was sunny Lydia insisted they walk in the park. At first he refused, and they argued, and then he followed her because it was easier.

The next time it rained he listened to the patter and thought about the different places where droplets hit pavement or earth and splashed open, and about the spaces and lulls between the little wet impacts. He could hear that the world was large and shot through with weightlessness. He got up and came into the kitchen, and he got a glass of juice, and he went into the living room and stood near the window and watched the rain come down on the yellow traffic lights and on the cars and taxis that they stopped and allowed to move forward as the signal changed from red to yellow to green, on the scaffolding of metal and olive-painted wood, the small passersby half-hidden by umbrellas, their wet dogs and sodden paper bags. He still felt nothing for the city but it seemed to have room for his sadness.

The schedule is helping, said Lydia.

Yes, he said, although he was not sure.

Lydia woke him and put him to bed. She encouraged him to respond to the occasional messages he received from Beau and to limit his time on social media. On good days he was tender and talkative. She was proud of him and tried not to think about his father. To make this easier she hired two hulking movers who removed the rest of Tom's belongings from the apartment.

It rained again, and the sound was flat.

The weather cleared. He knew he could make Lydia happy by pointing at the newly red leaves of trees.

One day she said, Let's go to Burger Heaven. I haven't been to Burger Heaven in ages.

All right.

They walked through the park. He said the trees were beautiful. She agreed and noted the blue sky and crisp air. They took the 6 a couple of stops downtown.

At the diner a waitress led them past strangers to a teal vinyl booth in the far back corner. They sat and looked at their menus. They could hear jovial talk.

Lydia pressed her napkin to her mouth, then put it in her lap. I'm glad this place is still here, she said.

She pointed out the white-and-black tile floor. He said that he liked it. She asked him what he wanted to eat. He wasn't sure yet. He wished he had not come here and was glad they were hidden away in the farthest possible booth. She noted the light fixtures. She paused for him to speak and then told him what was supposed to be good on Netflix.

There's this one where Jason Bateman has to move near a lake because he's ripped off a cartel and then he has to commit more fraud to save himself, and it also has what's-her-face.

Laura Linney, said Caleb.

Good for you, she said. Her voice sounded higher than usual.

It's called *Ozark*, he said. He bit his lip. There was no point in red trees or rain or the patterns of tile floors, and he was tired of pretending that it was wrong to know that. He blurted out, Are you surprised I know who Laura Linney is?

What would you do, said Lydia, leaning forward, if you'd defrauded a cartel?

I think it's his friend. His friend defrauds the cartel.

The waitress arrived, wrote their order on a thin white notepad, and read it back to them. Cheeseburger, coffee, veggie burger, Coke. They said that was correct. She left.

Veggie burger, said Lydia.

Yeah.

There was something playful in her tone, and he felt his face move toward a smile. This is a smile, he thought, this is the feeling of happiness. But it did not touch him. Slowly he let his face go slack and then he saw that she was disappointed.

I'd do whatever they wanted, he said, and so would you, so would anyone.

You're right. She turned her head to look out the big plate glass window. A stout woman with a blue hat and fat hands was walking past.

Who do you think that is, Lydia asked.

What do you mean?

Where is she going, what is she doing, who is she?

Are you giving me some kind of test.

It's a game.

You go.

But the woman had passed them. They could no longer see her.

Okay, said Lydia. If you pick someone.

A red-faced man had just rounded the corner. A newspaper protruded from the pocket of his quilted black jacket. He jammed his hand in alongside it and walked quickly with his neck stuck out. Caleb pointed to him.

Hmm. Lydia paused, and when she spoke again her voice was sweet and conspiratorial. I think he feels guilty about something he read in the newspaper. He thinks he should be a better citizen.

What? Caleb laughed and clasped his hands under his chin. He looked happy. He knew because Lydia looked pleased with herself. She continued.

He thinks he should do more to help others, but he doesn't, and he doesn't know why so now he's going to see his ex-wife, who plays the flute in an orchestra, to talk to her about how to improve.

And?

That's it.

He said he still didn't get it. Do another, he said.

You pick, you tell me who.

Caleb indicated a girl of about fourteen. She wore a lilac skirt. Her dark hair was in a single long braid down her back. She carried a white paper bag.

Oh she's very sad. Her friends have been terrible to her. Pick someone else.

Terrible how.

See, you do get it, you like this. You make one up.

An old woman was crossing the street, pushing a black wire cart full of plastic bags that bulged with groceries and bright plastic spray bottles and yellow canisters of wipes. Two women in jeans and puffy jackets chatted as they leant against the side of a building. Nearby a boy stared at the trunk of a tree. He put his face close to the bark.

That boy is looking at tree bark, Caleb said.

Okay, what else?

That's it.

That's not a story, that's just what he's doing.

He did not answer but shrugged. They sat in silence and drank coffee and Coke. The waitress poured Lydia a refill. She took another sip.

Okay, she said, I'll do one more. That lady over there, you

see her? The one in the black skirt. She works as a consult-ant and she gets paid tons of money to advise the oil and gas industry. She went to Antarctica last year to see it before it's ruined. You know you're not supposed to go. Because for the moment it's pretty much unspoilt. It's the last place.

The story, said Caleb.

So at work, before lunch, she found a secret memo, and she's going to confront her boss about it.

What's in the memo? he asked, because he knew it was the obvious question.

Lydia pursed her lips and screwed up her forehead. He laughed in recognition of her effort.

It's secret, she said. He smiled in spite of himself. She was very charming. They were happy.

Maybe, he ventured, maybe it says that her boss is going to Antarctica. And she's going to stop him, because she learned her lesson, she feels guilty.

That could be, said Lydia. Though if she wants to save Antarctica she should probably quit her job.

Or maybe, said Caleb, she's going to meet with a jour-nalist. Maybe she's leaking information from the oil and gas corporation, because she wants to make up for the damage she's done by working for them and by going to Antarctica.

That's great, she said, and nodded, her eyes wide and bright. He could tell that she thought that she had helped him and that she wanted him to know how proud she was. That's great, she said again. You see, if your father hadn't died we couldn't be together like this.

Do you still want that tattoo?

What tattoo? She was playing dumb.

The ghost we talked about. Like mine.

He could see her hesitate. Her eyes held something back. Why did she say yes? Afterward, he was never sure. She said yes and he got out the needle.

At the last minute she told him to wait and he thought that she was going to say again that she didn't want him to tattoo her. Instead she said, I don't want a ghost like yours, I want an eye like yours. Like the one on your back.

The pictures had killed his father. He had killed his father with the pictures. Diane in the pictures had killed his father. Lydia had killed his father. At night he killed his father with Lydia. In a picture a plush tiger killed his father. A wrong turn or rats or squirrels had killed his father. Caleb considered these possibilities. By Thanksgiving he was sure that he had killed his father with selfishness, just as he had killed Ellen.

His father had been beside himself with happiness when Caleb had asked him to drive hours to his makeshift home. If his father had not loved him he would be alive. So Caleb could also say that he had killed his father with love.

When Caleb went back to seeing Antonelli, the doctor told him that his feelings of guilt were inaccurate and abso- lutely usual.

Okay, said Caleb.

Dr. Antonelli asked if Caleb had thoughts of suicide.

How could he explain that if he left Lydia his father would be dead for no reason? And that was true whether Caleb left her by dying or in any other way. Somehow they would have to make up for fire and for the teeth of rodents. Each time he saw the eye on the back of her neck he felt ashamed because he had been angry when he made it.

Chapter Twenty-Three

In December Caleb and Lydia sat in the living room each evening, as Lydia and his father had once done. He drank soda water. Lydia was back on scotch. He wanted to join her but did not dare ask. She drank more these days.

One night they sat on the sofa his father and Diane had had reupholstered in black velvet. He told her a story his father had told him when he was a child. A rhinoceros was thirsty and went searching for water but only found gold. I never heard this story, said Lydia, where was I? He answered, You were there.

Another night she said, I want to redecorate.

No, he said, and did not explain.

Once his inheritance came through he took her to nice restaurants, where neither of them shied away from the glances of strangers. They went to sleep early. It made sense that he was tired, that she was tired. It had been a tiring year. She reminded herself that the year had been tiring whenever a disappointed arid glassy-eyed expression stole over his love for her. Most times it was not long before what looked like love was evident again. Dr. Antonelli had been very wrong. They shared mezze platters. On the way home they walked under barren trees and held hands. She still hated the maroon carpet more than anything.

Some nights he woke her up and clung to her body, told her never to leave him. I need you to promise me never to leave. She promised. As she touched his skin she thought,

Here his father burned, and here, and here. She found all the
spots.

The week before Thanksgiving a cream envelope arrived in
the mail. It was addressed to Caleb in delicate calligraphy.
The return address read ODLING-SCHWARZ. Sandy had
tucked a note between the wedding invitation and the RSVP
card. Caleb could feel Lydia read it over his shoulder as she sat
next to him on the black sofa.

What does she want? Lydia asked.

He almost told her he knew she could read the note from
where she was. Instead he said, She's inviting me, and you I
guess, to her wedding in my dad's place. He was going to go.

Lydia wrapped her arms around herself. What do you
think?

He put the envelope down on the coffee table and looked
at her. I think it's a bad idea.

Why?

It's not like she really wants us there. *He*'s the one she
invited.

But this is her way of honoring his memory.

Caleb ran a hand through his hair and said that he would
think about it. Lydia stood up, walked over to the armchair
and sat.

I don't see why you're even considering saying no, she said.
You want to stop her from honoring your father's memory.
Really.

I'm just, he began, and then stopped. He thought about
what it would be like to walk into the room as the living
reason his father was not walking into the room. But also it
was kind, what Sandy was trying to do. He was not sure what
was right.

Do you think he was fucking her?

Caleb looked at Lydia's bony fingers, spread wide over the rounded ends of the fat arms of the chair, and at the dark leather that showed between them. You don't feel responsible at all, he said, at all, do you.

At Lydia's insistence Caleb told Sandy they would come to the wedding. For Christmas Lydia got him a PlayStation. On New Year's Eve they went to bed before midnight.

The morning of the wedding Caleb said he could not go, he had been mistaken, it was a terrible idea. It took Lydia an hour of pleading and hair-stroking to convince him that they had to show up. On the downtown 2 she said that he had made them late and he said that she shouldn't have made him accept the invitation in the first place. By the time they arrived a man and a minister were already standing at the end of the aisle, waiting, and a cellist was playing, and guests turned their heads to see who was entering the church. Caleb kept his head down and they slipped quietly into the back pew. Before long small children walked down the aisle, dropping flowers on the carpet. Bridesmaids in gauzy mint-colored dresses followed. Everyone stood. Lydia looked back to see Sandy begin to walk forward. She strained her eyes to get a good look at the woman.

Sandy walked alone and wore a blue dress. Her hair was in the same blonde bob she had had when Lydia first saw her. She had a strong, pointed nose and a heart-shaped face that wore a playful expression. She looked straight ahead of herself at the fat kind-looking man waiting for her and seemed to take no notice of the guests. Her wine-colored lips pulled back in a smile that was for an instant wolflike. She looked up, then back at the groom, giggling.

She's flirting, Lydia realized.

Sandy passed her and Lydia could not see her over the shoulders of the other guests but in her mind she saw those near-purple lips pulling back, breaking into giggles, pulling back, breaking. Caleb put his hand on her lower back but she did not relax into it. He removed his hand.

The ceremony was simple and soon over. Afterward the man on Lydia's right said, What a wonderful wedding.

Yes, said Lydia.

At the reception there were white orchids everywhere. Waiters slid through the crowd offering champagne, potato chips in clear plastic cups, and shrimp on silver trays, which they angled so as to allow better access to silver bowls of cocktail sauce.

Everyone seemed very happy chatting in their small groups, thought Lydia. She got a drink and walked around the edge of the room, looking for people she knew. She saw no one so far. Caleb followed her.

I'm so happy for them, said a woman in a green dress.

Lydia stopped walking and let Caleb catch up to her. She slid her hand down his arm and tried to feel the muscles in his forearm, but she could not feel them through his suit jacket. She reached for his hand, which did not grasp hers.

I can't be here, said Caleb, his voice low. Lydia did not look up at him.

Nearby a man in a striped suit said that he had thought Belarus was part of Russia. Across the room a woman in a low-cut pink dress brushed her hair away from her face and shoved an hors d'oeuvre into her mouth. Lydia knew her but could not think who she was. The woman looked back at Lydia, swallowed, and tapped a man in a dark jacket on the shoulder. The man turned. It was Jim Delaney. Kathleen looked so different that Lydia wondered if Jim had left her for another woman, like Tom had, but then Kathleen waved and Lydia knew that she recognized her.

Lydia nudged Caleb.

That's Kathleen, let's go say hi.

Did you hear me, I told you I can't be here.

Lydia leaned in so that he would hear her over the sounds of conversation.

You know, she whispered in his ear, you look so sexy.

He looked at her. Their faces were very close. Lydia was pleased that he was looking at her and that he was so beautiful. Everyone around them and even Kathleen must surely see how beautiful he was and more than that how kind and sweet and gentle and in love with her. His eyes moved over her face with a soft sad curiosity that both flattered her and made her uncomfortable. Then they grew clear and steady and she wanted to get away from him. He flinched and turned his head to one side and looked off into the crowd, and she was relieved and wanted to hide her face in his shoulder and to hit him. Lydia was angry at him for spoiling her pleasure and angry at herself for having in her whatever he had seen.

A waiter came by with a tray. Lydia closed her eyes and said she did not want shrimp.

When the waiter had left she said quietly, You have to come. Kathleen has seen us both and it would be rude.

I'm going outside to smoke.

You don't have the coat check ticket, she said, you'll freeze, but he was already walking away.

She watched his shoulders, broad and slumped. Because of his yellow hair she did not lose sight of him in the crowd until he was almost to the exit. She turned and made her way through the crowd toward where the Delaneys had been, excusing herself, shoving past white-shirted chests and suit-clad arms and shoulders, excusing herself.

Oh my gosh, Lydia, said Kathleen. Hello. Jim, it's Lydia.

Jim was portly and diffident, as Lydia remembered him. He had the same thin white mustache and thick glasses with black plastic frames. Kathleen had done something strange with her makeup so that her eyes looked hooded and deep-set. Lydia felt uncomfortable.

I almost didn't recognize you.

I'm trying to experiment.

Next to them Jim looked into the distance and ate a potato chip.

How are you? Kathleen asked. Tom's service was so beautiful.

Thank you. I'm all right.

He was such a lovely man. I'm so sorry, it must have been very painful for you.

Lydia said that it was.

Even considering, said Kathleen, and stopped speaking. Jim smacked his lips.

It was, said Lydia again. It was all very difficult.

It must have been, I'm sorry I didn't get the chance to say hello at the funeral.

That's all right, I wasn't really in a talkative mood.

Of course, of course.

How've you been?

Kathleen said that she was very well. As she spoke Lydia began to feel the tension in her lips and hands dissipate. She had thought Kathleen might revile her, might refuse to say hello, but nothing was much different than it had been before. In fact Tom might have shown up any minute and

Kathleen would have greeted him with the same obvious pleasure. Lydia felt almost as if he might appear, as if he might stand next to her and listen to Kathleen talk about the work she wanted done at her garden in Rye as soon as it started to warm up and the trip she and Jim were taking to Greece before it got too hot. Kathleen wondered if Lydia had any tips.

I didn't spend much time in Athens, said Lydia. You know there were serious wildfires there last summer.

Not in Athens, said Kathleen, her voice rising.

No, I mean, I guess, they're wildfires, said Lydia, so I guess they're probably in the countryside, but not far. Tom would not have gone out into the cold and left her here like this. Anyway, she said, I'd look it up.

I will, said Kathleen. Her face took on a serious, grateful expression, though Lydia saw a sly flicker in her deep eyes. I think it's time for dinner.

Lydia looked around. Waiters had begun to beckon people toward the back of the restaurant.

I wonder if we missed some kind of announcement, she said. She turned back toward Kathleen, who was tugging on the sleeve of Jim's navy jacket as she whispered something into his ear. He shook his head.

Kathleen let go and asked Lydia what table she was at.

Seven, I think, but I'm not sure, Caleb might remember.

Well, we're eleven, said Kathleen, that's a shame. Great to run into you.

Abruptly she took Jim's arm and steered him toward the tables at the back of the restaurant. As they walked away Jim held his other arm behind himself so that his fist stood out against the dark fabric of his jacket. Then he opened his hand so that potato chips fell to the floor in his wake.

Lydia looked around for Caleb but did not see him anywhere and figured he must still be outside. Just before she reached the exit she saw the tall wiry man who had been sitting to her right during the ceremony, the one who had told her that the wedding had been beautiful. At first he did not see her. He was fixing his tie. She grabbed his forearm and told him that he was right, the wedding had been beautiful.

He turned to look at her and she wished she had not said it and that she had gone to get Caleb, who was surely freezing, standing outside all this time.

The man introduced himself as Tony Mulhouse. When they shook hands she thought his palm was too warm, and then she told herself that she shouldn't think that, that he had no control over how warm his palm was, the warmth of palms was not a matter of individual control and said nothing about him and she should not reproach temperatures but also he let go of her hand so slowly. Then he told her that he was a cinematographer.

Oh, said Lydia. I need to go find my boyfriend.

I thought you were a young mom, said Tony Mulhouse.

There was a small dark mole just below and to the left of his nose. As he smiled it disappeared in the crevice that ran toward the corner of his mouth, hidden by the flesh of a cheek. Lydia watched it reemerge as his face went slack.

I need to bring him to dinner, she said, and left.

As the bride and groom were welcomed to dinner with shouts and applause, as Sandy's sister told the guests tearfully that love was a matter of patience and asked them to raise their glasses, as everyone drank, Lydia looked around the room at enthusiastic partygoers who were just like her. She saw Kathleen and Jim at table eleven. Not far off Tony Mulhouse or a man who looked just like him from the back nodded as he cut his chicken. He seemed to take up a lot of space. Lydia cut her fish with the side of her fork.

Across the table Caleb was carrying on a conversation with an older woman in a purple dress. He seemed to be having a nice time. He belonged here, thought Lydia, just like she did; they belonged here together; they were just like all the other fish-or-chicken eaters, all these friends, minding their elbows and nodding. Lydia had been with Tom to parties just like this and never had she felt at home as she did now. She remembered how Bobbie and Dan Philbrick had treated her when she was young, how Bob Mackenzie had smirked at her years ago when Tom introduced her to him. Tonight Kathleen Delaney had been happy to see her. Caleb was so kind to the old woman across the table. Love was a matter of patience.

Chapter Twenty-Four

Lydia decided that she and Caleb would have a dinner party. Kathleen and Jim would come. Bobbie and Dan Philbrick would be there too, and Sandy and Mark.

Lydia wondered if Sandy and Mark knew Bobbie and Dan. If not she would introduce them. It would be like the dinner parties that Lydia and Tom had had, except that Caleb would sit where Tom used to sit and Lydia would be happy.

She could ask Caleb to pour wine although he would not have any himself. Probably not. Although she wondered whether or not abstinence was really necessary seeing as how he was so much better than he had once been and seeing as how he was in a completely different situation. And he was now older. Maybe he could have a drink if he wanted to. Only if he wanted, of course.

Drinking or not drinking he would charm everyone. Kathleen Delaney would look over at Lydia and raise her eyebrows as if to say, He's terrific. I never realized how terrific he is. You and Tom were good together, but I never realized how terrific you could be. Bobbie and Dan Philbrick would tacitly concur.

Lydia would tell the Delaneys that she had searched her notes and come up with several recommendations about where to eat in Athens. She would opine about whether or not the Parthenon was all it was cracked up to be. Lydia was a person who could be expected to know about the Parthenon. She and Caleb were having a dinner party.

Bobbie Philbrick responded to Lydia's email almost immediately with one line: Dan and I will not attend.

Kathleen did not respond to her email at all and did not pick up the phone when Lydia called. A week later she sent a text informing Lydia that while she had thought it best to be friendly at the wedding she found Lydia's relationship with Caleb completely inappropriate and hoped there was no misunderstanding. She hoped Lydia would never contact her again.

I hated your pink dress, Lydia texted back.

The next day Lydia heard from Sandy, who said that she and Mark had just returned from Argentina and would love to come.

Great, Lydia typed. She wondered if she should say that they would just be four in the end.

She could invite Bob Mackenzie, although she hated him. She could invite Liz and Marty. She could invite Jane. If they all came then that was a group of eight and if even two of them came it was still a party of six. Six was a party still.

She contacted all of them. None of them replied.

Sunday morning Caleb was in his boxers in the kitchen, leaning against the counter and drinking coffee, when Lydia walked into the room.

Do you want to invite anyone to this party?

I'm dreading it, you know that.

She poured a cup of coffee for herself.

It would mean a lot to me if you could invite some friends.

Who do you want me to invite?

Lydia thought. He was looking at her as if she did not understand something. He scratched his stomach and looked down, then raised his head to meet her eyes again.

I know, she said suddenly, I know you would have invited Ellen, and now you can't, and you can't invite Kenny either, and that must hurt, and that other girl.

I wasn't really friends with Kimmie, said Caleb, if that's who you mean, and I don't miss Kenny either.

She could tell he was still waiting for her to figure something out but she did not know what it was.

You're not suggesting we could invite Diane.

No. Anyway, she's moved back to Hawaii.

What do you mean, back to Hawaii?

That's where she's from, she missed it. I'm pretty sure her family's there. And the main office for her company is still there too.

Her what?

She founded a company. They make rash guards. And other clothes for surfing. She only came to New York for my dad.

Lydia noticed that her mouth was open. She closed it, bit her lip, closed her eyes, opened them, and dismissed the thought of Diane on the beach, happy among people who loved her. She looked up at Caleb.

You never asked, he said, shrugging.

You could invite Beau, Lydia said. Would you mind?

Caleb texted Beau that Lydia wanted to have a dinner party. On the 15th. Could he make it?

Hilarious, Beau texted back.

So is that a yes?

Hilarious is a yes.

Sandy, Mark, Beau, Caleb, herself.

She called Kathleen Delaney again.

Jesus, don't you listen, said Kathleen, and hung up.

Lydia Googled *tony mulhouse cinematographer*. He had worked on a few movies she had seen and disliked. He knows Sandy, she thought, I could reach out. Lydia thought of the mole near his mouth sinking into the smile that hid it. She would not invite Tony Mulhouse, did not want to invite Tony Mulhouse, but she opened a Twitter account and followed him.

She would not invite Tony Mulhouse to the dinner party, but when he direct messaged her and said that it had been nice to meet her at the wedding she responded that it had been nice to meet him too. He wrote back and asked if she would like to have a drink. Lydia did not respond immediately. In their bedroom Caleb was probably reading Reddit. He would read Reddit in their bedroom every evening for the foreseeable future. He was kind and good and young. He needed her.

She went into their bedroom. He was lying on the bed. He closed the laptop. She said, What if we got married?

What if, said Caleb.

Do you want to?

He bit his lip. For an instant she worried he might say no. Then he looked up and said, Let's do it.

Great, I don't think it needs to be a big deal, we can just go to City Hall.

Sounds good.

Great, said Lydia, and then she went back into the kitchen and messaged Tony that she'd love to have a drink with him.

Lydia met Tony Mulhouse at a bar with plush red velvet benches. He asked her what she wanted to drink. She asked for a glass of Riesling, although she never drank Riesling and had no idea what it tasted like.

Fine, said Tony Mulhouse, and ordered a Riesling and a scotch and two glasses of champagne.

I don't need the champagne, said Lydia.

My treat.

You know, I'm getting married.

Tony Mulhouse looked at Lydia with incredulity. His teeth were very white in the light of the dim warm lamps that hung from the ceiling.

You're fascinating, really.

Lydia said that Sandy had had a beautiful wedding.

Yes, said Tony. She saw mirth at the corners of his mouth.

Don't you think so, she said. Everything was crimson and plush, dim and lonely. There was something distinguished in his face and in the way he mocked her.

I just said I did.

Their drinks came. Lydia took a big gulp of wine.

Good, said Tony, I'm trying to get you drunk, and then he told her that he was joking, of course.

Of course, said Lydia.

So tell me about your young man.

What do you want to know?

Well, his name, his occupation, for starters.

Lydia said that his name was Caleb and that he was taking some time off from school to figure out what he wanted.

Fabulous, said Tony. And how does he feel about how old you are?

I don't know, we've never really talked about it.

Even better. Cheers, said Tony, picking up his champagne. I don't know why we didn't start with these.

Cheers, said Lydia, and picked up hers. How do you know Sandy and Mark?

I used to be married to Mark's sister.

Oh, said Lydia.

Briefly and not happily.

I'm surprised they invited you then.

So am I. Tony drained his champagne glass and switched back to his scotch.

I'm seeing them Friday, we're having them over to dinner.

Are you inviting me?

I wasn't. Do you want to come?

He raised his eyebrows.

Oh, said Lydia. You were teasing me.

Yes.

Embarrassed, she sat up straight. Under the table she moved her knee away from his so that they were no longer touching. Well, anyway, she said.

Anyway what?

She gave him the address. Drinks at seven. She told herself it didn't matter and felt confident and appropriate, like the woman who would sit at the head of the long table on Friday evening.

I'll probably forget all of that.

Just as well.

Anyway, Tony said pointedly, tell me more about yourself, fascinating woman.

Lydia said that she was a graphic designer. So I do layouts, logos, things like that. I used to do packaging but I stopped because I couldn't convince anyone to use sustainable materials.

Like what.

Certain types of cardboard, Lydia said, and glass, and bio-degradable plastics. She heard how weak she sounded and drank more.

So you're not an idiot, said Tony Mulhouse.

Excuse me?

I'm just wondering why you wanted to meet me. Because here you are, you're getting married to your young man, who is very handsome if you don't mind my saying so, I'm not blind, and you're clearly not stupid, and yet you wanted to come meet me for a drink.

You asked.

You followed me on Twitter. Why?

I don't know.

Do you want to come to my apartment?

She had not expected him to ask so soon, and she had thought that when he did he would to lean forward and say it playfully, as if in confidence, so that she could pretend that it was sweet. Instead he had been matter-of-fact.

He waited.

Sure, said Lydia. She drank quietly as he asked for the check. As he signed he said, You can leave that if you don't feel like finishing it.

It turned out that Tony Mulhouse lived around the corner. His apartment had cream furnishings and large windows.

With the bathroom door open Lydia, still lying in bed, could see Tony remove a shirt from a nearby hanger and place it on the ironing board that stood already unfolded near the sink. Tony plugged in the iron and let it heat.

Sorry, he said, I have to get to work early tomorrow and I'm very particular about these things.

That's all right, said Lydia. As he stood near the board and waited she looked at his naked body. She had not really looked at it before. He had sinewy legs. She thought of Caleb and Tom and felt sad and stupid.

Tony was ironing now. I'd better watch out, he said, I could neuter myself if I'm not careful.

Lydia did not respond. She was thinking of how kind Caleb was, how curious.

You were wrong, she said to Tony.

About what?

She didn't want to tell him and he did not ask again. She smelled starch in the air. He put the ironed shirt back on the hanger and hung it from the bathroom door, then picked up a pair of navy trousers.

I'm really bad at doing these, he said, and began to press them. Especially bad.

Lydia listened to the iron move across the fabric and wondered why she had not left yet. She noticed that on Tony's bedside table was a copy of Freud's *Civilization and Its Discontents*.

Are you reading this?

What?

Tony poked his head out of the bathroom. Oh, no, he said, of course not, it's just there.

Oh.

Do you have any advice about how to iron these?

No.

He went back to ironing. Lydia sat up.

I ought to get married too, said Tony, so I can get someone to do this for me.

Lydia got out of the bed and looked for her underwear. When she got home she spent a while in the shower and crawled into bed next to Caleb. It was still not late.

Did you have a nice drink with your friend? he asked.

Yes.

Chapter Twenty-Five

In the morning Lydia made Caleb French toast. That day she lay in bed with him watching the last season of *The Sopranos*. Once they had finished the last episode she praised his theories about the cut to black.

What if Tony had a panic attack, said Caleb, so it ends the way it starts.

That's a fantastic insight, she said, trying not to flinch. You're probably right.

Or what if Meadow's in league with the guy in the Members Only jacket.

That could be it too, said Lydia. Absolutely.

He looked at her and away and she could not tell if the cast of his eyes was amused or suspicious so the next day she bought him rugelach. She watched as he untaped the lid of the box and wondered if his bewilderment was the same as it had been the week before or if the sad gentle surprise on his face was a reaction to how quiet she had been when she came home later than expected. Maybe she had been too quiet and he had noticed.

She was nervous around him all the time. If he suspected anything he did not mention it. Soon she resented the pleasure on his face when he poured syrup on his pancakes.

Beau came over early on the day of the party and wandered jauntily around the living room. Haven't been here in a while, he said, chuckling.

Lydia offered Beau a drink.

Sure, he said, and shrugged. Do you have vodka?

Yes, said Lydia, and realized she disliked him and disliked Caleb when he was around him. They made childish jokes. Caleb declined the drink she offered with incredulity, as if she had been ridiculous to offer it.

Sandy and Mark would show up soon and she would not be ridiculous. At the same time she wanted to apologize to Caleb always.

When Sandy and Mark arrived Lydia asked if she could take their coats and then noticed that Sandy only had a light jacket.

This weather, said Mark, who was not wearing a coat at all.

Some weather, said Caleb, leaning on the dining room table. Lydia wrinkled her nose. This weather, some weather. Some weather, this. She wished Caleb had not said that and was not smiling at Mark so amicably. She could not say why she found that smile so irritating. This weather, some weather, what weather. But now Caleb was looking at her.

Actually, said Lydia, this is becoming normal.

Mark and Sandy introduced themselves to Beau.

Cool, he said, amused, and did not say his name.

Lydia said, This is Beau. Now I've made beef and I've totally forgotten to ask if anyone's a vegetarian, so I hope it's all right, but if it's not we've got vegetables and other things, so —

The only thing I don't eat is duck, said Sandy.

Beef's great, said Mark.

I'm so glad, said Lydia. She was aware of a falseness in the way she spoke and did not like it but did not know how to change it. There was the self she heard and saw in the mirror and who was touched when people touched her body. She had been thinking since Tony Mulhouse that most of her self was a space within that form. Across it hard things clacked against one another like billiard balls, reeling across soft manufactured expanses, hitting walls, unable to find pockets, hitting themselves and one another again, startling themselves. And yet she was responsible for herself. She did not know how, but she was supposed to be responsible. She felt a frightening loose feeling, smiled thinly, and said, Have you been here since we redecorated?

You know, I've never been here, said Sandy.

Oh right, said Lydia. I must be confused.

Must be, said Mark.

Yeah, said Caleb.

Wow, man, said Beau, laughing, I'm sorry, I can't get over this.

They took their drinks into the living room and sat. For a minute no one said anything. Caleb leaned forward as if listening avidly. Lydia coughed and wondered who he was imitating. He cracked his knuckles and she flinched. Beau suppressed a laugh. Sandy seemed at ease as she looked around the room, breezy in the face of awkwardness. Still no one said anything.

You know, said Sandy, I feel for some reason I should say I pride myself on not being judgmental.

Beau stood back up and leaned against a wall, wide-eyed.

What a horrible woman, thought Lydia, what a horrible woman.

What I mean is, said Sandy, I consider myself a free thinker.

So Mark, said Lydia, I don't think I ever heard what you do.

He's in springs, said Sandy, leaning back into the black sofa.

What kind of springs?

All kinds. But we have a special focus on die springs. For heavy machinery, clutches, brakes.

Business good? said Caleb. For the first time Lydia wondered what it was like for him to be here, in his dead father's redecorated apartment, entertaining his father's acquaintances.

Very good, said Mark. With this economy –

Mark and I have different feelings about the president, Sandy interjected.

Oh, said Lydia, and drank.

Mark thinks this economy is worth it, and I think he's a disgrace. The president, of course, she said, laughing. Sandy glanced at Caleb and said, But your father agreed with me.

Right, said Caleb.

What can I say, said Mark, my 401k is in great shape and I love it, so sue me.

There are more important things, said Sandy. You're lucky I love you.

The room was silent again. Caleb moved his foot and the sound of his shoe scraping the wood floor was childish and excruciating. Beau pulled out his phone.

Lydia asked about Argentina. Sandy said they'd had the best time. In Buenos Aires they had wandered past beautiful painted houses. Sandy had not been able to convince Mark to tango but he maintained he'd enjoyed watching her.

I had a great time, he said, I'm just not a dancer.

Then they had gone to Mendoza and spent a few days drinking wine.

It was perfect, except I wish we could have stayed longer. And I do sort of wish we'd gone to Evita's grave.

She was a terrible person, said Mark.

She was lobotomized, said Sandy.

At the end of her life, so how is that relevant?

Wait what? said Beau.

Who's Evita? Caleb asked.

It doesn't have to be relevant, said Sandy, it's just very sad. She explained who Juan and Eva Perón were and that toward the end of Evita's life her husband had had her lobotomized without her consent in a secret room in their palace. And no one knows why, she continued, taking a sip of wine. It might have been because she was in extreme pain from cervical cancer and they thought the operation would help, or it might have been because her politics were becoming more and more extreme and lobotomies were supposed to calm the personality.

By *extreme*, said Mark, Sandy means she was secretly buying thousands of machine guns to arm militias of workers. Lest you think it was some harmless difference of opinion. She could have caused a civil war.

Yeah but you can't *lobotomize* someone. Anyway, said Sandy, smiling, we had a great honeymoon, though I wish we'd seen more, but I always want to do everything and it's just not possible.

Sandy, said Lydia, I've been wondering, as a person of faith — I can't help but notice your lovely necklace — how do you feel about all of these evangelicals embracing Trump even though he's, you know, he lies, he breaks promises, he's cheated on his wives, and everything. Do you find it shocking?

Lydia felt a bright surge of accomplishment and pleasure at her own charm. Then Sandy grasped her necklace with one hand and said, Oh, I'm not religious. It was my grandmother's, that's all.

Oh.

I certainly don't believe in God. Do you?

No, said Caleb, I don't.

Well, neither do I, Lydia said.

Heaven, said Sandy, what a racket. As far as I'm concerned there's nothing after this. You just check out, and that's that.

I think dinner's ready, said Lydia.

Oh, I'm sorry, Caleb, said Sandy, I shouldn't have said that.

You're right, though, said Caleb. My father thought the same thing.

Shall we eat? said Lydia. Beau put his phone away. They all went into the next room, where they ate salad and beef and potatoes and spinach and talked about the difference between the stock market and the real economy. They wondered aloud whether the economy would fall apart imminently or when the planet did.

We'll be dead by the time it gets bad, said Mark. Or the three of us will, he said, indicating Lydia and Sandy and himself.

No we won't, said Sandy.

I think Elon Musk is going to get us out of here, said Beau. We'll all go to Mars.

I mean, Mark said, I understand the idea of Medicare for All, but where does the money come from?

No one mentioned Medicare for All, sweetheart.

Caleb said that Elon Musk wasn't going to help them.

Did you know, Beau continued, that there's this group that wants to send people to Mars, I don't think it's Elon Musk's thing, it's another group, but they're taking applications for four spots and they've had like tons, like hundreds of thousands of applications, but the thing is you never come back. Ever. And you can never have sex.

Mark laughed and drank.

No, seriously, Beau continued, because they, uh, they think it will make everything more complicated on the mission, and also they're not equipped for Mars babies.

Martians, said Lydia.

You know if we do go to Mars it'll be like a tiny group of people, said Caleb, you know most people are going to die here. There's no way out, people are too selfish.

Lydia looked at him. He took another bite of beef and chewed. It was very quiet. Caleb swallowed and then said, Anyway the kids born on the spaceship wouldn't really be Martians. I mean like Marvin the Martian is a Martian.

Marvin the Martian is a cartoon, said Lydia.

Beau, are you in school? Sandy asked.

I go to NYU.

Beau said he wanted to major in business. Mark asked him whether he wanted to go to business school once he graduated.

I think so.

That's fantastic.

Sandy, Lydia said, why don't you eat duck?

Mark exhaled and shifted in his seat.

Oh, I don't mind saying, said Sandy. It's an old story.

Awful story, said Mark.

I had a pet duck as a child.

Well that makes sense, then, said Caleb.

I had a pet duck, and her name was Quack Quack. I grew up in a pretty rural area, not on a farm but we had a big yard and a little coop at the edge of it. Every morning I would go see if she had eggs, and play with her, and pet her. She was a wonderful duck. But then one evening, I was about nine, and we were having dinner. And halfway through dinner my mother said, You know, this is Quack Quack.

Caleb stopped eating.

No, said Lydia, smiling.

It was a joke, right? asked Beau.

No, said Sandy calmly. They'd cooked my pet. I ate my pet, and I had no idea until we were halfway through.

She picked up her fork.

How awful, said Lydia.

That's sick, said Beau. It's twisted.

You're so sweet, said Sandy. It did hurt me. But they did their best and I don't really think about it anymore, I just don't eat duck.

How awful, said Lydia again. Is that why you walked down the aisle by yourself?

No, they're dead.

Oh.

I just can't get over how mean it is, said Beau.

To her astonishment Lydia saw that he was blinking back tears. Here, she said, let me get you a tissue.

I don't need it, he said, blinking faster.

Anyway, said Sandy, I was glad, we were all on very good terms before they went. I feel good about that.

There was a pause.

I'm so sorry, said Caleb.

Thank you, said Sandy, well, I know you understand.

I'm so sorry, said Lydia. Caleb glanced at her. Beau wiped his eyes on his napkin.

After chocolate cake the guests thanked her and said goodbye and called the elevator. Lydia said that she was so glad they had all come. As soon as the elevator door closed she turned to Caleb, who was yawning and running one hand through his hair, and said, What do you think of Sandy, because if you wanted to fuck her I'd be okay with it.

Caleb let his hand drop.

What made you think of that?

I don't know. But afterward I want you to do something for me. Afterward, when she's asleep, I want you to take her necklace. Lydia heard the words rush out of her mouth and was surprised at what she was saying, but Caleb's eyebrows were not rising and his eyes were not wide. She kept talking. The cross necklace. I don't like it, I don't want her to have it. It's not fair.

His face was still calm. He looked at once younger and older than she had thought he was. But he was not disgusted with her, and he was not surprised. She wished he had been and saw that instead he pitied her. She began to cry. He wrapped his arms around her. She wiped her snot on his shirt. He said, You're very tired, let's go to bed.

Lydia was in the bathroom splashing her face with cold water when the doorbell rang. Caleb was in their bedroom. She tied the belt of her bathrobe around her waist and went to the door. Tony Mulhouse was downstairs.

Lydia answered the intercom and said, You're late, the party is over.

I've brought you something.

We don't want it.

Who is it, she heard Caleb shout.

Lydia had no idea what to say to him. Look, she said to Tony through the intercom, I really, really don't want you here, it's going to screw everything up for me, and I don't want whatever you have.

Oh relax, said Tony, just buzz me in. I'm not so stupid, and anyway, relax.

Who is it, said Caleb again.

The apartment was so big. We should have moved somewhere else, she thought, we should have gone somewhere new. Caleb walked up behind her, put his hand on her shoulder, and pressed the buzzer with his free hand.

Thank you, they heard Tony say, and then through the speaker they heard the inner door to the building close.

Caleb went into the living room. Lydia did not follow him. When she heard Tony knock on the apartment door she opened it immediately and said, Look, we're very tired, so I don't know what you're angling for, but if you're thinking, if you came up here with any ideas –

Don't be ridiculous. Have you been crying?

– we are not into that. We don't do that.

Anyway, I've brought you this, said Tony. He held up a tall dark bottle with a red cap and a red label, on which was written CYNAR in large white letters. Behind the word there was a small image of a green artichoke.

What the hell is that.

Read it, Tony said. You say it Chee*nar*. Some people say *Sigh*nar, but they're idiots.

Are you actually insane.

I thought we could have a drink, said Tony, you invited me to the party.

By now Caleb had come into the entryway. Lydia did not turn to look at him but knew that he was there and felt that he was somehow preventing her from seeing Tony clearly, like a scar in the back of her eye. If he would go back into the living room she would be able to handle Tony. She did not know how she knew that he was leaning against the wall and had his hands in his pockets, but she did.

It's a digestivo made from artichokes, said Tony.

What?

An after-dinner drink. It's an amaro. A bit like Campari, but better. It's Italian. It made me think of you.

I'm not Italian.

You could be. By the way, I don't know what you're worried about, he already knows.

Lydia had been wrong about where Caleb was. He was very close behind her. She heard him say, You're the guy from the wedding.

Right, said Tony. That's who I am. Is that your kitchen? Let me know where I can find some small glasses and some ice. He walked briskly past them.

Lydia felt Caleb's hand on her upper back and flinched. She could not look at him.

What are you doing, she said to Tony, you're ruining everything.

I'm pouring drinks, that hardly counts as ruining anything.

He doesn't drink.

She heard a voice behind her say, I want to.

Tony looked at her and threw up his hands for effect. You heard the man, he wants a drink. Now if you could help me with the glasses.

He was opening the cupboards one by one, closing them, moving onto the next. Lydia did not move. Caleb walked past her into the kitchen, opened the cupboard at the back of the room, took out three glasses and placed them on the stone top of the island. Lydia heard the hard sound when they touched down and then the rumble of machinery and ice as he pulled the freezer open. Tony watched, his eyebrows raised.

See, he said to Lydia. He poured the drinks and put a cube of ice in each. The liquor was dark brown. Caleb picked up the glass nearest him, took a sip, and spat. He screwed up his face. From the working of his jaw Lydia could tell he was trying to get the taste off his tongue. Tony laughed.

Let's go sit, he said.

Caleb, you don't have to drink this, Lydia said. She walked

toward them, picked up her glass, and led them into the living room.

Caleb and Tony both brought their glasses. They sat.

It's very late, said Lydia.

Cheers, said Tony, to love.

Fine, said Lydia, and raised her glass. She watched Caleb try the drink again. This time he only grimaced a little. She drank too. It did not taste like anything she could identify. She had thought it would be bitter and it was, but not very much. She swallowed. She took another sip and swilled the liquid in her mouth and tried to think what it tasted like and failed again. Tony leaned back in the armchair.

This is a great chair. How did you two meet, anyway?

Lydia told him. Caleb drank slowly and listened to Lydia's voice and Tony's laughter.

Tony kept saying, That's stupendous. After two drinks he told them that in the morning he had to take his mother to a doctor's appointment and left.

As Lydia and Caleb were washing out the glasses she said, So it doesn't matter to you, what I did.

Does this go in the refrigerator, he said.

That night she lay awake for hours and listened to his breathing and the sounds of passing traffic. Finally she slept. When she woke up she was alone in the room. Warm light poured toward the empty bookshelves and over their clean surfaces. She heard Caleb's footsteps in the hallway and did not get up. What she had said about Sandy and the necklace came back to her, and she remembered Tony saying stupendous, they were stupendous, and she buried her face in the pillow. She regretted all of it and especially how she had wiped her nose on Caleb's shirt. Eventually he came into the room and said,

Let's go for a walk.

Now?

It's late already, he said. She washed her face and got dressed quickly. He was going to leave her, she thought.

Do I bring a coat, she asked him, or is it still weirdly warm?

It's still pretty warm.

She chose a navy cardigan and put it on. They went into the elevator and down and outside and began to walk east toward the park. She did not know what to do with her hands and felt sick.

I want coffee, she said, so they turned onto Columbus and got two cups of coffee and an everything bagel with cream cheese. Then they kept walking east. Before long they entered the park, where confused birds were singing. They left the drive and turned down a winding path. They could see past the bare trees on either side. Maybe Caleb did not have anything he wanted to say after all.

Then he coughed. Casually, almost sweetly, he said, I want to just say something about Tony.

What, she said, and stopped walking.

It's not a big thing, he said, beckoning her onward so that she started moving again. Just in the future, I'd rather you tell me in advance. When you're going to do something like that.

Someone had dropped a black leather glove on the ground. He picked it up and put it on top of the railing. It slipped and he tried again and got it to stay.

You mean, she said slowly, when I'm going to fuck someone else you just want me to tell you beforehand and then it's fine.

They could still see the street outside the park. A yellow cab stopped at a traffic light.

Yeah, he said. Let's get further in and then see if we can find a bench.

But I'm not going to, she said.

But if you do.

They passed a large boulder and the path twisted back on itself and they found themselves again at the drive that cut through the park. A carriage drawn by a slow tan horse wearing blinders passed in front of them. They crossed the road. They walked around an area of plain gray–brown dirt that in the summer would be a softball field. He pointed to a bench. They made for it.

So you want to open up the relationship, she said.

Not exactly, he said. More like I'm telling you how I think about it. And just asking you for a heads–up next time.

Well, I don't agree. Lots of people have open relationships but everyone involved has to agree to open up, and I don't agree.

You won't tell me beforehand, is what you're saying.

They sat. He unwrapped the bagel and offered her half. She took it.

I'm saying I won't do it. Again. I won't do it again.

I would just rather think I'll know. It helps me.

You're not listening, she said, and ate. Then you'll tell me too, she said abruptly.

If what?

If you want to have sex with someone. Like Sandy for example. You agree you'll tell me in advance.

No.

She looked at him in shock. His cheeks were pink and in front of her his gaze followed the movement of something she could not pick out.

No you won't tell me. So you know what I'm doing but I'm in the dark. So I have to worry but you don't.

No I'm not going to be with anyone else, he said, and began to eat.

A pigeon hopped up to their feet, looking to see what they'd dropped.

But it's not fair, she said. I mean it's not fair to *you*.

A week later Caleb and Lydia got married. Lydia's white sundress had been in her storage unit and so had not been lost in the fire. She wore a sweater over it. There were no guests. The next year Caleb finished high school online. During the worst of the pandemic they stayed indoors together, and when it was over he went to Hunter College, where he made friends who did not know how he had met Lydia. She kept telling him that if he took a lover it would be all right, and he said that he would not discuss it.

Well then I won't either, she said, you can trust I won't.

Tell me beforehand, he repeated.

He slept in his childhood bed, and she was alone in Tom's and listened for footsteps in the night. She heard none. Occasionally she met a man she would have liked to sleep with, but when she was on the point of going home with him the memory of Caleb's simple request stopped her.

She grew angry. A few years later Caleb told her she had to quit drinking. She refused. The tattooed ghost and tattooed eye faded. They moved west. If he fell in love with someone else or wished he had fallen in love he never told her anything about it.

PART THREE

It happened slowly, and then it happened all at once. It happened all at once, and there was more left to happen. Her joints began to hurt. She tired easily. The lines on her face grew in number and deepened and each day it seemed there were still more of them. In a magazine she read an interview with a plastic surgeon who said, The moment you see something that bothers you, that's the moment to do something, because if you wait the damage will be done and the change will be there to stay. She did nothing. She could see in the mirror the change that was to her already irremediable and weeks or months or years or days later she was surprised when there was yet another change. She got more cellulite. She sweated at random intervals and stopped menstruating. Her breasts sagged. Her arms sagged. Her joints hurt more. She forgot things. Her hair thinned.

The water encroached further and the earth burned faster and more wildly. In many places it was so hot that sweating was inadequate. Children could not cool themselves and cooked to death in their own chubby bodies. New regulations were enacted due to the cooking of the children. It was expensive to comply with the ordinances and corporations lobbied and the laws regarding the matter of the children's overheating were amended and then were struck down. More people sweated to death and elsewhere people froze and others drowned in search of a place that was neither frozen nor too hot nor bereft of ozone nor beset by dust nor lost to the empire of newly vigorous microbes causing suppurating infection or liquefaction of innards or fever. Those who did not drown en route were often turned away. The water encroached further and the people who had turned the others away went looking for home. Caleb and Lydia were lucky to be in the right place at the right time.

Caleb's hair had turned white in his forties and thinned over the years that followed. He remembered that his father's hair had not thinned. Lydia did not say anything about Caleb's hair and he did not say anything about hers.

Around the time the small lines on his face had begun to deepen, the flooding in their area sped up. Soon they and twenty other families were on one of a few pieces of dry land in an inland sea.

Most of the day Caleb sat alone at his job at the grocery store and waited for someone to come in to buy something. When he rang up purchases he had brief cheerful conversations. Then he went home and made dinner for Lydia. He had learned to cook in his thirties and he still enjoyed it even though he had to adapt the recipes in his tattered cookbooks to the available ingredients. Lydia missed tomatoes.

Often she went for walks during the day and once or twice she found eggs and brought them home. She said they had been hidden in the rushes and joked that she was lucky the bird didn't return at the wrong moment and catch her in the act. He fried them. For dessert they shared an orange.

What a treat, she said, and cut the round fruit open with their best knife.

The first time he saw her she was descending the steps from the giant silver bridge down to the island. She leaned forward under the weight of a large camping backpack. She took each big step down with trepidation and then brought her other foot to meet the first one and stood for an instant righting herself and looking out at the place where she would soon arrive. She looked past him. He wondered if she had been traveling a long time. On that day the water's extension toward the horizon was calm and flat and tender. It had rained the night before but it did not rain now. He looked down at the water and watched her reflection descend the limpid mirrored bridge and saw the sea shiver as she pushed her hair out of her face. He did not think she could want help from him.

When she got to the foot of the bridge she took her rucksack off and rested it on the last step and sat next to it. He looked past her carefully and pretended not to watch her wipe the sweat from her face with one forearm. The supply boat would be coming any minute and he would load the flour and onions and mushrooms and whatever else into the van and take it to the store.

Hey, mister, he heard her say. Can I ask you a question?

Now that he let himself look at her he could see that her face was covered in freckles.

Sure, he said. She was pushing her long hair away from her face again and he heard how casual he sounded.

Is this a good place to look for work?

To be honest there's not much work here.

She nodded. She fixed her hair again.

Where do you work?

He liked her eyes. He told her he worked at the grocery store. She asked if he could use any help. He was on the point of telling her that he didn't run the store, he just worked there and so couldn't hire anyone, and anyway there was no need of a second employee given how rarely customers came in and how little there was to buy. Instead he said, Sure.

The grocery store consisted of two aisles and one register in the empty echoing cavern of the old supermarket. They sat in the dim light from the one long bulb they were permitted to keep on overhead. Her name was Jody, and if she could get things to work here she was going to send for her son, who was with her sister in Wisconsin.

No sense dragging him out here otherwise, she said.

Caleb agreed.

No sense at all, he said.

He paid Jody an advance out of his own money and later that day convinced Tonya Brooks, who lived in the blue house near the estuary, to rent her the spare room. It had been empty since her daughter's death from cholera.

That night Lydia did not return from her walk until the moon was far up in the sky and dinner was cold. When Caleb asked where she'd been she would not at first give an answer. She sat at the table and clutched the handle of her spoon. After a long while she said that it was a beautiful night.

That's true, he said.

The next day Jody helped Caleb open the store, although it was barely enough work for even one person. They pulled an extra chair up next to the register and talked about the landscapes they remembered from their childhoods. Jody was from Arizona and had never been to New York City or the surrounding area and Caleb had never been to the Southwest. Nevertheless he loved hearing her talk about red striped cliffs and multitudes of stars.

It's a shame those cliffs aren't there anymore, he said.

Oh they're there, she said, we just had to leave.

Each day he looked forward to seeing her. She did push-ups in the aisles when no customers were there. They went for walks together on their breaks. He told her more about Lydia than he had ever told anyone. After two weeks she went to Wisconsin to pick up her son. He missed her constantly.

That Wednesday he was alone in the big dark supermarket all day and then in the evening Lydia did not come home. He was terrified and wished he could tell Jody about it or ask her what to do and so he snapped at Lydia when she came in drenched with rain. Afterward he apologized and touched the side of her face. She reminded him that it had been a while and they went into the bedroom. In the middle of the night he awoke to find her crying. I keep getting lost, she said.

Isaac, when Jody brought him, was playful and earnest. He had soft tan skin and a neat buzz cut. In the vacant aisles he invented oceans, forests, savannahs, rainforests, tundra. He hoisted himself into the tan shelving and shimmied along on his belly, hissing, and Jody came running when the sound of buckling metal panels echoed too loudly and in too quick succession. Isaac was fine but Jody was afraid. You can be a snake on the floor, she told him, so he lay down and tried to slither along the linoleum toward the one register they still used and its defunct black conveyor belt which now functioned only as a table. Even from the other end of the room Caleb could hear the fleshy *thwap* of the boy's little belly where the linoleum would not let it move forward. The boy tucked his shirt again under his body and pulled himself forward repeatedly with one elbow. This took some effort. Isaac forgot to hiss and bit his lower lip.

He looks like a commando, said Caleb, crawling like that.

Snake, said Isaac.

Other times Caleb and Jody heard hard slapping noises in irregular rhythms, some single and halting and some in quick triplet sequence, and they knew the boy was playing hopscotch in one aisle or another with the edges of linoleum squares for guide. When he complained of boredom Jody would set up a scavenger hunt with the flour and sugar and canned corn and applesauce jars that went largely unsold in the lighted and stocked part of the store where Caleb sat. The difficulty was, she told Caleb later, that there weren't many places to hide things in the rest of the store, seeing as how the shelves were empty. He was not a stupid boy and he found things easily. If she tried to hide things behind one set of shelves he walked to the next aisle and saw the box of salt or can of peas sitting plainly on the floor on the other side of that same metal structure.

The best hiding spots were: under the bottommost shelf of each unit, which was only slightly raised from the floor; behind the square fan; peeking over the edge of the fourth shelf, which was above Isaac's head but not out of his reach; behind the obsolete freezer unit or tucked into the tangle of its cord.

Why not inside the freezer? said Caleb once, and Jody said she did not want to encourage Isaac to go in there. She feared that if he slid the clear door shut he might not be able to get out and would eventually suffocate.

What about inside the fan? said Caleb. You could stick a packet of yeast in there.

I don't want him thinking it's smart to stick his fingers in there.

It's off.

Most of the time.

After the first few scavenger hunts Isaac developed a search method. First he would walk the aisles briskly, marching up one and down the next and scanning the shelves and ground for anything obvious. Then he would turn around and retrace his steps, looking up to see if any small item was hidden on the shelf just above him and if he could catch its corner with his eye. Then he'd check behind the fan and behind the freezer. He brought his few treasures to the front of the room, and then Jody congratulated him and put what he had found back where it belonged.

He became quickly adept at finding the packets of yeast or pieces of cheesecloth his mother hid under the bottom shelf.

You only *half* hide things, he said, I see them sticking really far out.

But I don't want to tuck anything further underneath that big unit, Jody said to Caleb, what if he tries to reach in there and his arm gets stuck? Or what if he tips the whole thing over onto himself?

Before long Isaac got into the habit of searching the shelf over his head by touch only. He reached up and trailed his hand along its edge as he walked obstinately through the aisles, stomping his feet as loudly as he could.

Once, in the yard behind the store, Jody found a pile of the plastic and metal innards of devices no longer in production, little chips with copper-colored dots and green processors and one big silver battery. She considered giving Isaac the old trash to play with.

Why not, said Caleb. I'm sure none of it works anyway.

Aren't batteries dangerous? said Jody.

I'm sure it's fine, said Caleb. It can't be charged. It looks very old.

Late at night, to avoid the law and righteous bystanders, Jody walked down to the water and threw the chips in. She watched them sink and threw the battery after them. It made a heavy sound, and it was gone.

The next time Isaac got bored Jody took him out onto the bridge and walked about an hour toward the rest of the world. When he got back he told Caleb how much he had enjoyed seeing the drowned cities from above.

How far did you get? said Caleb.

As far as Missoula, said Jody.

Jody read Caleb the recipes printed on the backs of packages of flour. Her tone was wry and light. When she glanced up at him he looked down at the thin ridges in the motionless conveyor belt. One day, when Isaac was playing in the back of the store, she slid her chair close to his and stopped speaking.

He began to count the ridges but they were too small for him to be sure of their number.

She was watching him, he could feel it, she was reaching toward his shoulder with one hand.

He coughed and stood up. Then she walked over to the shelf of baking supplies.

Do you want to me to read you what's in imitation vanilla, she said.

Mapes, who owned the store, was a tall thin man with a ponytail and harsh gray eyes. He did not live on the island but came by every few weeks to see how things were going. He would come by any day now and Caleb would get him to hire Jody. He did not know how, but he would see to it that Mapes understood that he had to hire her.

Where do you work? Lydia asked Caleb. He reminded her.

Mapes was waiting at the store when Caleb got there one Thursday morning. He took a quick look around and said things looked all right and asked if there was anything he needed to be aware of. In halting, tense phrases Caleb told him about Jody and asked him to give her a job.

Mapes said, Sorry, man, I don't need another employee.

But Jody had already been restocking shelves, sweeping floors, bagging groceries, doing inventory, replacing weevily bags of grain so as to maintain the satisfaction of the customer, making conversation, locking up.

Well, I didn't tell you to bring anyone new in, said Mapes. He adjusted his hat and his ponytail.

Caleb described how Mrs. Kelleher had smiled at the way Jody bagged her onions and canned broth, and who smiled at onions? Jody was exceptional. Jody was charming. Charm was good for business.

There's nowhere else to buy food around here, said Mapes. And I don't need two of you sitting around there all day.

She has a child, said Caleb, think of the child.

Mapes had the mill to see to and the boats to check up on. He outlined the upshot. If Caleb wanted to quit, Jody could have that job. But if Caleb didn't want to quit, then the job was Caleb's and not Jody's. In any case there was only one job, because there was only enough work at the supermarket to merit one employee. Child or no child.

Before Jody dropped Isaac at her sister's, they'd been hiking all through the Upper Midwest and into lower Saskatchewan and back. They'd found a patch of forest where the branches and trunks and needles were the color of rust and stayed there for two weeks until fellow travelers stole their malaria net.

I brought him here too soon, said Jody when Caleb told

269

her that there was no job for her at the supermarket.

No, no, he said.

I might have to leave, she said, if I can't find something else.

No, he said.

He took her to the community center but the bulletin boards were empty. He booked her an hour on the computer later that day and in order to kill time until the machine became available they walked by the shore. They picked up the floating spiny bodies of urchins and wondered if they were edible given the metals rumored to be in the water and threw them far out. Isaac had hoped they could be skipped like rocks and as much as Jody tried to explain that the variable depths and prominences of their sharp exteriors made this unlikely he was still disappointed when they went straight under. The regional employment office portal showed no work available.

They went to collect Jody and Isaac's things from the rented room and carried them to Caleb's house. He said, This way you won't need to pay rent anymore.

That evening Caleb and Lydia and Jody and Isaac shared a tense celebratory dinner of cabbage and the expensive rice that grew in filtered water. In the morning Caleb went to see Tonya Brooks and paid the debt that Jody had incurred.

Late one night he got up to get a glass of water. Jody was awake and Isaac was asleep next to her. Caleb was very quiet. Silently Jody beckoned him out the front door and they stood on the porch. There was no wind and the nearby grasses were still.

Why don't you want to touch me? she said.

What?

She repeated herself. If it's because you don't want me to

think you expect it then you don't need to worry about that. She spoke quickly. Her eyes were bright and he had to look away. I want you to, she said.

It's not that, said Caleb, that's not it, and went back inside.

The next day at the grocery store she asked if she had done something wrong.

No, he said. He turned red and could not speak.

Jody helped cook. Jody fixed the tiles when they fell off the wall of the bathroom. Caleb watched her mix putty. They squeezed past each other in the narrow hallway.

Lydia wanted to go to the Met. Lydia wanted someone to 3D-print her a kitten. Lydia wanted advice on the radio-activity of various fracture zones in the seafloor. Lydia wanted a salad.

With tomatoes, she said, and sliced red onion, and butter lettuce. And a hard-boiled egg.

Lydia wanted to know why they were in this strange house and when Tom was coming home. She wanted her mother. Jody said they should take her to see someone.

The doctor asked Lydia to remember three words in order, to touch her nose, to touch his finger, her nose, his finger, her nose, his finger, as the finger moved from side to side. Then with her other hand. Then the days of the week in reverse order.

Starting from what day? Lydia wanted to know.

Sunday, said the doctor.

Then to repeat the words.

Afterward, the doctor took Caleb aside. There were things that they could have done, he said, years ago, there were at one point medications that he would have loved to prescribe, not to mention other interventions, stem cell and so on, but the labs that had escaped submersion were busy with pain-killers and treatments for contagious diseases.

Fox, melon, garden.

That night Caleb told Jody what would happen and asked if she thought they should tell Lydia everything.

Would you want to know? she said quietly.

The moon was big and round behind her. The moon was the same size it had been on nights with full moons when he was a child. Its light picked up flyaway hairs around her face.

No, he said. I would not.

She nodded. Me neither, she said. They sat there. He heard things moving in the grass.

So we won't tell her, he said. She nodded again. She reached her hand toward his.

The next morning Isaac showed them how the ants that came up through the rotted wood planks of the porch ran their forelegs again and again along their black antennae, pulling.

That's amazing, said Jody. Caleb agreed that it was. They all watched the ants for a long time.

Soon summer came. Lydia forgot her way home more and more often. One day Jody found her on the far side of the island, sitting on the ground with her arms wrapped around her bent knees. She was looking out at the cattails that grew near the shore.

Later, when Isaac and Lydia had both gone to sleep, Jody told Caleb about the people she had seen asleep on the bridge over the drowned highways and cities and farms and homes and cemeteries of the previous world. She could not tell if they lived there or were only resting or if they did not know whether to go to the mainland or the island, forward or back.

I want a kite, said Isaac.

It was late morning and the day was very hot. Caleb and Jody were sitting on the porch, finishing their dandelion coffee. Isaac drank his water loudly, then set the glass down.

Sorry, Jody said, we don't have a kite.

Maybe you could make one, said Caleb.

Out of what? the boy wanted to know.

You just find two good long sticks.

Isaac ran down the porch steps and off through the grass. Caleb and Jody watched him crouch under the stand of cottonwood trees and begin to pick branches up off of the ground, which was covered in fluffy white seedpods.

I'll get him an old pillowcase, said Caleb.

Sit, sit, said Jody. I want to make more coffee anyway. I'll get it.

I can make coffee, said Caleb.

No, you sit here with him, said Jody, and went inside.

The house was quiet. Jody put the ground dandelion in the pot, added water, set it on the stove and lit the flame underneath. Through the window over the sink she could see Isaac trying to get the sticky white cottonwood seeds off of his hands and legs. Then he took the two long branches he had found and went back toward Caleb and the porch.

Jody heard a door open behind her. She turned around. Lydia was standing in the hallway. She wore a blue robe and her bleary eyes were wide.

Who are you? she said.

ACKNOWLEDGMENTS

I want to thank Neil Griffiths and Damian Lanigan for asking me to write a novel, and for approaching its manuscript with keen editorial insight, great sensitivity to language and character, frankness, and unfailing dedication. Thanks to James Tookey for his astute observations on the text and inspired, assiduous work in many essential roles. Thanks to Jasmin Kirkbride for her patient copy-editing, Luke Bird for his elegant cover, Charles Boyle for his text design, and everyone involved in the production of the book.

I would like to thank Marc Jaffee for his excellent advice, perceptive reading, and longstanding friendship. For their encouragement and support, I am grateful to Sharon Kivland, Yve Lomax, Jonathan Miles, Ian Kiaer, Rebecca Jagoe, Gilda Williams, Alida Kuzemczak-Sayer, Sam Williams, Emma Bäcklund, Stefan Zebrowski-Rubin, Catherine Taylor, Michael Caines, Nina Trivedi, Valerie Hammond, Maureen Gallace, Jane Avrich, Marty Skoble, Manca Bajec, and many others. Special thanks to Sarah Cameron, who brought me to Greece, and to the late Marielle Vigourt.

Thanks to all who work at Burley Fisher Books in Haggerston and at Paragraph in Brooklyn, NY. I wrote most of this book at these wonderful spaces.

Thanks to my family for more than I can say here.

Thank you to our Founder Readers.
We are immensely grateful for your supoport and faith in us.

Kirk Annett

Andrea Barlien

Linda Barton

Therese Bernbach

Willa Bews

Kevin Bleyer

Geof Branch

Celia Brayfield

Sarah Brearley

John Brewin

Peter Burgess

Karen Burns

William Butler

Joseph Camilleri

Russell Chant

James Clammer

David Clarke

Jeff Collins

Joe Cooney

Matthew Craig

Alan Crilly

Ian Critchley

Stafford Critchlow

George Cronin

Kevin Davey

Gaynor Doyle

Kevin Duffy

Anthony Duncan

Timna Fibert

Sam Fisher

Marita Fraser

Emma French

Paul Fulcher

Graham Fulcher

Joseph Gallivan

Neil George

Sarah Goldson

Victoria Goodall

Susan Gorgioski

Bryan Gormley

Charlotte Green

Louise Greenberg

Paul Griffiths

Anne Griffiths

Ortelio Grillo

Ian Hagues

Daniel Hahn

Paul Hannan

Alison Hardy

Jack Hargreaves

Sonia Harris

Katy Hastie

David Hebblethwaite

Rónán Hession

Dirk-Jan Hoogerdijk

Stephen Hopper

Hugh Hudson

Bex Hughes

Robert Hughes

Joe Hutson

Dylan Hyson

Roy Immanuel

Jarkko Inkinen

Bijan Jalili

Daniel Janes

Alistair Jenkins

Dan Jenkins
Stuart Kirschbaum
Marina Klimovich
Justin Kurian
Alida Kuzemczak-Sayer
Simon Lewis
Duncan Lewis
Chiara Liberio
Alex Lockwood
Catherine Lowden
Anil Malhotra
Sarah Manvel
Kelsey Marcus
Oscar Mardell
Andrea Mason
Charlie Mawer
Jack McSweeney
Eloise Millar
Geoffry Missinne
Ian Mond
Zosha Nash
Armen Nersessian
Amanda Nicholls
Vilma Nikolaidou
Steve Noyes
John O'Donoghue
Declan O'Driscoll
Anna Paige
Krista Parris
Debra Patek
Keirstan Pawson
Hannah Piekarz
Robert Pisani
Ben Plouviez
Jonathan Ruppin

Josephine Sacks
Mimi Sahu
Dan Simon
Alan Simpson
Arabella Spencer
Han Smith
Jolene Smith
Valarie Smith
Peggy Starbuck
Elizabeth Stubbs
Daryl Sullivan
Sue Thomas
Tessa Thornley
Matthew Tilt
Pat Tookey
Simon Trewin
Nina Trivedi
Paul Tyrell
Mark Valentine
Jeroen van Dooren
Pauline Van Mourik
    Broekman
Xiaowei Wang
Emma Warnock
Venetia Welby
Sam Whaley
Wendy Whidden
Phil & Anne Whitehurst
Crispin Whittell
Christine Whittemore
James Wilson
Lucinda Winter
Lisa Wohl
Marcus Wright
Stefan Zebrowski-Rubin

First published in 2021
by Weatherglass Books

002

Text design and typesetting by CB editions
Cover design by Luke Bird
Printed in the U.K. by TJ Books, Padstow

A CIP record for this book is published by the British Library

ISBN 978-1-8380181-2-2

www.weatherglassbooks.com

Weatherglass
Books